QUEEN
OF
LIGHT

USA TODAY BESTSELLING AUTHOR
MEG ANNE

Cover Art by Anna Spies of Eerilyfair Book Covers

Editing: Hanleigh Bradley

"Look at how a single candle can both defy and define the darkness."
— Anne Frank

"The scariest monsters are the ones that lurk within our souls..."
— Edgar Allan Poe

QUEEN
OF
LIGHT

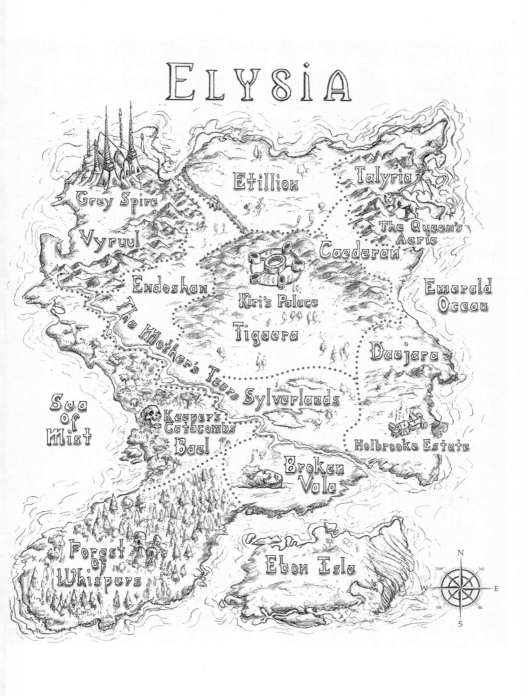

CHAPTER 1

*T*hree towering figures stood facing each other in a loose semi-circle. The ruby red of their robes was the only discernible color in the darkness. From afar the color seemed like a bloody smear against the inky black of the cave's wall. Up close, the splash of color only served to emphasize the seemingly empty space within the recessed area of their hoods.

There was no outward sign that the figures were aware of the storm raging just beyond the cave's entrance. They were unmoving even as a flash of lightning filled the cavern with its blinding glare while an answering crash of thunder echoed along its length.

"The pieces are almost in place."

"It won't be long now."

"She is finally ready to become who she was always meant to be."

"Our salvation."

"Perhaps."

Two of the figures twisted their heads to face the one standing between them.

"But it has been foretold."

"It is but one of two paths."

The leftmost figure's robe rippled, as if the person within was fidgeting restlessly.

"For all that we See, we cannot Know."

"Not until it has come to pass."

"There is always a choice."

The figure in the center dipped its head in a nod. *"And so you understand."*

The wind howled as the storm raged on.

"We will wait."

"And bear witness."

"Where is the Vessel now?"

The central figure's shoulders shook with what might have been laughter. Without waiting to see if the others would follow, he turned and began to make his way deeper into the catacombs.

"She celebrates life before she must greet death."

"SWEET MOTHER, YES!" Helena screamed as Von drove into her with one final, toe-curling thrust.

Von's eyes glittered with wicked satisfaction as he leaned down to kiss her before rolling onto his side and pulling her limp body against his. "We should just stay locked in here tonight and skip the dog and pony show."

Helena let out a snort of amusement as she twisted her head to look at her Mate. "That dog and pony show is your brother's mating ceremony."

"Yes, but I much prefer our *mating* ceremonies." There was no mistaking his innuendo or the sexual promise shining in his silvery gaze.

Despite barely being able to keep her eyes open, Helena's blood quickened at his words. "You're trying to kill me," she finally declared.

"But what a way to go."

They chuckled together, sharing another brief kiss. Von moved to lie on his back, and Helena followed him, curling into his side and resting her head over the still thundering beat of his heart. With her fingers lazily tracing the scrolling lines of his Jaka, she sighed and said, "I should probably go down to check on things. There's not much time left before the guests start to arrive."

Von grunted, holding her tighter.

Knowing better than to try to protest, Helena let her sleepy eyes take in the room. Last time she'd stayed at the Holbrooke Estate, they'd set her up in one of their guest rooms. This time she was sharing Von's childhood room, and it amused her to see the evidence of the boy he'd once been still littered around the chamber.

"So how many women know about your penchant for drawing?" she teased.

Von raised a brow. "My what?"

Helena gestured toward the crudely sketched portrait of what she assumed was a Daejaran wolf.

Von followed her hand before bursting into surprised laughter. "Oh, that. Nial made it for me. When he was four."

"And here I was thinking I finally found something you were terrible at." Helena's words were playful, and her smile grew at the thought of the proud little boy showing his big brother what he'd drawn.

He scoffed. "If I *had* drawn it… hell, if it was just a bunch of stick figures holding swords, and I told you I'd made it especially for you, you'd do the same thing."

"What's your point?"

"That the value is not in the skill."

"Obviously."

Von peered at her curiously. "You wanted to take it, didn't you? When you thought I had drawn it?"

"Maybe."

His chest rumbled with his laughter. "Do you want me to draw you a picture, *Mira*?"

"Only if you use stick figures."

They laughed again.

"And what did you mean *my women*?" he asked once their laughter had faded. "Just how many do you think have been in my room?"

3

Helena's cheeks grew warm. "Well, I mean… clearly you have a past. You don't learn how to do *that* without experience."

"Helena, look at me." His warm voice grew serious. He didn't continue speaking until her eyes met his. "You are the only woman I've ever allowed into my room, at least in any kind of romantic capacity."

The pleasure and relief that filled her at his admission almost surprised her. "But surely you had conquests…"

"Aye, but never here." At her confused expression, he elaborated. "It saves you from enduring a series of uncomfortable conversations. Not to mention it's a lot harder to leave once you've finished when it's your room."

Helena shook her head with mock disapproval. "Quite the lover even then."

Von gave her a wry smile. "Love had nothing to do with it, and there was never a reason to stay."

"Never?"

"Not until you."

Helena could feel the sincerity of his words filling her through their bond. "Lucky me," she murmured, moving to kiss him.

"No, Helena. Lucky me," he corrected, brushing a stray curl behind her ear before closing the distance between their lips.

Before their tender kisses could go any further, a knock sounded at the door.

"Your brother is looking for you," Ronan called from the other side.

"He probably needs advice about what to do after the ceremony," Von muttered dryly, making no move to get up.

Helena gave him a saccharine smile. "If you've seen the way Serena looks at him when she thinks no one's watching, you'd know he doesn't need any help in that regard."

"How could you possibly know that?"

"It's the same way I look at you."

Von's fingers wove into her hair as he pulled her down for a searing kiss. Ronan had to knock three more times before the lovers finally made it out of their bed to greet him.

"About damn time," he said without any heat. Ronan's blue eyes were twinkling with amusement as Von punched his shoulder by way of greeting.

"Fucker," he said beneath his breath as he walked past the newest member of her Circle.

"Bastard," Ronan returned, saluting Von's retreating back.

"Heard that."

"Meant you to."

"See you down there," Helena told Von, staying behind. She wanted a moment alone with Ronan before the ceremony.

"Don't take too long. You know I can only handle my mother in small doses without you as my buffer."

Helena's answering laugh followed Von down the hall. "Poor Margo."

Ronan lifted an inquiring brow.

"Seeing both of her son's happy and whole is proving to be too much for her. She can't seem to go more than ten minutes without bursting into tears. Von is finding it... trying."

"Only a woman cries because she's too happy."

"Careful, Shield."

"What? It's true."

"I'm starting to think Von didn't hit you hard enough."

Ronan snickered. "He's just lucky I stopped punching back."

"Because you know you'd have to deal with me."

Ronan's answering smile was warm. "Can you think of a better reason?"

Weaving her arm through his, they started walking. Helena considered his question for a moment before replying, "No. Self-preservation is a powerful motivator."

"Indeed, it is." They walked a bit further in companionable silence before Ronan sighed and said, "Just ask. I know you want to."

Not even pretending to misunderstand him, she blurted out, "Are you sure you're okay with this?" Helena had hoped she'd be able to read his feelings through the Jaka, but all she could sense was a tangle of conflicted emotions. Her eyes searched his face, looking for physical signs of how he was doing, but it was a neutral mask. "If this is going to be too much for you, I can find some errand to send you on."

"And leave you unprotected? Not a chance." His words were gruff, but he raised his hand to place it over hers and squeezed. He appreciated her offer, even though he would never take her up on it.

"I am hardly unprotected, and I know several men who would take great offense at the implication."

"Maybe if they'd stop losing all their sparring matches with me, I'd have a little more faith in their abilities."

Helena laughed, remembering how the remaining men in her Circle had all found a reason to take her aside and complain about Ronan's morning practices throughout the course of the week. She knew his words were a cover, Ronan didn't doubt Von's ability to protect her for an instant.

"Are you sure?" she asked again in a softer voice.

Ronan was silent for a long stretch. When he finally spoke, his voice was so soft she barely heard him. "It's time."

Time to really let go. Time to say goodbye. Time to move on. Yes, it was time.

"Then let's go."

THERE WASN'T enough space in the Holbrooke's home to fit all Nial and Serena's guests, so they'd decided to hold the ceremony outside. Even if that hadn't been the case, and had it been her decision to make, Helena would have decided the same. It was beautiful being among the trees and mountainside. The roaring sound of the crashing ocean waves was a perfect soundtrack as the sun began its descent through the sky.

Further decoration was unnecessary, given the vibrant beauty of their natural surroundings, but a small pavilion had been erected and swathed in fresh flowers. The scent of roses and jasmine wafted in the mild breeze.

Ronan had left her once she'd made it outside, citing a need to check on his men. Helena scanned the yard, looking for someone that appeared to be in charge. Technically it should have been her, seeing as how the ceremony was her idea, but frankly she was tired of making decisions and gladly passed all decision making on to the couple. It was their day, after all.

Helena's thoughts began to wander, and she closed her eyes only to find Rowena's icy stare waiting for her. She shuddered and shoved the thought away, forcing herself to take a deep, centering breath. The Circle and their new allies would deal with her soon enough. Today was not a day for worrying about such things. It was a day for celebration, probably the last they'd have until the war was over. Today she would focus on love and life; two of the Mother's most precious gifts.

She sent a caress down the bond, wanting her Mate to know that she was thinking of him. An answering ripple of warmth greeted her, washing away the chill her thoughts of Rowena had caused.

Helena looked back at the pavilion, watching the fragile flower petals flutter in the breeze. In a few short hours, she'd be standing there, speaking the words that formally commemorated what two souls had already acknowledged. It would have been nice to be able to stand on the sidelines and simply be a guest for once. But that was not who she was, or who she was meant to be. Not anymore.

Perhaps it never really was.

"Mira?" Von asked, sensing her disappointment.

"It's nothing."

She felt his curiosity as if it was a tickle up her spine, but he did not question her further.

"Isn't it perfect?" Serena asked, joining her.

"That it is," Helena answered with a smile. "Aren't you supposed to be hidden away until the ceremony starts?"

"Alina just finished helping me get ready and I couldn't stand being cooped up any longer. That woman is truly gifted. I've never felt so feminine in my entire life." Serena laughed as she said the words, the warrior in her appreciating the irony. For years she'd had to pretend that she wasn't soft so that the men around her would take her seriously. Today she could set that instinct aside and embrace the purely female part of herself. Still chuckling, Serena asked, "Isn't this dress divine?" She performed a small twirl, holding her arms out to let her simple lilac gown billow around her.

Helena's smile grew, completely understanding the sentiment. She was no stranger to Alina's ministrations, or her miracles. "You look beautiful," Helena agreed, but it was not because of the dress or her upswept curls that had been held back with a garland of flowers. Serena was glowing with the intensity of her joy. She was a woman in love; one who had been lucky enough to find her mate. It was a rare and beautiful gift that none of the Chosen would take for granted.

"Thank you!" Serena beamed brightly before her lips twisted in a grimace. "I'm just ready to get this over with."

"Don't say that," Helena urged, placing a hand on her friend's arm. "Cherish every second of today."

Serena's jaw clenched and her violet eyes hardened. She heard the words that Helena did not say: they were on borrowed time. Rowena could strike at any minute, although given her less than subtle invitation, it appeared that she was in the process of setting the stage for her next salvo.

The blonde woman took Helena's hand in hers and squeezed, hard. "You're right. It's just my nerves speaking."

"I think that's normal," Helena replied, remembering the way her stomach had felt like it was somersaulting within her the day she and Von made their vows.

"You're probably right."

"Aren't I always?"

"Hardly."

They shared a look before bursting into laughter.

"Now that's what I like to see," Nial said from behind them.

They moved to make room for him, Serena peering at him almost shyly as he took in the sight of her.

8

"Beautiful," he murmured, his storm-gray eyes shining with a possessive intensity Helena instantly recognized.

Knowing that neither of them remembered she was still standing there, Helena quietly stepped away, giving the couple a few stolen moments of solitude before their ceremony began. She smiled softly as she watched the way that they fussed over the other, their tender caresses and heated looks making her long for something she couldn't name.

CHAPTER 2

a few of their new allies had arrived in Daejara early. Rather than have them remain segregated in their various camps, the Circle had made the call to include them in the festivities. There really was no better way to cement a new partnership than with a raging party and copious amounts of alcohol. It was clear that help was definitely required in that regard.

Helena winced at the reminder. Anduin and his Storm Forged had been the first to arrive. She'd barely closed the door behind the Stormbringer when Reyna and the Night Stalkers began to knock. To say their initial meeting had been uneasy was an understatement. The two leaders had taken one look at each other standing in the Holbrooke's hallway and any trace of warmth they'd had when greeting Helena drained away. Their distrust was palpable. Even Kragen's ever-present grin vanished when he noticed Reyna's hand move to the dagger sheathed at her hip.

To be fair, the move had not been entirely uncalled for. One of Anduin's party had made a snide comment about how it was a surprise to see that the Night Stalkers were let out of their cages during the day. Helena's own hand had itched to slap the self-satisfied smile off the man's face while around him others shuffled uncomfortably. If not for

Timmins stepping in, Helena wasn't sure they would have avoided the two groups coming to blows.

Helena let her eyes find Reyna in the crowd, noting the stiff way she was perched on her seat. She sighed. It seemed that not much had changed in the last four days.

Following her gaze, Von's lips twitched up in the ghost of a smile. *"Lucky for us, Reyna chose to wear a dress without weapon sheathes."*

Helena fought the urge to laugh. *"If you believe that then you aren't half the master strategist you think you are."*

"All right, fine. At least the Storm Forged are seated well away from the Night Stalkers."

"That much is true. It's almost like someone had the foresight to do that on purpose."

"Who can we thank for that?"

Helena bit back a grin that would have seemed entirely out of place to those not participating in the current conversation—namely everyone else. *"I'm not sure, but when you find him, can you give him a big kiss from me?"*

"Hey now," Von said, his eyes catching and holding hers from where he stood, just to the left of the pavilion, *"those kisses belong to me."* The iridescent rings around his pupils seemed to glow in what was left of the sunlight.

Seeing the physical evidence of their connection made her heart swell with primal satisfaction. It wasn't just her kisses that belonged to him. It was her very essence. They were soul-bound, tied together in a way that only death could ever rip apart.

Helena winked at him. *"You can collect them later."*

"Count on it."

Returning to their initial conversation, Helena said, *"I can't believe I thought getting the Forsaken to agree to join us would be the hard part. I didn't even stop to consider how we were going to convince everyone to work together."*

"Hopefully tonight's party will be the first step in bridging that gap."

"From your lips to the Mother's ears…"

"From my lips to—"

"Shhh!" Helena cut him off, already feeling the telling heat of a blush rising to her cheeks. Now was definitely not the time to think about that. Not with so many eyes on her.

Guests slowly began to take their seats, their mingled voices swelling like a wave about to crash. Helena stood beneath the pavilion, smiling in greeting as familiar and unfamiliar faces alike caught her eye.

Von and Nial's parents were seated in the first row with Margo already dabbing at her eyes. Helena could feel Von's mental eye-roll at the sight, which only made her smile grow. Just beside the couple, filling out the row, were the rest of the Circle. Despite being impeccably dressed and on their best behavior, her men looked entirely out of place amid the other guests. It wasn't just the sheer size of them, although Kragen and Ronan were clearly blocking the view of everyone sitting behind them. More than one guest had sat down only to immediately begin craning their neck around the towering wall of pure muscle in an attempt to get a better view. Not one of them had been successful. Finally, they'd simply given up entirely and left the seats directly behind her Sword and Shield empty.

No, it was not their size. It was less obvious and more intangible than that, like an aura of violence that was never quite abated even during times of peace. There was just something about them, especially when all together, that made it impossible to forget who they were and what they were capable of. Not that Helena ever worried, they were hers after all, but given the sidelong glances thrown their way, others were certainly aware of the not-so-subtle threat. Smart of them to remain on guard, really. Even now.

Kragen caught her looking at him and gave her a wide grin, his dark eyes crinkling with his amusement. He seemed to know exactly what she was thinking and reveled in the suspicious stares. Upon further inspection, it appeared that all of her Circle did. They were proud of the fact that they made others nervous. That was why, even though they were not doing anything to provoke or encourage the stares, they were doing absolutely nothing to mitigate them either. Not even Timmins, who was usually too well-behaved to give in to such a blatant display of male ego.

Helena snickered. Timmins thought he had them all fooled, but these past couple of days he'd been running around in a near panic when he could not find the sacred text he'd brought from Tigaera. It contained the ceremonial words required to bind two souls during a formal mating ceremony within its ancient pages. He'd finally snapped when Helena had shrugged and said she'd wing it.

"One does not 'wing' the Mother's sacred words!"

"Maybe you don't…"

He scowled at her. "Helena, this is the most hallowed of ceremonies. We need that book."

"Timmins, calm down. You're looking apoplectic."

He huffed and snapped his lips closed.

Helena placed a hand on his shoulder. "Timmins," she started in her most soothing voice, "I've been improvising for the last year and the Mother hasn't struck me down yet. Tomorrow will be no different. In the end, they are just words. It is the intention of the two being bound that matters."

Timmins looked no more convinced, but the fight left him. "If you say so, Kiri."

"I do."

Timmins let out a long-suffering sigh. "Better you than me."

Helena punched him lightly on the shoulder. "That's the spirit."

He scowled and rubbed his shoulder. "You spend entirely too much time in the company of your Mate and Shield."

Helena was smiling with the memory of her Advisor. Few, if any, saw him in those rare moments of uncertainty. Helena secretly cherished them. Knowing that not even he had the answer or solution to every situation made her feel infinitely better about the fact that neither did she. Perfection was an impossible task, even for the Mother's Vessel.

Ronan was the personification of male disinterest. His arms were crossed and he was leaning back in his chair with his long legs sprawled out before him. Helena didn't buy it for a second, but she was likely the only one. If it wasn't for their connection, she too would be unaware of the undercurrent of tension simmering beneath that aloof countenance.

Sensing her eyes on him, he shifted his gaze up from his leather boots toward her. Helena raised a brow in silent question. Ronan's lips lifted in the ghost of a smile, understanding that she was repeating her offer from earlier, and he discretely shifted his chin in the barest of shakes. *No.*

With a small nod of understanding, Helena turned her focus at last to Joquil. Her Master had returned to his long-drawn-out silences since arriving in Daejara, but something had changed since revealing his secret. While quiet, he did not keep to the sidelines, as if ready to flee at a moment's notice. There was a new determination that glimmered in his amber eyes. *He's no longer afraid of being cast aside,* Helena realized. He finally felt accepted. Seeing the almost easy way he interacted with Reyna's people, Helena thought that being amongst his countrymen had something to do with that as well.

Helena made a mental note to speak with Reyna about the ways of the Night Stalkers. Perhaps there were some traditions she could bring back to Tigaera that would help her Master feel more at home.

The subtle strains of the music shifted, letting the guests know that the ceremony was about to begin. Helena pulled her wandering thoughts back, refocusing on the task that lay before her. By the smug cast of Timmins smile, Helena was certain he was mocking her. She could almost hear his taunting, *"Not so sure about winging it now are you?"* She barely restrained herself from sticking her tongue out at him.

The music continued to build as the guests of honor took their respective places. Margo's happy sniffling could just be heard over the lilting melody. In deference to the Great Mother, and as a symbol that they had been blessed, the couple wore her color. Nial looked devastatingly handsome in his fitted suit of pale purple as he stood beside his brother at the bottom of the pavilion. Helena could not recall a time she'd seen the younger Holbrooke look quite so blissfully happy.

Toward the back of the crowd, Serena stood with her arms woven through each of her parents'. The long length of her lilac dress rippled in the soft breeze, causing it to flutter behind her like a banner. Her head was tilted down as her father whispered something into her ear. From the quick grin and shake of Serena's head, Helena thought she knew what he had asked her.

As Serena's violet eyes lifted back up they met and held her mate's. She did not look away, did not so much as blink, as the trio made their way down the aisle. Neither did Nial. In that moment, Helena wasn't sure if it was Serena's graceful steps or the force of Nial's will that carried her down the aisle. With his back to her, Helena could not see his face, but there was no disputing that he was impatient for her to reach him. Nial could not stand still. He kept shifting his weight, like he was about to step forward and then had to fight against the urge to lift his foot. A small, private smile played about Serena's lips. Maybe she could also sense his desire to rush toward her. Or maybe it was just the knowing smile always shared between two lovers.

The music reached its crescendo just as Serena and her parents arrived at the base of the pavilion. A hush settled over the crowd as Serena's father lifted her hand from his arm and placed it in Nial's outstretched palm. The two stood there, gazing at each other, utterly oblivious to everything else around them. Helena waited as long as she could before softly clearing her throat to get their attention.

Nial and Serena wore matching blushes as they spun toward her.

"Sorry," Serena mouthed, while the guests chuckled.

"I'm not," Nial added, loud enough for the guests to hear. Their laughter turned to approving hoots and hollers.

"Perhaps we should get started before our two lovebirds sneak away." The cheering continued for a few moments longer before finally settling down.

"Nial, Serena," Helena began, looking at each of them as she said their names, "we are gathered here today under the ever-watchful eye of the Mother so that you may publicly declare what your souls already recognize. Today, you will take the vows that will bind your souls together."

At that, Nial looked down at Serena with a look so full of love and devotion, Helena felt tears prick her eyes. Feeling the tide of emotion rise within her, Von ran a phantom hand along the length of her back, infusing the caress with his strength. She shot him a grateful look and continued.

"From the time we are children, each of us learn that somewhere in this world the other half of our soul is waiting for us to find it. It does not take us much longer to realize how rare a gift it is to actually do so. When any of the Chosen find their true mate, it is a cause for all of us to celebrate, which is why we gather to bear witness to such a joyful occasion."

Helena paused to address Nial and Serena. "Did you two prepare your own vows?"

"We did," Nial affirmed as Serena nodded beside him.

Addressing the crowd again, Helena raised her voice. "Now they shall share the words in their hearts."

Nial took each of Serena's hands in his. "Serena, the first time I laid eyes on you I knew. It felt like all of the air left my lungs, and there was a moment when I forgot how to breathe because I was so lost in you. I do not love you just because you are strong, or beautiful, or that you know how to set me in my place, even though you are all those things. You are my equal. The part of me that had been missing my whole life even though I never realized how empty I had been until you were there to fill the void. I was told many times that I was not a whole man because I could not walk. But I can say with complete sincerity that I was not a whole man, because I had not yet found you."

A lone tear caught the sun as it shimmered against Serena's lashes before sliding down her cheek. Nial paused to brush it away.

"Serena, loving you has made me a better man. I do not know if I will ever be worthy of the gift you are to me, but I shall spend whatever time the Mother grants us endeavoring to be."

Serena's breath caught on a sob, and her lower lip trembled as Nial's words washed over her. "You are," she whispered to him, before swallowing back her emotions. Nial's thumbs brushed the back of her hands as she composed herself.

"Nial, it is no secret that I have been twice blessed by the Mother. I never thought to ask her for my mate, because I had been loved so completely that I never had a reason to want for more."

Ronan sat straighter in his chair, his red braid and blue eyes shining bright in the afternoon sun.

"At first, I fought my feelings for you, even as I sought every opportunity to spend more time with you. I was terrified of what it said about me that I had already known love, and still I could feel the depth of emotion that I did for a man I had known for only a handful of days. It wasn't long before I realized that what is between us is not something as simple as love. It is completion."

Nial's eyes darkened, his own breath catching.

"The Mother loves to test us. She gave me her greatest gift, but it was up to me to recognize it and to accept it. It was the only way to truly earn her gift, to earn you." Serena's voice had gone husky with the depth of her emotions. "And so, I had to walk away from the life I had built in order to run toward one I never even knew I wanted. I do not say this to suggest that loving you is a burden, only to say that I would sacrifice anything to be with you. Whatever the price, I will pay it. My place, my future, my life is with you. For as many days as the Mother gives us, I am yours."

Nial's hands moved to cup her cheeks as he brought his lips down against hers. There were a few heartfelt sighs as members of the audience secretly wished to experience that kind of love, even as others snickered and whistled suggestively.

"Pssst," Helena stage-whispered. "We're not quite done here."

The couple pulled apart with a chuckle and turned toward her once more.

"I have no desire to draw this out longer than necessary."

"Thank the Mother," Nial fervently swore.

The crowd laughed appreciatively while Helena shook her head with mock disapproval. Once everyone had settled, Helena continued, "Since you are of the Mother, and it is her grace that brought you together, we celebrate being her Chosen with the offering of a gift." There was an air of hushed anticipation as the crowd refocused on the couple, eager to see what the mating gifts would be.

This was always the most anticipated part of any Chosen mating ceremony. It was, in fact, the single most defining moment. It had seemed silly to Helena as a child that giving someone a present held so much more importance than declaring your love and acceptance of them. She had finally begun to understand the importance of the act once her mother explained it to her, but it wasn't until she actually received Von's gift that she truly understood it.

The traditional gift giving was similar to what happened during the Kiri's search for her Mate, at least in terms of the meaning behind the act. For a Kiri, tradition mandated that each of her suitors present a gift as part of their declaration of intent, and she took it to show that she was recognizing their suit. For the rest of the Chosen, gifts were exchanged to symbolize the actual moment when two mates fully accepted the bond, and each other.

Using their power, a combination potentially as singular as a fingerprint, the gifts were unique to the individuals being joined. They would create the most meaningful, and usually spectacular, present that they were able. Something that highlighted their individuality, as well as the person they were offering it to. In a mating ceremony, that exchange of such a personal and unique gift was symbolic of the sharing of one's self. No two gifts would, or in fact could, ever be the same.

The only difference in Helena's case was that, as Kiri, she was not required to create or provide a gift. As the Mother's hand-selected representative, she *was* the gift. Or that was what tradition said anyway. Now that she was reflecting on it, Helena was a bit dismayed to realize that she had never taken the time to make a mating gift for Von. Knowing what the magnolia had come to mean to her, that she refused to travel without it no matter where they were going, Helena made a silent pledge to remedy the situation as soon as possible. It was the least she could do for the man she loved.

Helena looked over the couple, toward her Mate. He was already looking at her, his eyes warm as he too remembered that moment on the dais. It was the first time she'd publicly declared that he was hers. Something that had taken all of five minutes for her to do after meeting him, although in truth, she had known the first time those gray eyes bore into hers.

His smile was soft and gently mocking as he said along their bond, *"If I would have actually thought I had a chance with you, I would have tried a little harder to give you something special."*

"I wouldn't change a thing. It's my most precious possession... well, after you."

She saw laughter sparkling in his eyes. *"Helena, it's just a flower. Hardly anything to write home about."*

"It's not just a flower," she insisted, offended at the implication. *"It proved that even when you thought it was just for show, you took the time to ensure that your gift would be something meaningful to me in particular. For a mercenary, it was an especially tender gift. It alluded to your true nature, even as you tried so hard to hide it, proved you were thoughtful and kind, that you could be gentle. When I saw that pristine white bloom cradled in your scarred hand, I saw the hands that would cradle and protect me. It will never just be a flower, Von. It was,"* she paused to correct herself, *"it is a promise. A promise about the kind of Mate you will be and the sort of life we will have together."*

His eyes had darkened with emotion as she spoke, the iridescent rings shining in sharp contrast against the stormy gray. She watched as he swallowed, seeming to be at a loss for words.

"If I had known that you were out there waiting for me, I would have left everything behind and walked to the ends of the world to find you."

"Had I known, I would have met you halfway, if only to shorten the journey."

They shared a long look, their love on clear display had anyone bothered to spare them a glance. Fortunately, everyone else was too busy watching Nial and Serena. The crowd was too eager to see what they had created for each other to notice the secret moment between their Kiri and her Mate.

Von finally dragged his eyes away from hers as his brother turned toward him. Nial's hands shook slightly as he held one out for his brother to place a wrapped item into.

Removing the slightly crinkled paper, Nial turned back to Serena. The item in his hand sparkled as it caught the light. It was small, barely taking up the full space of his open palm. Helena's vantage point allowed her to see what many others could not. Nial had crafted a figure with remarkable detail. Without having to be told, Helena knew it was Serena as she appeared to him. The small woman was gorgeous and fierce, her eyes glittering with challenge, even as she grinned with wicked amusement.

Nial ran his finger gently along the back of the figurine. The small figure shivered and came alive with a yawn and stretch. Serena gasped in wonder as the figure began to move on her own, her delicate golden curls fluttering on an invisible breeze, while the small mouth twisted with a war cry.

As if conjured by air, another figure appeared, this one a winged and fanged creature of legend. It could only be one of the Macabruls. Each one of its black scales glittered like jewels as it let out a silent roar. The tiny Serena wasted no time, launching itself into the air in a flying spin, using a sword that glowed with ruby flames to make quick work of the beast. As the sword made contact with the long serpentine neck, the Macabrul disappeared in a cloud of glittering smoke. The figurine landed in a crouch, before standing back up and brushing a few lingering pieces of dust off her silver armor.

Serena held out her hand and the tiny warrior fearlessly stalked toward the new territory. Sensing that she was home, the little figure dropped her sword and let out a big yawn before promptly curling up in a ball and falling asleep.

Serena looked up with wide-eyes, unable to speak.

Nial was one of the few true magic masters, there was no question of his ability. He had brought together each of the four Branches he commanded to create life out of nothing. And not just any life, a representation of his mate and her various accomplishments.

It was stunning in its detail and mastery. There were few, if any, who would be capable of ever crafting it's like.

Serena curled her hand protectively over the figure, letting out a watery laugh as the figure began to snore.

"It's beautiful," she whispered.

Nial shrugged, looking pleased and embarrassed. "It's you."

Serena appeared nervous as she called forth a Daejaran warrior who was standing just off to the side.

The man carried a large object that had been covered with a white sheet. At Serena's nod, the man gently set down the item on a table that had been set up for the purpose and pulled away the sheet.

"So that I may protect you even if we are apart," Serena whispered, as Nial's mouth fell open.

Serena was not a master of four Branches as her mate was, but she was skilled in her own right. A warrior first and foremost, Serena had created a suit of armor. It was not a traditional chest plate of leather and metal. Helena recognized the color immediately, it was the deep stormy blue of his eyes. Nial would be easy to spot amongst a crowd, probably part of Serena's intention.

"A small punch of power, if you wouldn't mind, Kiri," Serena requested.

Helena raised an eyebrow in surprise but called up her power. A ball of dancing flame quickly took shape in her palm. At Serena's nod, Helena released the fireball, launching it at the armor. As it made impact, the plate began to glow a deep and pulsing violet. There was an audible hiss and the fire disintegrated, leaving the armor entirely unharmed.

The crowd let out startled gasps and then burst into roaring applause.

"I know that our duties will not always allow us to stand together, but at least when you wear that, I will not have to overly worry about your safety."

Nial looked between his new armor and his mate, clearly moved by her words and her gift. "You honor me," he whispered.

Sensing their need to be together, Helena moved into action. "Now that that's out of the way, let's finish this up. The Mother brought you together, it will be up to the two of you to ensure that you cherish her gift and help it thrive. From this day forth, your souls will forever be one."

The crowd exploded in cheers.

Leaning forward, Helena whispered, "Now you can kiss her."

With a roguish grin she knew too well, Nial bent down and claimed Serena's lips in another searing kiss. Helena looked away, her eyes moving toward her Mate.

As far as ceremonies went, it was very different from what she and Von had shared. Even still, Helena would not change a thing. From the heat in his silvery gaze, Helena knew that her Mate felt the same.

"I love you."

Von's eyes softened and his smile grew. *"And I you."*

Using magic to enhance her voice, Helena spoke over the roar of the crowd. "Now for the part you've really been waiting for! Let's eat!"

Nial and Serena were impervious as their guests made their way to the tables overlooking the cliffs and the raging ocean below, still too busy taking their fill of each other.

CHAPTER 3

*R*onan stared into the bottom of his mug, surprised to see that it was already empty.

"I do not get the impression that you are celebrating."

Ronan looked up into eyes the color of forest leaves. "Reyna."

She dipped her head in greeting and gestured again toward his cup. "Do you want another?"

"Need and want are two very different things."

"So, this is definitely not a celebration."

Ronan's lips twisted in a mocking smile. "There are days you think a wound has fully healed only to find that you have simply grown accustomed to the pain."

Reyna's eyes glittered with understanding. Gesturing toward the empty seat next to him she asked, "May I?"

"By all means."

Reyna swept her skirt to the side and gracefully lowered herself into the chair. The movement was so smooth Ronan was reminded of the way shadows slid across a forest floor.

He eyed the dark-haired woman beside him. Her hair was still a wild mix of braids and long curls, but her face was wiped clean of the Night Stalkers' iconic face paint. In its absence her skin glowed, complementing the golden flecks in her eyes. Ronan would say that she appeared more feminine, but that wasn't strictly true. Reyna had never appeared anything but feminine to begin with. It was more a sense of being tamed, although one only need look in her eyes to see the wildness was barely leashed. She was a feral creature, more suited to the starlit shadows of the forest than the glittering decadence of a ballroom. Ronan let his eyes wander along her body, appreciating the way her dress showcased her curves, even as he wished she was wearing her black leather instead.

Reyna coughed pointedly.

Ronan was slow to pull his eyes up, only grinning when she shook her head at him. He shrugged, not bothering to apologize for getting caught.

"There are many men who have felt the sharp edge of my blade for daring to look at me that way." Despite the threat, amusement laced her voice.

"Lucky for me, you don't have it on you."

The words had barely left his mouth when the shadows around them rippled and Reyna's hand, now gripping a golden dagger, was at his throat. "Don't be so sure about that."

Ronan lifted a brow, but otherwise showed no reaction. "Point taken."

Reyna smirked and vanished her dagger. "Now, about that drink." With a slight lift of her chin, Reyna was able to get the attention of a server. The boy scurried over, using Air to keep his tray of drinks stable while he dodged the partygoers. Reyna plucked two glasses off the tray and dismissed the boy with a brief, but warm, smile.

She was already taking a sip from her glass as she held the other out to Ronan. He couldn't help but appreciate her sense of priorities. Apparently, he was not the only one who needed something to dull the edges tonight.

Ronan had just begun to drink deeply from his glass when Reyna said, "You were the lover she referred to."

Ronan began to choke on his ale, barely getting his mug on the table as he coughed up the amber liquid. "You don't pull any punches, do you?"

Reyna lifted one shoulder. "What's the point? I am just stating the obvious. Your relationship wasn't a secret, was it?"

Despite wishing someone else was at the receiving end of her interrogation, Ronan had to admire her no-nonsense approach to conversation. At least you would always know where you stood with the lady.

Ronan wasn't sure which question to answer, so he remained silent.

"The Night Stalkers do not have such a narrow view of mates."

Ronan raised a brow, waiting for her to continue.

"It is foolish to believe that there is only one person in the world that you are supposed to love."

"The possibility of a mate does not impede your ability to love another," Ronan stated flatly. The irony of his statement was not lost on either of them. He was clearly proof.

"That's not what I meant." Reyna took another deep gulp, her glass now more than half empty. "It is only that we are constantly evolving. The person that was right for me ten years ago, is not the person that will fulfill me now."

"Your true mate grows with you. They are the piece that completes you." It was Ronan's turn to drink deeply. Setting his empty mug down, he added, "Although it is said that you will not find your mate until you are ready to accept them."

"Is that not true of all lovers?"

"You're missing the point."

"Am I?"

Ronan sighed with exasperation. How could he possibly explain something he'd never experienced? Instead of admitting defeat he went on the offensive. Scrubbing a hand down his face, he groaned. "Woman, you are exhausting."

Reyna's laugh was deep and throaty. He felt it move over him like the gentlest of caresses. His body was quick to respond. Ronan looked at his lap in surprise. That was unexpected.

She shifted in her seat, placing her hand lightly on his arm. "I did not mean to insult your beliefs, Shield. I was just trying, perhaps in a misguided way, to let you know that you are not doomed to be alone just because she was not your mate. You may have lost the one you thought was your forever, but that doesn't mean there is not another, or even many, that will bring you happiness again." Reyna's eyes had turned a bright, glowing emerald as she spoke.

Ronan's mouth went dry.

"You will find her, when you're ready."

The words, so softly spoken, settled something that had been loose within him. Ronan wasn't sure he was ready, but for the first time, he wanted to be.

"Thank you," he said, his deep voice barely a whisper.

Reyna offered him a small smile and settled back into her seat. The loss of contact chilled him, and Ronan found that he wasn't quite ready to let the conversation, or the company, go just yet.

"So why are you drinking tonight?"

The warmth left Reyna's eyes, leaving them almost black. Her smile turned sarcastic as she replied, "Can't you tell? Preservation, same as you."

Ronan's brows dropped low over his eyes. "What do you mean?"

"If one more ignorant bastard makes a comment about me or my people, I will gut them. I do not want to risk your Kiri's wrath by killing one of her people."

Anger rose swift and sure, warming him with the intensity of its heat. "One of the Chosen dared insult you?"

Reyna's expression softened, the hard line of her mouth curling upwards. "No, not one of the Chosen."

"The Storm Forged?" Reyna nodded, causing Ronan's frown to deepen. "I'll take care of it."

Reyna's brows lifted in surprise. "If I recall correctly, I am not the one you are supposed to be protecting, Shield."

Ronan snarled. "You are Helena's friend. I protect what is hers."

Reyna stared at him thoughtfully, her face an inscrutable mask. After a long moment, she finally said, "Then I will gladly accept the help."

The urge to protect and defend raged within him, but now was neither the time nor the place. Seeking a return to levity, Ronan asked, "Out of curiosity, whose preservation? Yours or theirs?"

Reyna's smile was so filled with the threat of violence that Ronan already knew the answer.

"Fair enough," he said with a chuckle, grabbing two glasses of ale as another server walked by. "Here's to preservation."

"I'll drink to that!" Reyna clinked her glass with his, eagerly tipping it back.

Ronan watched in stunned amazement as the Night Stalker drank, and drank. The way her throat worked as she swallowed threatened to distract him. Realizing she was going to drain the whole glass, Ronan quickly followed suit. She slammed her glass down on the table only seconds before he did.

"Now what?" Her eyes glowed with challenge and perhaps the smallest amount of inebriation.

"Now we dance."

Reyna sputtered. "What?"

Ronan was already standing and holding a hand out for her to grab. "It is a party."

"Do you even know how to dance?" she asked, uncertainly placing her hand in his.

Ronan's answer was a confident smile. "Only one way to find out."

"If you step on my toes..." Reyna threatened half-heartedly, seeming distracted by Ronan's roguish grin.

Feeling devious, Ronan leaned down and whispered in her ear, "If I step on your toes, you can take it out on me any way you want to." With that he made his way to the dance floor, pulling a dumbstruck Reyna behind him.

HELENA WATCHED Reyna trailing behind Ronan with amusement.

"What's that face for?" Von asked.

"I'm just trying to recall the last time Ronan looked so relaxed."

Von turned his silvery gaze on his best friend before laughing softly. "That's not relaxed, *Mira*. That's determined. Your Shield is on a mission."

Helena studied Ronan a bit more closely, noting the calculating look in his eye as well as his single-minded focus on the dark-haired Night Stalker. "Does the name of his mission start with an R?"

Von's dimple flashed, letting her know that she had arrived at the correct answer.

Ronan dancing wasn't a sight Helena thought she would ever encounter. Like everything else he did, his moves were testosterone laden and aggressive. There was no other way to classify the way he rolled his hips up and into his partner. Reyna's shock was short lived as she began to move her hips and shoulders to the beat, giving Ronan a run for his money. For each seductive move he made, she made another in kind. Both tried to remain unaffected, but it was clear from the heated looks they sent one another that neither was immune.

"I'm not entirely sure who is pursuing who."

"Does it have to be one or the other?"

Helena shook her head. "I'm just curious which one is going to try to take credit for the win."

Von let out a bark of laughter. "That is the kind of argument that leads to the bedroom and is never entirely resolved."

"So, they're both winners."

"Exactly."

Von and Helena shared a long, heated look, memories of their own time in the bedroom passing between them.

"How much longer do we need to stay down here?" Von asked, brushing a kiss against her lips.

"A while yet, I'm afraid," she answered, regret heavy in her voice.

Von scowled. "My little brother is grown and yet he continues to annoy me."

"You can't blame him. It's your position as my Mate that requires your presence more so than yours as his brother."

He gave her a scorching look. "I shall try to suffer in silence, my love."

Helena laughed in his face. "You're about as likely to remain silent as Darrin is to walk through that door."

"You wound me," he said as he wrapped his arms around her waist and pulled her back to his chest.

"That doesn't feel like a wound to me."

"The longer it's neglected, the more that it aches."

Helena knew that she had started it, but she was not prepared for the effect his words had on her. "Mother's tits," she gasped, pressing into him.

Von leaned forward, under the guise of adjusting her necklace, and pressed a trail of kisses along her neck and shoulder. "You're the one that won't let us leave," he reminded her with a final nip at her ear.

Helena blinked a few times, trying to pull herself out of her Mate's seductive web.

Von chuckled, stepping away from her. "So, what else is required of us tonight?"

Helena gave him a blank look, letting his words echo about her mind as she tried to make sense of them. "What?"

"What else do we need to take care of before we can go to bed," he repeated, his smile making it clear that sleep was the last thing on his mind.

Helena racked her brain, trying to remember what specific duties she still had to perform. After the ceremony, they had made their way to the tables that had been set up for dinner. The meal had been relatively informal, with plates being passed around the table for guests to take what they wanted before passing it on. After the guests had finished eating, there was a round of increasingly inappropriate toasts, one of which Helena had made. Then about twenty minutes ago, the musicians had started up again, opening the dance floor for the rowdy guests. As far as she could recall, there was nothing left for her to officially do.

"Now that I think on it, I guess we're technically done. Although it's frowned upon to leave before the newly mated couple."

"Who would dare tell you when you are allowed to leave?"

Helena gave him a pointed look.

Von sighed, but his disappointment was short lived. When he began to smile, Helena knew that he was up to something. With a mischievous lift of his brow, he stepped away from her and started making his way toward his brother, who was currently spinning Serena around the dance floor.

"What are you doing?"

"What every good brother should."

"Von..."

He winked at her over his shoulder but did not slow down. Nial gave his brother a wide grin as he approached, his smile faltering only slightly as Von grabbed his arm and pulled him to the side before whispering in his ear.

Nial laughed and nodded, eagerly returning to his curious mate. In a similar fashion, Nial bent down and whispered something that caused Serena's eyes to go dreamy. She nodded, looking up at him from under her lashes. With barely a glance at the rest of their guests, Nial and Serena slipped away.

"There," Von said, returning to her side. "Can we go now?"

Helena's mouth fell open. "You did not just send your brother to bed on his mating night."

"I told him it was bad form to keep his mate waiting." There was nothing but smug satisfaction in his voice.

"You are terrible," she informed him, unable to keep her laughter in check long enough to maintain her pretense of chastisement.

"No, my love. Simply a man of action."

Just as Helena was about to agree, Margo walked over to them.

"Your brother ran off without dancing with his mother!"

Von stared at her with frustrated amusement. "I suppose that means you're looking for a stand in?"

"But of course!"

Von held out his arm, letting his mother weave her own arm through it before he led her to the dance floor.

"So close," he said mournfully through the bond.

"We have all night, my love."

"From your lips..." he said, repeating her words from earlier.

Helena's laugh was muffled by the sweeping strains of the music as Von began to dance with his mother. It was with joy, and perhaps a small bit of wistfulness, that she stayed there to watch them, knowing as she did that their window for such simple pleasures was swiftly closing.

CHAPTER 4

GREYSPIRE

"The scouts have returned."

"And?" Rowena didn't bother to turn around and address the man directly.

"They remain in hiding. There has been no sign of the Kiri or her Circle."

"Incompetent fools," she hissed, letting her pointed nails rake across the glass as she looked over her shoulder.

There was a discernible wince on the handsome face, but it passed quickly. It was only the sound, and not her displeasure, that caused the reaction. Rowena could tell because there was no sign of fear in the golden eyes that boldly stared back into hers. There hadn't been since the day she had met him standing defiantly at the door of his stone palace. *This one believes he is my equal. Brave*, Rowena decided, impressed despite herself. Although she would never tell him that. It had been years since anyone mistakenly believed the same, but he would learn. Eventually. They always did. No one was her equal.

Not even the Endoshan heir.

When given the choice to join her or die, the same choice she had offered each of the Chosen she had come across, Kai-Soren surprised her by being the first to willingly accept... albeit for a price. For months Rowena and her army had marched across Elysia, taking by force what he freely offered. She could have Endoshan, but only if he stood at her side. An alliance, he said, to be forged by marriage. An easy enough promise to make, and not one she had any intention of keeping. But he didn't need to know that. Not yet.

Kai-Soren had already proven to be a useful ally. For all their power, there was much his Endoshans could do that her Shadows could not. Most notably, the Endoshans could move amongst the Chosen unnoticed. Rumors were beautiful things, both powerful and effective. It was easy enough to convince the others that Endoshan had been lost. One bloodied runner had been enough to convince the Etillions, and from there, they had handled the rest. Just like that, an entire territory was under her control with no more effort than a simple, "I accept."

Rowena couldn't wait to see that aqua-eyed impostor's face when she saw she didn't control the Chosen as completely as she believed. As it did every time she thought of that little bitch sitting on her throne, Rowena's anger multiplied. She turned to face Kai-Soren fully. The window had frozen where her hand had been, small fissures appearing in the glass as it began to shatter beneath the assault. He didn't even spare the cracking glass a glance, his eyes remaining steadily leveled on her.

"I am displeased."

"I can see that."

A cold smile made her lips tilt up. "Would you like to see what happened to the last man who displeased me?"

There was a flicker in the golden eyes. She had struck a nerve. *Good. He is learning already.*

"How may I remedy the situation, my lady?"

Rowena tilted her head, considering her answer. After a long-drawn-out silence, she shrugged. "It is no matter. The bitch will come to us."

Kai-Soren bowed his head. "As you say."

"We will be ready when she arrives." It was an order, not a question.

"Yes, my lady. They will not leave alive."

"I cannot think of a more pleasing betrothal gift."

The smile that twisted his lips matched hers for depravity. "Nor I."

MEANWHILE, IN DAEJARA

THE MORNING after Nial and Serena's ceremony found her in yet another crowded room, although this time there was a decided lack of smiling faces. Helena's eyes moved from face to face, trying to gauge the level of unease. She grimaced. Getting these stubborn fools to agree to work together was going to be no small feat.

Overnight, the last of her allies had arrived in Daejara. At least those that were still alive. She frowned with the memory of Endoshan. There was little love lost between her and the Endoshan heir, that much was true, but she would not wish Rowena's brand of justice on anyone.

Sitting uncomfortably in the room were the representatives for the Night Stalkers, the Storm Forged, the Daejarans, the Calderans, the Etillions, and the Sylvanese. The only allies not accounted for were the Talyrians, and that was more for logistical reasons than anything. Although, if she was being honest, Helena would feel more confident if Starshine and her teeth were close at hand. The threat of a Talyrian bite worked almost better than anything else to keep others in line. Helena flexed her hands, the tips of her black claws making a brief appearance. They would have to do. She smirked at the thought of acting as the Talyrian enforcer. She had a feeling Starshine would have been equal parts proud and amused.

Each territory had been allowed no more than three representatives to be present. Always the exception, the Circle was fully accounted for. Sitting beside her Mate, representing Daejara, were Nial, Serena, and Effie. The latter was a ghost of her former self. Helena had been shocked when Effie insisted on being the third as she'd barely left her room since they had buried Darrin. Helena wished she'd had more time to spend offering comfort to the woman so clearly consumed by mourning. There was little she would refuse the petite blonde; she would give anything to help keep her busy and distracted.

The Calderans were next. Tinka and Khouman were present, along with a new female with bright red braids liberally streaked with gray. She was as small as Tinka and as fierce-looking as Khouman. Helena would guess that she was the one calling the shots for Calderan.

Beside them were the Etillions. Helena recognized Amara and Xander from her brief and unfortunately memorable trip to Etillion. With them was a younger man who looked like he might be related to Amara. A brother or cousin perhaps. He was struggling to keep from staring at the cerulean-skinned woman seated beside him.

Helena couldn't blame him. The Storm Forged were certainly alluring with their tinged skin and colorful hair. Anduin sat between two turquoise-haired women whom Helena did not recognize. She mentally applauded his efforts at diplomacy by not bringing the troublemakers who had been causing problems with the Night Stalkers.

On the other side of the Storm Forged sat the Sylvanese. The trio looked familiar, but she could not say with certainty which she had met before, if any. They were another group that she would guess were all related in some capacity.

Rounding out the table were Reyna and her Night Stalkers. She sat beside Ronan with Ryder and another dark-haired man. All three of them appeared battle-ready, their swirls of paint and fitted leathers a clear, and not very subtle, message.

The room was warm, and Helena regretted asking Margo to light the hearth in the massive stone chamber. She had thought that the amber glow would help create a welcoming atmosphere, but the dribble of sweat she felt roll down her back mocked her. *So much for atmosphere.* Calling on Air, Helena wrapped the cool current around herself.

She was just about ready to call the room to order when a quick knock rapped on the door. Not waiting for permission, the door opened to reveal Miranda.

"Kiri, I request permission to attend on behalf of the Keepers."

At the mention of the notorious historians and secret-keepers, the room fell silent.

"Permission granted." Helena could see no reason to exclude her, and Miranda had already proven herself an asset. If she wanted to use her title to gain access to this meeting so be it, Helena would take all the help she could get.

Effie went to make space beside her at the table, but Timmins had already stood and offered his seat to the Keeper. Miranda gave Timmins a smile of thanks and lowered herself into his vacated seat.

"She just needs to fuck him already and put the poor bastard out of his misery."

"Who says she hasn't?" Helena replied, watching her Mate's head swivel to better study her Advisor and the Keeper. There had always been a palpable energy between those two, but it seemed more pronounced now. Solidified perhaps. Helena lifted a brow, something had certainly changed between them, and she was almost certain they'd finally acted on the sexual tension they'd been fighting since they'd first met.

"Shall we get started?" Helena asked.

There were a few murmurs of assent, but the group otherwise remained silent.

"Shortly after I returned home from the Vale I received an invitation. One I plan to accept." Helena lifted a hand to silence the protests that were already rising. "Before you say anything, yes, I am aware that it is a trap. However, there is no better time or way for us to infiltrate her defenses and strike."

"She will be expecting you to, Kiri. You cannot think she won't," Khouman said.

Helena nodded her agreement. "She will lay her trap well, but she will be expecting the Kiri."

Her words were met with looks of confusion.

Helena elaborated, "She does not know that I can alter my appearance. I have been working with Joquil on ways to extend that power to others."

"You expect to sneak in without suspicion," Anduin said, admiration coloring his voice.

Helena shrugged. "It wouldn't be the first time."

"What do you need from us?" Reyna asked.

"A distraction."

"How big?" Ronan asked with a dangerous grin.

Helena smiled at him before addressing the others. "I want to strike before she can. We need to do as much damage as quickly as possible."

Kragen rubbed his hands together gleefully.

"In the confusion of the attack, I want her and her generals separated from the chaos so that they cannot assist. It should give us time to take out the bulk of her army."

"A Talyrian strike?" Von asked, already picturing how they could maximize the casualties.

"She won't expect it," Helena replied as she considered the suggestion.

There were nods of agreement around the table.

"You cannot expect to go in alone," Reyna pointed out.

"I was hoping some of the Night Stalkers could join me. Your people are the most adept at subterfuge and close-range combat."

The Night Stalkers' answering grin would have been chilling if they had not been mirrors of her own.

"Rowena will not stay idle," one of the Sylvanese warned.

"Which is why the rest of you will need to be ready. Ronan, Von, can you work with the others to create a plan? When Rowena realizes what is happening, she will not hesitate. The full force of our army will need to be prepared for that eventuality."

The men nodded.

"My people can provide cover until we are ready to reveal ourselves, Kiri," Anduin offered.

"I am certain you will live up to your name, Stormbringer."

He dipped his head in agreement.

"Do you remember the layout of Greyspire?" Ronan asked Von.

Her Mate's eyes went hazy. "Enough."

Helena's lips tilted in a frown as she recalled his capture. The tendril of Von's unease she felt snaking through their bond did little to dilute her rage at the reminder.

"Do you really think she does not expect you to try to strike, Kiri?" Amara asked, looking worried.

Helena's eyes went iridescent. "Rowena underestimates me. She forgets that as the Mother's Vessel I am more than a figurehead. I am the Mother's wrath every bit as much as I am Her love. It is time to show her my claws."

There was a ripple of panic throughout the room as her words affected them. To some degree, they had all witnessed her power, but none had seen her fully unleash it with the intent to destroy.

"Sometimes to cleanse, first you must burn," Miranda reminded them in her midnight voice.

"Then let the world burn," Von said, his voice steel.

"There are many kinds of storms," Anduin added, bloodlust making his pupils flare.

"We are yours to command, Kiri. Wherever you lead us, we are with you," Serena said. The rest of the group murmured their agreement.

Helena smiled gratefully at her friends, new and old.

"When do we leave?" Joquil asked.

"Three days."

If anyone thought it wasn't enough time, they didn't say so.

CHAPTER 5

'When attempting transformational magic, it is essential the weaver knows the most minute details of their subject. The better the understanding, the more authentic the transformation. Any discrepancy could be the tell that gives away the magic. Detail is everything in transformational magic.'

*H*elena slammed the musty tome closed with a frustrated sigh. She was not readily finding the answers she needed, and they were out of time. So much of what she knew about her power came from intuition. She thought of what she wanted and her power responded. True, it wasn't always perfect, but it was instinct and therefore so much simpler than trying to make sense of half-hocked attempts to explain what she was supposed to think and feel. Magic was emotional for her. Not scientific. Trying to force it like this had left her frustrated, not to mention unsuccessful, for days.

It was imperative that she find a way to hide the small group of Night Stalkers and Chosen who would join her inside Rowena's party. But there was the rub. She was not the only one that had to take on a new form. For each person that joined her, she needed to create a new identity that made sense amongst the other partygoers. Someone who would not cause others to look at them askance. That sounded easy in theory, but how could she turn someone into another person she had never met? It was one thing to create something entirely new, but the need to blend in severely tempered any creative license.

Shapeshifting was tied to detail and an intimate knowledge of what you were trying to transform into. The problem was Helena didn't know who she was supposed to make these people become. They needed to be unremarkable and easily overlooked. Faces in a crowd that were easily forgotten as curious eyes looked on and toward something more interesting.

Helena rubbed her forehead, closing her eyes in an attempt to alleviate her pounding headache.

She heard the library door open but didn't bother turning around.

"I seem to find you as I left you, Kiri."

"Then perhaps you have returned too soon, Keeper," Helena replied, her voice low and laced with tension.

Miranda's hand perched momentarily on Helena's shoulder, a display of comfort or perhaps understanding. The older woman moved around the ancient table, taking a seat across from her.

"Perhaps you are thinking about this the wrong way."

Helena opened an eye to glare blearily at her. "Spare me your riddles and speak plainly."

Gesturing toward the bevy of open and unopened books that littered the table, Miranda asked, "Must they be transformed? Is there not another way to hide amongst a crowd? Deceit does not always have to be in the details, but their absence."

Helena continued to glare, even as the words worked their way around her brain. There was a truth to them that she could not quite ascertain. It was as if the answer was hidden just out of reach. A fact which only increased her ire. Something in her face must have given that away because Miranda had the grace to dip her head and murmur an apology.

"I do not pretend to know the answer, Kiri. I am not half as gifted as you. It is just, sometimes thinking of a problem from a new angle can present the solution we could not initially find."

Helena could not help but agree. "That is certainly true, Keeper."

"I find that talking through the situation with another can sometimes present other avenues to explore."

"Are you offering your services, Keeper?" Helena asked with a wry smile.

Miranda's midnight eyes glittered, but her smile was nothing less than respectful as she replied, "Always, Kiri."

"How many times must I insist that you call me Helena?"

"You are my Kiri, first and foremost. When speaking of matters of politics and war, it is only appropriate to address you such. When we speak as two equals then you can be Helena."

"Is that not what we are right now?"

Miranda's smile was kind but tinged with sadness. "I'm afraid not, Kiri. Not when we discuss such important things."

"Not even if I consider you my equal?" Helena pressed.

The Keeper reached out a hand and laid it gently on hers. "It would seem I am not the only one with trouble remembering her lessons."

Helena's smile was puzzled. "I'm afraid I don't follow, although I am more than certain you must be correct. There is much I seem to forget, as Joquil and Timmins so often take pleasure in reminding me. Would you care to enlighten me on which lesson it would seem I have forgotten this time?"

"Dearest Kiri, only the most important one."

Helena's brows dropped in a deeper frown.

Taking pity on her, Miranda laughed and sat back in her chair. "Only this: None are your equal."

Her words had the air of prophecy even though she had not taken on any of the physical traits often associated with the Sight.

Helena sat up straighter in her chair. "Not even my Mate?"

Miranda shook her head slightly, a small smile still playing about her lips. "Not even he that completes you. You alone are the Mother's Vessel. That is a power no other can match, and so they will seek to thwart it for their own gain."

"You are speaking of the prophecy, aren't you? The one warning of my corruption?"

Miranda shrugged. "It is one of many warnings, although I was not being specific."

A niggling voice had Helena asking, "What do you know that you are not saying, Keeper?"

Miranda's eyes lost their amusement as a newfound respect entered their glittering midnight depths. "The Sight is not perfect. There is always room for misinterpretation, as you are aware."

Helena nodded.

Looking away and into the dusty stacks of books that sat on the library shelves that surrounded them, Miranda remained quiet for a long moment. As she watched and waited for an answer, Helena was reminded of one who rifled through the pages of an old book, as if seeking a specific passage.

When Miranda spoke again, it was not the words of prophecy, but yet another warning. "Do not underestimate the Corruptor. She values that which you have and will seek to use it against you and what you hold most dear. Even now she spins her web, knowing that her prey will find it irresistible."

A heavy sense of foreboding settled in the pit of Helena's stomach. There was nothing the woman said that she did not already know, and yet... the sense of inevitability was exhausting. There was no getting around Rowena or her traps. Helena did not know what she planned, only that she did. It was hard to be prepared for the unknown, but given her opponent, she had to try. It could be the difference between victory or the bitterest defeat.

"Do not despair, Kiri. The future is not yet written. There are many pieces to move and choices to make."

"It is not despair I feel, Keeper."

Miranda's answering smile was full of pride. "Good. Then all is certainly not lost."

The words did little to bolster her.

"Helena," Miranda said more softly.

Surprised to hear her name after the Keeper's earlier comment, Helena looked at her in confusion.

"Do not be afraid of what lies in the darkness, only of getting lost in it. Your strength lies in being able to navigate both darkness and light. Make sure you keep sight of your compass, so that you may find your way back." With that, Miranda abruptly stood. "I should take my leave so that you may return to your studies. Remember what I said, Kiri."

There wasn't a chance for Helena to question her further. Miranda left as quickly as she had arrived, although her words lingered long after she did.

Helena let out a few choice curses before warily muttering, "Which words would you like me to remember, Keeper? You leave me with many."

Eying the stack of books she'd been studying, Helena decided to focus on the first bits of advice: approach her problem from a different angle and talk it through with someone else.

"Mate?"

Von's voice, when it found her, was tinged with concern as he responded to the despondency in her own. *"Mira?"*

"How do you conceal something in plain sight?"

She felt the swift shift of emotions as he processed the question and considered his answer. *"Cloaking it?"*

"You mean invisibility?"

"That is the easiest way."

"But not always practical for people that must move about a room."

"Ahh…" he replied, understanding the purpose of her question more fully.

"If I cannot transform my party to appear as expected partygoers, how can I make them fit in? What is both seen and unseen?"

"Scenery?" Von replied flippantly.

"Your wit is limitless," she said dryly. But his answer did spark an idea. Scenery was in fact something that was both seen and unseen. It was noticed and summarily dismissed. If she would not be

transforming the others, perhaps there was a way for her to make them blend into the background. *"Is blurring a thing?"* she asked, her excitement working its way into her mental voice.

"I do not think that I have heard of it," he admitted.

"But it is not impossible?"

"What you are speaking of, on the level on which you are speaking, would require not just a spell cast upon individuals but an entire group of people."

"Like when I can use my emotions to control the emotions of others?"

"Well... yes. However, in this case you would be convincing a room of people not *to look closely at something, instead of influencing them unknowingly with your emotions."*

"Purposeful intention rather than emotional ripples. Interesting," she replied, already making notes on the piece of paper that had until now only been used for errant doodles. *"This just might work."*

"Happy to help," he teased, sensing that her focus was no longer on their conversation.

Morning gave way to afternoon as Helena's plan took shape on the paper beside her. When she was finished, the room was dark and her hand was cramped, but she knew what she was going to do.

Helena's smile was triumphant and fierce as she spoke to the darkness. "You are not the only one that plots, Corruptor. You should be more careful what you wish for; your invitation has just given us the opening we needed."

CHAPTER 6

$\mathcal{T}$he sound of drills rang through the courtyard. All signs of the mating ceremony had been removed and in its place a training ground had been erected. If it was not for the cliffs just off to the side and the soft call of the gulls as they flew above the crashing waves, Helena would not have realized she was standing in the exact same spot as she had only days prior.

It was the last day before they would make their way to Vyruul and whatever secrets awaited them there. Ronan and Von had agreed that given the different ways of fighting each of the groups employed, it was important that their army could recognize friend from foe on the battlefield. More than that, they needed to be able to combine their skills and work together.

Even now, a few days into the training, it was still more contest than collaborative effort. Helena winced at Ronan's roar. "Again! Are you deaf or just stupid? How many times do I need to say this? Expand your cover to those around you so that they can sneak up on their opponent as well. You keep jumping ahead and end up leaving them with their asses flapping in the breeze."

"Better your ass than your dick," Kragen commented in a bland tone.

"True, although your ass is a bigger target," Von replied mildly.

Nial barely covered his snicker with a cough as Serena glared at the three of them.

"It's not our fault," a dark-skinned girl of no more than seventeen whined. "Their thrice-cursed wind keeps blowing away our cover."

The nearest of the Storm Forged scowled at her. "Perhaps your little shadows are not strong enough if a breeze can knock them off course."

Green fire blazed in the girl's eyes as she rounded on the man. "Would you like to put it to the test, stormy bastard?"

"Smoke-stained bitch."

Ronan moved fast, his arm already extended so that his palm loudly smacked the chest of the Storm Forged who launched himself at the young Night Stalker. Reyna grabbed the girl from the back of her cloak and pulled hard, catching her before she could wrap the familiar cloak of darkness around her body and attack. The girl stumbled back a few steps while the Storm Forged rubbed at his chest. Both mumbled apologies but continued to glower at each other.

"We're doomed."

Von's chuckle met her like a warm caress on a chilly night. She tingled as it wrapped itself around her.

"We're not. They will learn that they despise the enemy more than each other when the time comes."

"Can that time come now?"

Von ran a hand along the length of her braid, tugging slightly when he got to the bottom. *"Perhaps they simply require some inspiration."*

Helena worried at her bottom lip as she thought on his words. *What sort of inspiration would suffice? Surely not another speech. Words didn't seem to have a lasting effect on them.*

Von carefully extracted her bottom lip from her teeth, using his thumb to stroke it. *"You distract me when you do that."*

She looked up at him through her lashes, smiling cheekily at the hunger burning in his eyes. *"And you distract me when you look at me like that, so stop it."*

"You first."

Helena stuck her tongue out at him.

"Not helping..."

Helena bit back a smile as she moved away from her Mate and toward her Shield. For what she had in mind, it didn't seem right to act without informing the Commander of her intention. She waited for him to finish correcting the maneuver of another group and waved him over.

Ronan had pulled his hair into a knot on the top of his head. Loose tendrils were stuck to his cheeks and neck, giving the appearance of bright streaks of blood across his tanned skin. Helena shuddered, focusing on his eyes to rid herself of the image.

He wiped sweat off his forehead with the back of his arm as he greeted her. "Hellion."

"I have an idea."

Ronan raised a brow. "Can it wait until after practice? Today is our last chance to get this right."

She glared at him. "It's about practice, you ass."

He winked at her. "Oh, well. In that case, do tell."

Helena rose up on her toes and whispered her plan into his ear. He looked at her in surprise before he said, "Mother's tits, that's devious and fucking brilliant. Why didn't I think of that before?"

She shrugged.

"By all means, go for it." He grinned with anticipation as he gestured for her to proceed.

"Should we give them warning first?" she asked as she considered how they might react.

Ronan folded his arms. "Part of being the army is being ready at all times. They cannot expect the enemy to politely tap them on the shoulder and say 'how-do' before they attack. Practice should be no different if they are to actually learn from it."

Helena couldn't help but agree with his assessment. You were never really ready for a battle until you were already in the thick of it and even then, ready wasn't exactly the word she would use.

"Here goes nothing. Let us hope they rise to the occasion. And that nobody dies," she added as an afterthought.

"That's all we can ever hope for." Ronan chuckled.

"True," she agreed before unleashing unholy hell amongst the lot of them.

BY THE TIME Helena was done, what had once been a brilliantly beautiful afternoon in Daejara was now under siege by thick roiling clouds and huge cracks of lightning. The storm was furious, but that was not the major concern at the moment.

Running at their army from every direction were dozens of skeletal Shadows. Their vacant snaking eyes and gaping mouths just as gruesome as the real thing. Since coming up with her plan for Rowena's party, Helena had been practicing casting mass illusions. Given the terrified sobs of the cowering girl before her, she would have to say she was getting better.

There was certainly nothing fake about the screams that met her ears as Helena and her Circle moved away from the chaos her magic had created. If the troops wanted to get out of this in one piece, they would have to work together. There'd be no help from any of their leaders.

Helena would have loved to say that the group came together seamlessly, but that was not remotely the case. All of Ronan's drills may as well have been instructions on etiquette at a tea party for all the effect they seemed to have. Before her, the Storm Forged, Night Stalkers and Chosen fought like three separate entities, which they technically were. The problem was that the conflicting styles were actively working against each other instead of complimenting each other.

The goal was for the Storm Forged to control the weather, using it to help conceal the Night Stalkers and the various groups of Chosen to help them evade notice. The Night Stalkers were supposed to extend their shadow cover to further assist the Chosen while they snuck up and attacked. But none of those things were happening.

The Chosen seemed to have entirely forgotten that there was a plan. They made absolutely no attempts to maneuver within the confines of Night Stalkers' or Storm Forged's concealments. Instead, they were running full out at the beasts, hurling their weapons or balls of power at the Shadows, and generally making beautiful targets for the Shadows to easily dispatch. Not that anyone was actually harmed. As part of her spell, Helena wove in a stun effect that held the person immobile if the Shadow made what would have been a killing blow, rendering them incapable of continuing the drill.

When more than half of the army was frozen in place, Helena let out a disgusted scream. "Enough!" With a flick of her wrist, the illusions vanished, but she held onto the storm, letting it rage above them as if contained by an invisible barrier while she retained the immobilization, wanting the lesson to sink in along with their failure.

"Is this a game to you?" she hissed, her voice echoing with the effects of her storm.

The people blanched. No one had ever seen her anger directed at them like this before.

Her Circle moved into place behind her, and Helena knew without looking that their expressions of displeasure were likely mirrors of her own. Anduin and Reyna moved to stand with her without hesitation, showing with the movement that they recognized and yielded to her authority, both leaders in sync for the first time since their arrival in Daejara.

One of the men that had not been hit by a Shadow snickered, thinking that her words were not meant for him. Helena lashed out, using Air to create a hand that gripped him at his ankle and pulled, causing him to fall hard on his ass. Those around him were too stunned to laugh.

"Is your pride worth more than your life? Than the lives of those around you? Are you so naïve that you truly believe your way is the right and only way to defeat our enemy?"

Her words rang about the field, the silence and humiliation of the troops absolute. For all their attempts, not one of them had brought down a single Shadow.

"No, Kiri," a girl whispered, her voice carrying in the silence.

"Are you sure? Because based on what I just saw, not one of you gives a damn who wins this war. Should we give up now and save ourselves the effort?"

"No, Kiri," more voices called out, growing stronger with their conviction.

"Prove it," she roared, releasing her hold on the storm and the people giving them only a heartbeat to stand as the Shadows flared back into being.

This time the groups worked together, and while it was not perfect, it was a start.

"This will be a lesson they won't soon forget," Reyna murmured thoughtfully as she watched yet another of her Night Stalkers get stunned.

"I wanted to make a point."

"Oh, you did," Anduin said. "One with a very sharp edge."

"Death would be the best they can hope for if they don't learn this lesson," Ronan added.

"If Rowena wins, death would be a mercy."

Helena's words caused Reyna to visibly shudder. "I will continue to work with the Night Stalkers. They will not disappoint you again."

"And I with the Storm Forged."

It took over an hour for the group to best half of Helena's Shadows. Even then more than half of the group had been stunned. Feeling merciless, Helena merely snapped and shouted, "Again!"

After three more attempts, the groups were finally working together, able to coordinate their attacks to best subdue and attack the Shadows without suffering any casualties. It took them less than an hour to finally take down all twenty-five of the illusions.

When they were done, Helena's army panted and shook with exhaustion. She had a feeling that no one would complain about what a demanding Commander her Shield was again. She'd just proven she was far worse. Hopefully, they'd all live long enough to complain about it.

"Or thank you for it," Von added, picking up on her thoughts.

She looked at him over her shoulder and smiled slightly. *"Somehow I doubt anyone ever remembers that part."*

"As the one who is usually in your position, I can confirm the accuracy of the statement. However, you do not need them to thank you for being demanding in your training. Or right about its necessity. Take comfort in each and every heart that still beats at the end of the war."

Helena nodded, her smile grim. *"I will."*

Ronan moved to her side with a whistle as they watched the troops disperse for showers and a hot meal. "I think you just put me out of a job."

She snickered. "Hardly. The last thing I want to do is wake up at ungodly hours of the morning to have people run drills."

Ronan laughed, but the amusement faded from his voice when he spoke. "You've just proven that you can prepare them in ways I never even thought of. They learned more from you today than they have from me in days of practice."

"They would have failed if not for those days of practice."

"They did fail," Ronan pointed out.

"Only because they refused to follow your commands. Once they did, they were successful."

Ronan was silent while he considered her words. "I suppose you're right."

"Of course, I am."

He raised an eyebrow but grinned when he saw that she was laughing.

"Perhaps you can just stop by every now and then and put them in their place?"

"Isn't that what I always do?" she teased.

Ronan let out a loud bark of laughter that had the rest of the Circle looking toward them. "I'll be damned. You totally do."

She winked at him, leaning over to whisper conspiratorially, "Don't tell Von, but I learned it from you."

"I heard that."

"Of course, you did. But he needed the compliment more than you did."

She felt Von's mental shrug. *"I'm not worried, Mira. If you learned it from him, it's only because he learned it from me."*

55

Helena shook her head, his twisted male logic making her laugh. *"It's always a competition with you two."*

"Oh, it's no competition."

She rolled her eyes, amused despite herself. *"If you say so."*

"Do you think we're ready?" Reyna asked, her husky voice uncharacteristically subdued.

Helena shifted focus, turning to look fully at the other woman. "As ready as we can be given the time constraints that we're under."

Reyna frowned but nodded. "We still have a few days before the party."

"True, but we will be trying to move into place undetected. Many of us will be separated. There will not be time to practice all together like this again."

"No, but that does not mean they cannot continue to run their Commander's drills on their own." Her gaze flit to Ronan for confirmation.

"Only if it is safe to do so. We cannot risk detection," he replied.

Reyna nodded her agreement.

"The Storm Forged can help with that. I will ensure it," Anduin offered.

Reyna looked up at him in surprise. "We will be glad of the assistance," she replied.

Anduin held out a hand. "I apologize that our people got off on the wrong foot. I hope that there is still a chance for friendship between us."

Reyna was slower to offer her hand, but she took his and nodded. "As do I, Stormbringer."

With that Anduin walked away, leaving Helena, Reyna, Ronan, and Von still standing in the clearing.

"Well, well, Hellion. It looks like you are a miracle worker after all," Ronan said.

"After everything she's done, *that's* the miracle?" Von asked.

"You know better than anyone the harm that years of prejudice can cause. They are almost impossible to bridge."

Von nodded. "Aye, I do."

"All Helena had to do was whip everyone's ass and prove that they were ignorant fools, and now they want to make nice."

"Is that what I did?"

"What would you call it?" Ronan challenged.

"I..." she paused, shrugging. "Practice?"

Her friends laughed.

"Whatever you want to call it, it was an important first step toward victory. We knew that we could not defeat Rowena on our own. Now you have an army that is willing to work together. If nothing else, I'll drink to that," Ronan said, as they began slowly walking back toward the house.

"And I," Von agreed.

Helena smiled, feeling more relieved than she had in months. "I suppose you're right. That is worth celebrating."

"Care to repeat that?" Ronan asked, holding up a hand to his ear.

Helena punched him in the shoulder. "If you missed it, it was your fault you weren't paying attention."

Reyna snickered.

"Hey now, don't go taking her side."

"Who said I was on your side to begin with?" Reyna asked, arching her brow.

Ronan gave her a dark look and shook his head. "You think you know a girl."

Reyna wove her arm through his, pulling him in the direction of the kitchens. "Come now, let me mend your wounded ego with a glass of ale."

"It's like you know me," Ronan said, placing a hand to his heart.

"Or the quickest way to earn a man's forgiveness, at the very least."

"I can think of better ways," Ronan said with a wink.

They continued to bicker playfully as they walked. Von and Helena watched them in silence, turning to one another once they were alone.

"Do you really think it will help?" she asked, finally letting the fear and doubt she'd been trying to hide show to the only person who would understand.

Von placed both of his hands on her shoulders. "I do, *Mira*. A group that bands together will always be stronger than one that does not." He took her hand and lifted it so that it was in front of her face. Wiggling her fingers, he said, "A hand can cause harm like this, but it does much more damage when it strikes like this." As he said it, he balled her hand into a fist. "You have taught them to strike as one. They will be more powerful because of it."

"Then let us hope they remember that when the time comes."

"They will," Von said confidently.

"How can you be so sure?"

His eyes glowed as he said, "You reminded them what their failure meant. They had to watch, over and over, as their friends fell in battle. It will haunt them."

"I didn't mean—"

He cut her off. "It was an important lesson, Helena. One you should never feel guilty for. You saved lives today."

She took a deep breath, letting his words soothe the part of her that could still hear the cries of fear. Some of their party were seasoned warriors, but many in their ranks had never seen a battle firsthand. Not at this scale. They had been safely tucked away living in relative peace their entire lives. Ronan's lessons had not sunk in, because they had not fully understood the importance of what he was trying to teach them.

Now they did.

When she thought of it that way, she much preferred that she was the one causing the nightmares rather than Rowena. Because at least if it was her, they were all still alive.

CHAPTER 7

"*I*t begins."

The three robed figures stood at the edge of a cliff overlooking the twisted stone that made up Greyspire. Their hoods were lowered as they stared down at the snow-covered fortress. Wind whipped at their cloaks, revealing the snaking navy runes that pulsed and moved along their skin.

"It is yet another step down a long and arduous path."

"The outcome will be telling."

"She cannot go back now."

"She never could."

"The choice was made long before she entered this world."

The central figure lifted a skeletal arm and pointed in the direction of the forest. *"The Vessel is near."*

The men on either side tilted their faces up, the pits of their eyes staring vacantly up into the glittering night sky.

"So much power."

"It tastes so sweet."

"Pure."

"For now."

They lowered their chins and turned their faces to look in the direction of the forest, as if they could see the woman of whom they spoke. Perhaps they could.

"The darkness swells around her."

"A storm about to strike."

"Ready to devour us all."

"She sits at its heart."

As one, they took a step back from the cliff, moving out of sight. Before they faded into the cavern at their backs, the central figure stopped and sniffed the air.

"Our daughter will be joining us soon."

The others turned, the gesture sharp, indicating surprise at the announcement.

"You are certain?"

"There is no doubt."

"That is joyous news indeed."

"Shall we stay awhile longer to greet her?"

"No. This is not the place for it."

The men nodded, and the trio disappeared into the inky darkness.

"THAT'S THE LAST OF THEM," Von said.

Helena eyed the newest arrivals, wincing in sympathy as some immediately hunched over and began to empty out the contents of their stomachs. Travel by Kaelpas stone was certainly not for everyone, and the first time was especially difficult.

"Have we heard word from the others that they are also in place?"

Von dipped his chin. "Aye."

Helena took a deep breath, letting the wintery pine scent fill her lungs and settle her. The weather here was so different from Daejara. Usually a trip like this would take weeks, so a person had time to adjust to the change in temperature, but only moments ago she had been in Daejara's much more temperate clime.

She shivered at the frostbitten air. "I forgot how cold it was here."

"You were a bit preoccupied last time."

Her lips quirked up. "To say the least."

Von frowned as he stared at the castle. "I do not like that you are going back in there without me."

Helena's heart twisted in her chest. She didn't like it either, but she needed him handling things out here. Their bond gave her a direct line of communication to what was happening outside and would allow her to signal them when it was time to strike. There was no one else who could relay the message for her.

The castle was still, there was no hint that a party was already underway inside.

"Tell me again that this will work," she pleaded, using the bond so that no one else would hear her uncertainty. Right now they needed her to be fearless, even though that was the last thing she was feeling.

Von ran a hand along her back, moving it to wrap around her hips and pull her back to him. He rested his cheek along the top of her head. *"I cannot promise we will not fail. No one can. But if we are to fail, we will take down every last one of them on our way."*

"Your pep talk could use some work."

He chuckled. *"Would you rather I lied?"*

"No," she said honestly, sighing.

"We are as ready as we can be."

Helena nodded, her expression grim. She was not afraid to face Rowena, the heartless bitch certainly had it coming. She'd taken enough from Helena. First Von, then Anderson, and finally Darrin. The time to repay her cruelty was more than overdue. It was the thought of having to say goodbye to more people she loved that had her stomach twisted in knots.

Her mind ran through the plan one final time. Everyone knew their roles. She'd split up the Circle so that at least one or two members were paired and overseeing a portion of the army. Reyna, Ryder, and seven others in her contingent would be joining Helena, along with Kragen. No one in the Circle was willing to budge on that point. They would not send their Kiri into Rowena's trap without at least one of them by her side. With Von needed outside and Ronan leading the main charge, her Sword was the obvious choice.

Von would be stationed on the nearby cliffs with Starshine and the rest of the Talyrian pride awaiting Helena's signal. Ronan's melee force would be hiding in plain sight, Anduin and Reyna's people concealing them with a combination of their unique abilities. The sheer number of people Anduin and Reyna's forces were concealing was beyond impressive. Ronan, Nial, Serena, Effie, and the rest of the Chosen and Forsaken fighting force had already begun to move into place so they would be ready when Von took to the skies. Helena knew where everyone was situated, but even still, she could not make out any sign of them amongst the snowy banks leading up to the castle.

Timmins and Joquil would be staying in the forest and heading up the ranged team. They would remain hidden until the battle began, supporting the fighters with their magic to help pick off any of the outlying threats. Miranda and the Etillions were with them, their skills more suited to ranged attacks than hand-to-hand combat.

"Everyone seems to be in place, I guess that means it's time for me to do the same."

Von remained silent behind her, his concern and love washing over her in a soothing wave. She curled into his embrace, laying her head on his shoulder and feeling his heart beat in time with hers. The world fell away. The Talyrians' snarls, the nervous chatter, the call of the birds. For a series of heartbeats, the only people in that forest were her and her Mate. There were no words to say, the bond making speech unnecessary. Hope. Fear. Love. It was all there swelling around them.

Helena forced herself to step away, knowing she had to be the one to make the first move. Von would never willingly walk away from her. Not after everything they'd been through. His eyes bore into hers, flaring gold as the intensity of his emotion took over.

"I'll be waiting for you in the sky, my love."

"Don't have too much fun without me, Mate."

"I could never." He smiled, but it didn't reach his eyes.

Helena leaned forward and pressed a fast kiss to his stubbled cheek. Tears made her eyes blur, so she spun away and all but ran toward the spot where Reyna was waiting for her. As she passed Midnight, she stopped and looked the massive cat dead in the eye.

"If you let anything happen to him while you're up there, I will geld you myself."

The Talyrian snarled at her and backed away.

Her eyes moved to Starshine. "Keep them safe for me, beautiful girl. If all goes well, I'll be joining you soon."

Starshine pressed into her, the peaty smell of fire and smoke filling her nose as the velvety fur rubbed against her skin.

"Let's go," she said thickly, not pausing to wait and see if she was followed, and not sure why leaving them felt so much like saying goodbye.

The others fell in line behind her, moving away from those that were staying behind. When they were a good distance away and not yet in sight of the castle, Helena called her power up. It rose quickly, greeting her like an old friend.

Illusion magic was a complicated blend of Spirit, Water, and Air. The power that rose felt like being submerged in a warm pool of water. She let it flow along her skin, feeling the subtle changes of her body as the transformation took place. Once it was complete, she pushed it out, watching as it washed over the rest of the party. *Smoke and mirrors,* she thought. She could see the bodies standing before her, but her eyes felt the pull to look away. Strong magic indeed, if even she was affected by its lure.

With a little bit of effort, she was able to fight the pull and focus on her friends. There was nothing specific that had changed about them, although it did appear as though their faces were slightly blurred and their dark attire was hazy at the edges, as if their bodies were trying to blend in with the forest around them. With one final pulse of magic, Helena made subtle changes to their clothing, turning their leather armor into more appropriate party wear.

Pleased with the results, she nodded and turned her attention back to herself. While none of them would be attending the party as themselves, the role she had to play required that she stand out a bit more than the others, which meant that she needed to take slightly more effort on her appearance.

As she released a breath, Helena ran her hands along her body, feeling her fighting leathers transform into a satin dress the color of midnight. It hugged her body, swishing as she moved. The top was a fitted corset, the bodice staying tight until just below her hips, where it flared out in black waves to the floor. To enhance the air of mystery, she added a netted veil that attached to a small feathered headpiece and obscured her face. She knew that they would receive masks once they were inside, but she didn't want to take any chances that someone would be able to see through the illusion and recognize her.

When she was done, she could feel nine sets of eyes on her. She looked up, wondering if something was amiss with her disguise.

"Von is going to kill me," Kragen declared.

Reyna whistled. "If discretion is your plan, you've chosen the wrong dress. I have never had a preference for women, but you're giving me ideas."

Helena laughed, color rising to her cheeks at the comments. "Let us hope no one feels the need to get too handsy."

"We will be nearby ready to relieve anyone of the offending limbs if they try, Kiri," Reyna promised.

Helena moved into position in front of them, the constriction of her dress making her usually long strides slow, while the hidden slits gave teasing glimpses of creamy skin as she walked. The flash of light against the dark material made her think of moonlight shining through the clouds.

Kragen looked up to the night sky, his calloused hand running over his bald head. "He might as well kill me now and get it over with."

Helena spared him a glance over her shoulder. "Don't forget who you serve, Sword. You have more to fear from me than him."

"That's what you think. When it comes to protecting you, he is more fearsome by half."

Helena smiled. He wasn't wrong.

"All right everyone, it's time to enter the viper's nest. Keep your eyes open and stay close to your partner. No one goes anywhere alone."

The others moved into position around her, and as one, they made their way up the path to the castle doors.

CHAPTER 8

*T*he shadow of Greyspire loomed over them, casting them in total darkness as they stood before the massive door. Helena lifted a hand to knock, but there wasn't a chance before it swung open on silent hinges.

Helena peered inside, expecting the foyer to be well-lit considering they were supposed to be some of only hundreds of guests that were in attendance, but she was wrong. There were only a few candelabras placed randomly throughout the room, their flickering reflections casting pools of light on the black stone floor. She shuddered, feeling like she was walking into a cave. Or a tomb.

"Lovely," Reyna murmured, her voice pitched low so that only Helena could hear it.

Remembering that she was not alone helped strengthen her resolve. She moved deeper into the chamber, barely recognizing it from her brief time here before.

Just as she started to wonder where they were supposed to go, a pale-faced boy appeared before them. His hair was almost as pale as his skin, giving him the appearance of a ghost. He kept his eyes downcast, not speaking, merely waiting for them all to gather in the entryway before motioning for them to follow. He led them slowly, seeming to float down the winding halls like a miniature specter as they made their way to the ballroom.

"Mother's tits, he's a creepy little fucker," Kragen said. She heard one of the others muffle their amusement. She didn't disagree.

Helena began to hear the haunting strains of music as they got closer. Fear danced up her spine at the sound. The sounds were harsh and sharp, a cacophonous melody that had the hairs lifting on her arms. This was not a joyous occasion but some macabre imitation of one. Helena let her eyes fall briefly closed. Everything was a distraction, all with the intention of ensnaring her so Rowena could strike. She could not allow herself to react. She let out a breath and opened her eyes.

The boy had stopped just outside of two blood-red doors. They were the only sign of color since entering the castle and Helena did not think that was a coincidence. There was no life here, only death and bloodshed. With a gentle shove, the boy pushed the doors, open spilling light and more music into the hall.

Helena flinched at the noise. The music sounded more like wailing cats than anything she would want to dance to. She risked a glance to her left, sharing a look with Kragen before stepping into the ballroom.

Nothing would have prepared her for the sight that greeted her. The ballroom was full of swaying bodies, with lavish masks and headdresses obscuring their identities. Helena was shocked by the sheer number of people in attendance. She had assumed there would be a significant number, but nothing close to the amount of people that were present. *Who are they? Where had they come from?*

Helena grabbed a random mask and took a moment to scan the room, trying to get her bearings. The monochromatic theme from the rest of the castle was echoed throughout, although splashes of deep violet and red did adorn a few of the guests' outfits and broke up the black. Each person had a unique mask that seemed to resemble a creature, although no one remained still long enough for Helena to identify any of them with certainty. A couple moved past her, giving Helena a brief glimpse of feathers and fangs. Macabruls perhaps, although why anyone would want to be one of those dastardly beasts, she could only hazard a guess.

Those that were not dancing stood along the sides of the room talking or engaging in other more intimate displays of affection. The public demonstrations were unlike anything she'd witnessed before. *Where am I?*

Helena's eyes lifted, noting the massive black crystal chandelier hanging in the center of the room, where it glittered like the darkest of night stars. Just beyond the sparkling monstrosity, sitting on a throne of twisted metal was a woman swathed in black. *Rowena.*

Her mask completely concealed her hair, its twisting horns adorned with ropes of expensive jewels. Icy eyes were all but invisible behind the lace and leather masterpiece. Her lips were an unsmiling ruby slash against pale skin. She stood suddenly, moving to stand at the center of the dais. Her dress rippled as it fell to the floor, it looked like liquid night, reflecting the candlelight that blazed about the room.

A man approached her, his mask similar in shape, although much less extravagant than Rowena's, the horns curling down and back instead of up and out. If one could show submission via headpiece, that was certainly the way. He lifted a feathered cloak from her shoulders, the feathers having created an elaborate fan behind her masked head before they began to lay flat against the rest of the cloth.

Without the cloak, her shoulders and neck were bare, save for the egg-sized pendant that hung above her breasts. Helena's breath caught. It was a pendant, so like hers, but it was white with snaking black lines. She shuddered, the similarity between it and the Shadows' eyes certainly no coincidence.

Rowena lifted her arms and the music came to a sudden stop. Helena and her friends moved to the sides of the room, trying to blend in with the others.

"What a perfect evening for a celebration. I can think of no better time to share my joyous news with you."

Helena stiffened. Whatever brought Rowena joy could hardly be considered a good thing.

The man had set down her cloak while she spoke and had just returned to stand beside her.

"Vyruul is pleased to welcome its newest citizens. Endoshan has proven itself to be as wise as it is mighty when it sought to combine its legacy with ours."

There were a few sporadic cheers throughout the room.

Endoshan? But they are all dead... aren't they? Helena reached for Kragen's hand, squeezing hard to convey her confused disbelief.

That was when the man spoke and fury pure and potent began to boil in her blood.

"Endoshan is singularly blessed to have you agree to join hands with us, not only in partnership, but in marriage."

Helena recognized his smug voice. It was the Endoshan heir. *What have you done?* She wanted to scream, but there was no point. The evidence was irrefutable. Rather than fight, he'd tied the fate of himself and his people to Rowena. Classic power move. The idiot clearly had no idea who he'd just tied himself to. Rowena was more likely to rip his head off than share one iota of her power with him.

"The papers were signed this morning. The deed is done!"

The crowd cheered again.

Helena began to shake with the power of her fury. What a mockery! This was no love-match. This was the desperate attempt of a man who didn't want to be second to a woman. *If he only knew...*

"Let us go into this new era together as equals. Vyruul, meet your King, my Consort, Kai-Soren!"

Behind her, Kragen snarled.

"What should we do, Kiri?" Reyna asked.

"Nothing yet," Helena grit out behind clenched teeth.

"Is this what she wanted you to see?" one of the Night Stalkers asked quietly.

Helena gave a quick nod. "It is probably just the first of many blows she hoped to land."

They shifted uneasily behind her, everyone aware that Endoshan's betrayal was indeed a massive blow. *If they surrendered to Rowena, are there others?* Helena tried to keep her thoughts from spiraling. Now was not the time to go down that particular rabbit hole.

"We have work to do," she said, pulling everyone's focus back to their mission.

With a subtle nod, pairs began to break off from the group. Their mission was to see what they could learn. If they found any of Rowena's Generals, they were to alert Helena immediately so that they could try to neutralize them. In a matter of seconds, Kragen and Helena were alone.

"Shall we dance?" he asked in a mild tone.

Helena gave a stiff nod. Dancing was the last thing she felt like doing. It would be almost impossible to fake the enthusiasm required to blend in with the others. But she would do it, because she had to. It was the only inconspicuous way to get closer to Rowena.

Her part of the plan was deceptively simple. Stay close to Rowena without getting caught while the others find and isolate the Generals. Each team would work on quickly dispatching their General, utilizing the Night Stalkers unique ability to sneak up on their targets. Helena wasn't certain how Rowena would react if they were successful, namely if she would be able to feel when one of her men was snuffed out. It was why the goal was to identify first. If they could coordinate an attack on at least four of the Generals at once, it would cripple Rowena's most powerful warriors and give them a complete advantage, even if Rowena immediately reacted. Assuming she could tell, Helena would be nearby to strike. If she didn't, the pairs were to locate the final General and take him out.

Once the Generals were handled, Helena would send the signal to Von to begin the attack outside. Without her Generals, Rowena would be thrown into chaos once the attack started, allowing the Chosen army to make a—hopefully—massive dent in Rowena's numbers.

That was, of course, assuming everything went perfectly. Helena was an optimist, but she wasn't naïve. Not anymore. She had Rowena to thank for that. It was a gift she actually appreciated. Which was why there was a contingency plan. One she fervently hoped they wouldn't need.

"Just don't step on my feet," she muttered as she took his hand and let him pull her into the crowd of bodies on the dance floor.

He scoffed. "Clearly you've never seen me dance, K—" he stopped before he uttered her title, shooting her an apologetic glance.

Helena thought back. "No, I don't think I ever have."

Kragen grinned down before grasping her wrist and executing a complex spin. Helena stared at him with wide eyes as they came back together.

"Just a different type of footwork," he said by way of explanation.

"And set to music," she pointed out.

He flashed her another grin and they fell silent, both turning their focus back to the present. Her eyes moved about the room, checking to see if any of the others had found their targets. A disappointed shake of Ryder's head left her frowning. It didn't appear that luck was on their side. Not one of the Generals seemed to be in attendance.

Where is she hiding them?

Kragen and Helena had finally gotten close to the dais. Rowena and Kai-Soren were speaking in hushed tones, their heads dipped in toward the other. Helena silently wished that the horns of their masks caught and tangled. She would have loved to see them try to work themselves free.

Minutes began to pass swiftly, making Helena grow anxious. So much rode on their ability to locate the Generals. Kragen and Helena danced to two more songs, before Helena finally pulled him off to the side near a table of refreshments. Not that she had any intention of imbibing anything Rowena had on offer.

Noting her maneuver, Reyna and Ryder closed in.

"If we can't go to them, we need to make them come to us. It's time for Plan B."

Reyna and Ryder nodded, before slipping back into the crowd to warn the others.

"Are you sure about this?" Kragen asked, a touch of concern coloring his voice.

Helena nodded, her eyes going iridescent. There was only one surefire way she could think of to draw those creepy bastards out.

Von is going to kill me once he finds out about this, she thought just as mayhem erupted in the ballroom.

CHAPTER 9

This time when Helena released her magic, it was not so quick to rise. She could feel it there, but it responded more like honey dripping off a spoon than water falling from a cliff. It was clear that she was starting to feel the strain of using so much power so quickly. Usually when she channeled this much magic, it was in short bursts, but she'd already been holding on to ten different illusions for well over an hour, and she was about to add two more.

Helena narrowed her eyes, zeroing in on the feather and fanged couple she'd noted when they first arrived. *They'll do.* She bit down hard on her lip to use the pain as a focus. It gave her the push she needed. Her magic shot out, the illusion falling over the couple like a shimmering curtain. It was a moment before anyone realized what she'd done, but a few startled shouts had heads turning quickly enough.

"My Queen, I see her!"

"It's the Kiri and her Mate!"

"Grab her!"

"Bar the doors, do not let them get away!"

The last insistent shout was none other than Rowena herself.

A mob formed and rushed at the confused couple who was furiously protesting the attention. "M-My Queen," the woman wailed, her arms lifted as if to protect her face from the clawed hands that sought to grab her.

The man beside her tried to squirm away, thinking only to protect himself.

"This won't do," Helena murmured, and Kragen grunted in agreement.

Helena needed the crowd to believe that this couple was, in fact, her and her Mate. She needed the doubles to play along just long enough that Rowena's Generals would come running for Reyna's people to intercept.

Not knowing what else to do, Helena attempted something that she had never consciously tried before. She turned her glittering eyes to the woman who was her twin. With every heartbeat, she pushed her will toward the woman. *You are the Kiri. That woman is your enemy. You do not fear her.* The false Helena's aqua eyes glazed over, and her expression and posture calmed.

"I do not fear you!" she shouted.

The crowd hissed at her.

"Because you are nothing more than a vapid little girl."

Rowena's statement was met by the crowd's cruel laughter. Fake Helena scowled.

"Is that really what I look like when I'm annoyed?" Helena asked Kragen in a low voice, momentarily distracted by her mirror-image.

Kragen chuckled but did not deign to answer the question. "Focus."

Helena took a deep breath and turned her attention onto the absolutely worthless excuse of a Mate who was frantically clawing at the door. *She is your Mate. It is your duty to protect her. Her life means more to you than your own.* This one was harder to convince. The man fought against her persuasion, his selfishness helping him resist the compulsion. *If she dies, you're next.* That did it. Suddenly, Von's twin spun around, roaring at the crowd.

"If you so much as touch her, I will have your heads!"

Helena fought a giggle. It was a Von thing to say, but somehow, he never looked quite so constipated when he was threatening people. It was as if the words were so foreign the man wasn't entirely sure of their meaning. She was willing to bet he'd never actually threatened anyone in his life. Or had to wield a weapon.

Helena sighed. She had chosen her targets on convenience, not talent. Given what she had to work with, and the fact that none of these people actually knew her or her Mate, her doubles were still effective. Even so, she made a mental note to check for temperament the next time she needed a realistic impersonator. These two would never get past a single member of her Circle.

Rowena lifted both her hands, her lips lifting in a smile too cold to be anything but threatening. "Perhaps we got off on the wrong foot. The Kiri and her Mate are my guests."

More snide laughter met the words, and Helena felt her eyes narrow with suspicion as she eyed the people around her. The crowd already knew what Rowena had planned, and they were eager to witness it.

Rowena continued to speak in a deceptively conversational tone, "Although I am surprised you didn't bring the rest of your Circle. They do seem to follow you like dogs after a bitch in heat."

Kragen growled low in his throat, his hands clenched into fists at his sides. Helena brushed her fingers along his arm, not needing her Jaka to feel the violence radiating off him. A shudder raced down his arm at the contact, his temper not easily calmed even with the silent reminder from his Kiri.

The fake Kiri smiled sweetly, not phased at all by the slight. *Good girl,* Helena thought, sending another suggestion her way. When the double spoke, it was with Helena's words. "Thankfully when they feel like a cuddle, I don't have to swallow the vomit induced by their stench. You should really consider putting your beasts down, they just don't look at all healthy. I mean, how can they be when they serve you? Oh right, they don't have a choice. I guess when the only people that willingly serve you are mindless corpses you have to make do."

The smile fell from Rowena's crimson lips long before fake Helena finished speaking. From where she stood, Helena could see a vein begin to pulse in Rowena's temple. The moment stretched on, but Rowena finally broke the silence with a tinkling laugh that sounded more like shards of glass hitting the floor than anything resembling true amusement.

"I think my pets have more than proven their use to me. If your Shield were still alive, he'd certainly agree, don't you think?"

The barb struck true. Helena's control slipped, her fury rolling off her in a tidal wave of power that caused those standing near her to falter and the floor to quake.

Heads spun toward where Helena and Kragen were standing with shock.

"Fuck," Kragen muttered, instinctively reaching for a weapon that wasn't there.

Helena regained control quickly, prompting her double to pull attention back toward her.

"Don't you dare speak of him unless you'd like me to return the favor with another of your pawns!"

The ruse worked. The crowd believed that the double had purposefully targeted that area of the room with "her" power, and the real Kiri and Kragen remained undiscovered. Sweat dripped down Helena's spine, her emotions not entirely settled. Darrin's death was an emotional wound that had yet to fully heal, if it ever would. Having Rowena so callously refer to it was a blow she could not protect herself against. That still did not mean she could allow herself to be swayed off course so easily.

"Perhaps it's time to begin tonight's entertainment."

Both Helena and her double's brows lowered over suspicious eyes. Whatever Rowena thought entertaining was surely anything but.

"Brace yourself," Kragen said.

"You as well," she replied.

For their part, the doubles remained silent while the crowd broke out into excited chatter that did little to reassure Helena.

"Do you think Reyna has found them yet?" Kragen whispered, eager to get away from the overzealous crowd.

Helena shook her head; there was no way to know until the Night Stalker found a way back into the room.

The sound of a door opening pulled everyone's attention to the dais. Two servants clad entirely in black brought in a child that was visibly trembling.

"Is that—" Kragen started to ask.

"That bitch," she seethed before he could finish the question. It was the child that had shown them into the ballroom. Helena knew then that Rowena had purposely given the boy that duty so that Helena would recognize him in this moment.

"Bring him to me," Rowena purred.

Helena and Kragen watched with wide, horror-filled eyes as the sobbing child was dragged to a slightly elevated platform just beside Rowena.

"Let me show you what my so-called corpses do for me," Rowena taunted, her colorless eyes staring down Helena's twin.

There wasn't time to draw in a breath before Rowena unleashed her power, the tainted Spirit magic twisting from her hand straight into the chest of the little boy. His back arched on a soundless cry as Rowena's mouth fell open and she began to feed off his essence. There was no other way to describe it. Within seconds of her power hitting him, the boy began to emit a dull white glow that Rowena quickly inhaled. The more of the glow that Rowena took in, the slower the boy's movements became until all he could manage were a few sluggish twitches of his fingers.

Nausea had Helena's stomach roiling. This was too far. No matter the plan, Helena could not stand by and watch while an innocent child was being tortured.

Rowena's head tilted back with a sexual moan of pleasure, and Helena snapped, losing hold of her disguise entirely. Shocked gasps filled the room at the sudden appearance of a second Kiri. Rowena's head flew back up, annoyance at the interruption clear in her sneer. Kai-Soren whispered something in her ear that had Rowena's head turning toward where they were standing.

"Helena," Kragen warned.

Power surged through Helena, her rage adding to her strength despite how much she'd already pushed herself. With minimal effort, Von and Helena doubles began to appear throughout the room. There were four new sets of imposters between one heartbeat and the next, and several others by the time she was done.

Rowena's eyes wildly scanned the room, trying to determine which of them was the real threat. "Kill them all!" she finally screamed.

Helena didn't waste any time. *"Now!"* she shouted to Von through the bond. Their window to gain the upper hand was rapidly closing, if they had any hope of salvaging this mission, they had to act now, Generals or not.

If he was surprised to hear the fear and fury in her psychic voice, he didn't comment on it. *"Get back to me, Mate,"* he ordered.

The doors flew open and Shadows began to pour into the ballroom, intermingling with the other partygoers. Helena didn't waste breath coordinating with Kragen. They'd already discussed their plan ad nauseam, and they'd fought together enough that they were already on the same page. Their first priority was to get out in one piece, but on the way, they were going to take out as many of their enemies as they could.

Throughout the ballroom, guests lunged at the various doubles, many of whom had no clue what was happening. Helena hadn't had a chance to establish any sort of enhanced connection like she had with the first duo. They tried to defend themselves against friends and family members that no longer recognized them, all while proclaiming their innocence.

Helena held no sympathy as she watched the first couple fall. Everyone in the room had stood by and watched as an innocent child had his life-essence drained from his body. They could all burn.

Not wanting to pull too much attention to themselves and the strength of their combined power, Kragen and Helena used a combination of fists and magic to clear a path as they moved toward the double doors in the back of the room. They worked together to make quick work of people who were clearly not fighters, their physical attacks rarely landing while the ones that did lacked any real power. Those that chose to rely on their magic lobbed colorful orbs that bounced off Kragen and Helena's shields only to fly back toward the attackers. Based on the complete lack of offensive and defensive skills, magical and otherwise, it was clear Rowena intended to use these people purely as fodder.

Helena spun to dodge another clumsy blow when she noticed the first of Rowena's Generals enter the room. Seeing where her eyes were focused, Kragen gave her a quick nod and used his bare hands to snap the neck of the person she'd just dodged. The lifeless body crumpled, but neither spared it a final glance as they stepped over it and toward the next person. Less of the partygoers were daring to approach the duo, sensing that they were the least easy of the targets.

Brawls were still taking place throughout the ballroom, all while the haunting music continued to play.

"I guess fighting can be set to music after all," Helena commented dryly, launching a ball of Fire at the closest Shadow.

Kragen grinned, picking up one of the candelabras to swing it into the face of another.

Helena's Shadow became a pillar of fire, its arms swinging wildly as it tried to extinguish the flames. It was a futile gesture. Her magical flames made quick work of the rotting flesh, but still the creature tried to save itself. Helena used Air to shove the burning Shadow into two others, knocking all three of them over in a pile of smoke and flame.

They were more than halfway to the door, still surrounded by hundreds of Rowena's guests. For her part, Rowena was throwing bolts of power into the crowd, not caring who they hit. Helena shook her head in disgust. The woman's callous disregard for life never ceased to amaze her. She valued nothing but power, everything else was simply a means to an end. Even the lives of her children.

Helena quickly scanned the room, her eyes searching for any sign of the Night Stalkers. Reyna and her people had to be close, especially with one of their targets finally in sight. Using him as her guide, Helena turned her focus back toward the General, who was busy launching acidic orbs toward the nearest of the doubles. Whatever the orbs made contact with immediately began to erode. As a result, there were massive smoking holes in the nearby floor and walls—not to mention the bodies—that were hit.

She called her power to her, preparing to neutralize him, when the air just beside the General seemed to ripple. If she'd have blinked, she would have missed the sight of Reyna's golden dagger cleanly slicing through his neck. The General blinked in shock before falling to the ground.

Reyna looked up, her face an impassive mask as her eyes found Helena's across the room. She shook her head, indicating that they had not found any of the others. Helena jerked her head toward the door, wordlessly communicating that it was time to go. Reyna turned into a blur as she complied.

So far they'd been lucky, and none of their group had been caught by Rowena's people, but they were pushing that luck each time they used their power. With one of Rowena's Generals removed, they'd gotten what they'd come for, at least to some degree.

Voices began to cry out as the battle raged on inside the ballroom.

"Greyspire is under attack!"

"The castle is ablaze, My Queen!"

"We are surrounded!"

Behind them, Rowena let out a blood curdling scream as she realized what had happened.

"It's time to go!" Helena shouted, gripping Kragen's arm as they set off at a dead run. "We need to get to the others."

They made for the door, hurdling over corpses and through the gaps in their race for the exit. Kragen used his bulk to smash into any obstacles, not allowing anyone or anything to slow them down. Helena followed close at his heels, sparing only a second to check behind her. What happened next felt like it happened in slow motion.

From her place on the dais, Rowena's eyes spotted the fleeing Helena. Her lips twisted in a snarl, and she threw an orb of pulsing black light at Helena. Helena tried to dodge but could not entirely escape the ball of corrupted power. She flew back, her body slamming into something hard. There was a loud crack and the feeling of liquid warmth rushing down her neck before the world turned black.

CHAPTER 10

"*N*ow!*" Even though Von had been waiting for the command, the sound of her panicked voice had adrenaline flooding his veins. The need to protect overwhelmed him, but he couldn't afford to distract her from whatever she was dealing with inside, so he did his best to rein it in.

"Get back to me, Mate!" He purposely used the tone he'd used with his men, the one that did not allow room for argument. He also gave the same order he'd have given any in his command: complete the mission and get back. It was a default mode that allowed him to focus on what he had to do, and not the mind-numbing fear he felt at the fact she had willingly walked back into that prison without him.

That was also the reason he'd used the title. It was a not-so-subtle reminder of her vow to him. She had promised him a life. Together. And he damn well intended to collect on that promise.

"Let's go!" he called in a loud whisper, knowing the Talyrians would hear him without problem.

He felt Midnight's muscles bunch and shift beneath him as the beast readied himself for flight. In less time than it took to draw in a breath, the Talyrian launched his powerful body into the air, his dark wings momentarily blocking the moon and throwing them all into darkness. They covered the distance from the cliffs to the castle quickly, Starshine's bright body acting as the beacon the others were waiting for as she flew close beside him.

The Talyrians were deadly predators, especially at night. The sound of their flapping wings almost entirely silent as they cut through the sky. Despite their size, and various coloring, their prey wouldn't know they were under attack until they felt the fiery breath of the Talyrian as it was upon them.

He loved his Daejaran Wolf, but there was nothing quite like flying through the sky on the back of such a powerful being. Between himself and Midnight, Von knew without a doubt that the Talyrian was the deadlier of them, and even his power paled in comparison to the Talyrian Queen. The fact that there were eight other Talyrians flying behind him filled him with confidence. The Shadows may have them beat in sheer numbers, but the Talyrians more than made up for that in raw power. It was a balanced fight at last.

They completed their circuit, the rest of the army now braced for what came next. Von channeled his rage, letting out a battle cry he knew would leave him hoarse for days after. Answering cries met his ears as the Chosen launched their attack. He recognized Ronan's deep growl, and even Effie's high-pitched shriek. All of them had lost something to this power-crazed bitch. It was time to return the favor.

The Talyrians roared, the combined sound so loud the windows of the castle rattled and shattered under the assault. Their fierce challenge was met instantly as bodies began to pour out of the castle.

Von stiffened in surprise. Even from his perch on Midnight, he could tell that those were not Shadows. The men moved with a precision that the Shadows' stumbling lurch, despite its speed, made impossible. Each new wave moved into position behind the front line, creating a wall that encircled the castle. For their part, Ronan's men remained cloaked by the Night Stalkers' and Storm Forged's combined efforts.

He nudged the Talyrian, signaling that he wanted to get closer. Midnight swooped down, breathing fire along the outer wall of the castle, causing it to go up in flames. The orange light cast an eerie glow on the field, but also helped Von notice what he'd missed.

Von hissed, outrage lifting his lip in a silent snarl. Endoshans. Their unique fighting leathers and curved blades were the only proof he needed of their betrayal. He wished for Helena's abilities then, wanting to rain down fire upon the backstabbing traitors. Sensing his desire, Midnight roared before aiming a jet of flame toward the closest of the Endoshans.

That was all Ronan's men needed. The Endoshans shouted in surprise as the Forsaken released their hold on their magic and thousands of the Chosen took shape before them. It was not long before the sounds of war met his ears.

The screams of the Endoshans were silenced only by the roar of the Talyrians and their resulting death. Nothing had prepared them for this battle. Outmanned and outnumbered, the Endoshans refused to retreat even as waves of their brothers were lost to Talyrian flame. They were warriors; casualties were expected. The Endoshans regrouped, pressing together as they faced off with the Chosen army.

One of the Endoshan's silver blades sliced through a Storm Forged's armor. The woman fell to her knees, screaming in agony. *Poison.* Von had heard tales of a lethal poison the Endoshan warriors used on their blades but had never felt its sting. The woman's cries faded away as she slumped on the ground, dead.

"Ronan!" Von warned, just in time for his friend to dodge another of the deadly blades. Ronan jumped up, lifting his knee and slamming his booted foot into the other man's wrist, shattering the bone and knocking the blade away. The man dropped to his knees, his limp arm cradled against his chest as he stared up into the face of death. Whatever he saw in Ronan's eyes caused his shoulders to slump in defeat moments before Ronan's blade swooped down to finish the kill.

Von continued to watch the battle from above, his eyes scanning the field but rarely straying from the castle doors for longer than a few seconds at a time. *Where are you?* He did not send the thought, but the longer he went without seeing Helena safe and whole, the greater his panic. The only thing keeping him sane was the fact that he could still feel their bond pulsing between them.

There was a loud crash and Midnight reared back, causing Von to slip down his back. He gripped the Talyrian tighter with his thighs and buried a fist deeper into the silky mane.

"Easy boy," he murmured, twisting his head to see what had caused the noise. As he watched more of Greyspire's outer buildings fell victim to the inferno, although it wasn't clear whose fire had started it.

From his vantage point, Von could see Timmins' group working to push the blaze away from them and toward the swarm of Shadows that were beginning to pour onto the field. It was hard to keep track of everyone after that, the bodies below him starting to all blend together under the dirt and blood.

A sharp tug along the bond left him gasping.

"Helena!"

There was no answer, only an endless stretch of silence.

His vision swam, and the metallic taste of blood began to fill his mouth. Von lifted a hand, surprised to find that his head was intact. Given the intensity of the pain, he thought it had been completely bashed in. Understanding dawned and his blood ran cold, terror clearing his mind of everything around him except for his connection to her.

"Answer me, Mate."

Still nothing.

Circling above a battlefield while on the back of a flying dragon-cat that was spouting jets of fire was hardly the time or place to try this, but he didn't care. Von closed his eyes, focusing on the golden tether that bound him to his Mate. Helena had explained how she had once found him while he'd been lost to the *Bella Morte* by following the strand until it led her to him. He was certain that his approach was not nearly as refined as hers, but by focusing on his visual representation of their bond, he instinctively understood what she had meant. It was similar to sending her a thought, except it was his awareness and not just his words that he directed to her.

He could feel the moment his consciousness left his physical body. There was a sense of weightlessness followed by the feeling of trying to force himself through a barrier of hot honey. It was not entirely unpleasant, but it required an intense focus to push himself through to the other side.

The first thing he felt was the pain. It was as if a white-hot blade had been driven straight through his skull.

"Mira!"

"V-von?" a tired, young-sounding Helena asked.

"Helena. Can you feel me?"

"Mmm," she murmured. He recognized the sound as the same one she'd make when rolling over to burrow deeper into his arms in the morning.

"Stay with me, Helena. You can't rest right now."

"Why? I'm so sleepy."

Von scrambled to make sense of her words under the weight of the pain. He was no healer, but if he had to guess, it was like her conscious mind was protecting itself by diving deeper into herself.

"Darling, you have to fight now."

That got her attention. There was a sizzle of awareness and then a sharp cry of pain.

"It hurts!" Her voice was more aware, but no less childlike. He needed to reach the Vessel.

"The Chosen are depending on you. They need their Kiri, and I need my Mate."

He could feel her struggling to awareness, and when she flinched away from the pain. *"It's too much."*

"What do you need?" But even as he asked, he knew. She needed to heal herself. Whatever injury she'd sustained was keeping her from knowing how to access her power and do it herself.

Von took a deep breath, hoping what he was about to do wasn't going to kill them both. He was only partially aware of his physical body and was mildly surprised he hadn't already fallen off Midnight. Focusing on the center of his power, he began to draw as much of it to the surface as he could. The process was similar to pouring water into an empty glass and trying to fill it all the way to the top without losing a drop, except that the glass could expand and so you are also trying to keep it from popping. It was a bizarre juggling act he'd rarely had an opportunity to perfect. So much of how he used his power had to do with short bursts of energy.

He continued to draw on his power until he felt full almost to the point of bursting. Then, with a quick prayer to the Mother, he sent it straight into Helena's injured body. There was no reaction at first, and Von began to worry he'd done something wrong. Her body was absorbing the power but didn't seem to be able to do anything with it.

Helena's sharp gasp let him know she was at least conscious again. Connected as they were, he could feel her sit up, their mental connect still secure although a bit foggy.

"Thank you."

"Whatever you need, Mira. You don't even have to ask."

His mouth, or was that hers, felt bone dry. *"Just a bit more."* Her voice was thin and brittle.

As she began to pull even more of his power into her, he realized why she hadn't been able to immediately heal herself in the first place. She had drained herself almost completely. Von could hardly comprehend the amount of magic she had used trying to keep the various illusions in place on top of whatever else she'd had to do inside. With the depth of her reservoir, his magic was probably akin to a drop in the ocean.

The pain continued to recede as she repaired whatever damage had been done. There was a blinding flash of light before Kragen's face came into view. Von drew back, confused to see him until he realized he was seeing through Helena's eyes.

"Thank the Mother," Kragen swore, checking over his shoulder before looking back down with concern. "Do you need me to carry you?"

Helena shook her head and pushed up onto her feet. "No, Von took care of it."

"Von?" Kragen's brows lowered, and he began to inspect the back of her head.

Helena slapped his hands away. "I'm fine. He gave me the power I needed to heal myself."

"Thank you again, Mate. That was an unexpectedly close call."

"I gave you an order."

He felt her amusement at his gruff reminder. *"We're on our way out now. Reyna and the Night Stalkers should already be outside."*

"I will have Starshine ready for you."

The flicker of amusement he'd felt at Kragen's reaction to her seemingly absurd explanation was quick to fade. Helena had put herself in a position where she'd been too weak to defend herself, and he hadn't been there to protect her. Everything in him that recognized Helena as his raged against the realization. He should have been there with her. She should never have put the safety of so many others above herself. She should have known better. She should have listened to him...

Von's lips lifted at the last one. Helena always listened to him, she just chose to ignore him and do what she wanted to do in the first place more than half the time. It was part of what he loved about her. She was as strong-willed, perhaps even stronger, than he was. Unfortunately, that did little to comfort him, knowing just how close to danger she'd been.

If Rowena had captured her during that moment of weakness, there was nothing that would have stopped him from walking in there and handing himself over just so that he could be with her. He was far too intimately aware of Rowena's brand of torture. He couldn't stand by knowing what she was doing to his Mate. Not if there was a way he could save her. With both of them under Rowena's control, there was very little hope for the rest of the Chosen.

Von shuddered. They'd come close, far too close, to losing everything.

CHAPTER 11

*R*onan had lost track of how long he'd been fighting. Time held no meaning in battle, every second stretching out into hours. Thanks to Von's warning, they were mostly able to dodge the poisoned Endoshan blades, although there had been more near misses than he'd care to admit.

He'd like to say he'd been surprised to see the Endoshan force face off against them, but he'd seen more than one man turn traitor to save their own ass. Unfortunately, all the training he'd drilled into his Kiri's army had been focused on fighting the brainless Shadows, not free-thinking men with poisoned blades. There was little time to worry about whether the lessons translated now. They were going to live or die on their own prowess.

Ronan was also thankful for the ranged team at their back. Between the Talyrians and Timmins' team, the heavy influx of fighters was seriously pared down by the time they ever reached him and his men at the front lines. They'd also been using their combined powers to keep the heavy smoke from the various fires out of the main battlefield. A handy trick, too bad it benefited the enemy as much as it did them.

Another Endoshan lunged toward him, and Ronan dodged the blow, using his momentum to spin around the man and shove him into one of his buddies with a well-placed kick to the back. One of Reyna's Night Stalkers finished the kill before moving on.

A sharp pain had Ronan spinning to the right in time to see a Shadow lunging for him. The walking corpses had joined the battle shortly after the courtyard went up in flames. He could only assume that was around the time Rowena realized they were there. Hopefully Helena and Reyna had made it out safely. He hadn't seen either woman since they'd parted ways in the forest. In the chaos, he hadn't had much of a chance to keep track of anyone.

Ronan continued to swing his blade, leaving a path of bodies in his wake. If ever there was something he was good at, it was killing people. A streak of black had his head twisting as his body braced for an attack that didn't come. Instead of facing a blow, Ronan's eyes landed on one of Rowena's Generals. The man had the same pale skin and stringy hair as the others, so it was impossible to tell if it was one of the same ones they'd fought in the Vale. At least until the bastard began to use whatever hell-cursed power Rowena's corruption had caused. That was the only way to really tell the fuckers apart.

The General lifted a pale hand, small gusts of wind lifting the oily strands of his hair. Ronan was already making his way over to him, knowing how fatal they could be once they got going. Rowena's man saw him and grinned, using a skeletal finger to beckon him closer. Ronan's brows lowered, and his lips curled in a menacing smile.

Game.

Fucking.

On.

He had already been a self-contained tornado of activity, his weapon swinging almost without pause, but after that taunt Ronan was unleashed. He used his shoulders, weapon, and fists to mow over anyone standing in his way, littering the ground with corpses and clearing the distance between them in a matter of moments. Just as Ronan's ax was about to swing true, the General laughed and vanished.

Snarling, Ronan spun around to see where he'd gone. *Slippery fucker must control Air.* That was going to make things more difficult.

The General was a good distance away, waving at Ronan before lifting his hand and circling his wrist. The dirt around him began to lift in the air, spinning around him faster and faster until it obscured him completely. The dust storm swelled in size, standing at least two times taller than Ronan himself, before the General released it by pushing it into a group of Chosen. The men and women flew back, flying through the air before falling down, some impaled on pieces of debris while others were killed by the force of their impact with the ground.

Ronan saw red as a murderous rage filled him. Pulling on every ounce of his power, Ronan launched himself into the air, lifting his ax above his head. The General watched him move through the sky. Winking, he vanished once more, half a second before Ronan's blade would have made contact with his face.

His weapon landed first, missing its mark. Ronan was next, landing in a crouched position that spared his body the effects of the impact. With a grunt he stood, pulling his weapon out of the earth, where it had gotten buried halfway up its hilt. Had the General still been standing there, he would have been rent in two.

There was nothing fun about the game of cat and mouse the Air General was playing with him. Ronan's frustration grew, his blood surging through his body as his heart pounded like a drum. This was more than just war now; it was personal.

The General laughed as he watched Ronan make his way toward him for the third time. However, this time he did not wait until the Shield was close before he blinked away. Ronan slammed his fist into one of the few wooden outer buildings that was still intact. The wood cracked, snapping in half and falling into the center of the building. The straw roof teetered at the loss of support before sliding down after it.

If he was going to capture the man, he needed to be smarter. Ronan stood still, letting his eyes follow the General's progress as he created more of his dust storms. There was no discernable pattern, the General moved freely, wanting only to create as much destruction as possible. The mass of bodies had definitely dwindled since the fighting had begun. There were no more groups of people, only small, scattered clusters. Except for one.

The Chosen's ranged team was still fully intact, having remained separate from the bulk of the fighting. If the General continued as he had been, they would likely be one of his next targets. Ronan zeroed in on the group. Miranda was standing closest to the edge, her face scrunched in concentration as she cast spell after spell. Ronan moved into her line of sight, trying to get her attention without alerting the General of his intention.

Using his blade and a nearby fire, Ronan aimed a beam of light toward the Keeper. Miranda flinched, her eyes squinting as she searched for the source of the light. Her eyes widened with surprise when she found Ronan standing still and staring up at her.

Once they had established eye contact, Ronan very purposefully turned his head toward the direction of the General and then back toward her. She followed his gaze, nodding in understanding when her eyes returned to him. Ronan didn't wait, trusting her to act on the knowledge.

Miranda didn't disappoint. She shouted something unintelligible to the others. Not long after, the group directed their attacks toward the General. Bolts of fire and lighting began to rain upon him, even as he blinked his way across the field. Finally catching on to their targeted attack, the General gave them a sinister smile and vanished.

Ronan used the distraction to conceal his race to the bottom of the ledge. He was just about to ascend when a glint of silver caught his eye. He crouched down, finding a discarded Endoshan blade. Ronan grinned, carefully picking it up. *Perfect.*

When he scaled the top of the ledge, the General had already beat him there. He'd created a wall of Air that held all the others within its center. He spared only a second to look at those held within. Inside, Timmins raged, his face nearly purple from his screams. The Advisor was throwing his fists against the invisible barrier as if he could break it down with the sheer force of his will. Joquil stood beside him, his eyes narrowed in concentration and his lips moving fast as he tried to counteract the powerful magic. But the thing that had captured his attention was what the General was doing to Miranda.

The Keeper was held up in the Air as if strung up by a rope, her hands clawing at her throat as the General called the breath out of her lungs. Miranda's feet flailed as she gasped and struggled to breathe. He was suffocating her with his magic. Ronan's blood ran cold. *Not again.*

The General's back was turned, so Ronan lunged, his borrowed blade ready to strike just as Miranda's eyes rolled back in her head and her struggling ceased.

"No!" Ronan roared, blindly swinging the poisoned blade. He didn't care where he hit the bastard, only that he cut through the skin. The poison would do the rest.

The blade sliced through the decayed-looking skin of the General's shoulder down to the bone, narrowly missing his neck. The pungent smell of rotting flesh met Ronan's nose as the General's arm swung limply at his side. Ronan had already recovered from the first attack and was prepared to strike again, even though he knew the poison had already entered the bloodstream. It was just a matter of time before the General met his final death.

But he didn't.

Miranda's body dropped to the ground, looking like a pile of discarded rags as the General turned his full attention onto Ronan. With another gaping grin, the General lifted his skeletal hand and shot the full force of his power into Ronan.

His lungs were on fire. Ronan gasped for breath, the blade dropping, forgotten from his hands as he struggled to breathe. He felt his booted feet begin to leave the ground, his toes scrambling for purchase. There was no relief. Dark spots began to dance in the corners of his vision.

Nonsensical thoughts began to flash in his mind, even as he continued to gasp like a fish out of water. Until there was only one.

Not like this. Mother's tits, it couldn't end like this.

CHAPTER 12

*K*ragen and Helena stumbled outside, the night sky painted a burnt orange due to the reflection of the flames. Helena's eyes immediately began to scan the horizon; she did not have to wait long to find what she was looking for.

Von was at her side almost instantly, using his power to blink off Midnight's back and over to her. His arms were around her, pulling her body against his before she had time to open her mouth.

"If you ever do anything that stupid again, I'll—"

"You'll what?" she teased, feeling more worn out than she cared to admit. Despite the influx of Von's power, she'd drained herself much more deeply than she had thought. It would likely take her a few days to fully recover.

"Think of something," he muttered gruffly, pressing a kiss to her forehead. She knew that it was his fear talking, she could feel it like a jagged edge scratching their bond. She had scared him, and he didn't quite know what to do with the feeling.

"I'm okay," she said aloud, for both men's benefit. "I promise."

Kragen was still looking at her with worried eyes, despite the number of assurances she'd given him.

Starshine landed beside Midnight and huffed, drawing Helena's attention over to her. As she turned her head, a figure climbing up the side of the cliff had her heart lurching in her chest. He was heading right toward the ranged group.

"Not so fast," Helena growled, her fatigue forgotten as the need to defend took over. "Let's finish this," she said to the others, squeezing her Mate's hand a final time before walking over to her Talyrian and climbing up.

Kragen gave a wave and took off at a run to join their people in battle.

Von was right behind Helena, vaulting up on Midnight in one fluid motion.

Starshine took flight, covering the distance quickly. As they closed in, the shock of red hair became clear, and Helena's eyes grew wide as she realized her mistake. The figure who had crested the ledge wasn't the threat, the skeletal man facing him was. Horror filled her as she watched Ronan levitate off the ground, a weapon slipping from his fingers as his feet swung helplessly.

Not again. She would not lose another of her Circle to these evil bastards.

Helena opened her mouth on a scream of absolute rage, the sky echoing her fury with jagged bolts of lightning and the answering crack of thunder. It sounded like the world was being split in two as Starshine and Helena streaked toward her Shield.

She drew on her power, preparing to unleash it on the General, but Starshine beat her to the kill. With a mighty roar, the Talyrian Queen swooped low, her jaws snapping closed over the General's head. She never stopped, flying a few feet away before landing and spitting out the General's head with a hiss. She pawed at her face, wiping away the smears of black blood that coated her otherwise pristine fur.

Helena scrambled off the Talyrian's back, rushing over to her friends. A distraught Timmins was on his hands and knees, Joquil next to him, trying to pull him up. Her Shield had fallen when the General's hold on him was released. Von had already dismounted and was beside the very pale Ronan, trying to help him sit up, but he was having none of it and was slapping her Mate's hands away with a scowl.

As relieved as she was to see that they were all well, her heart felt heavy as she knelt beside Miranda's corpse. Even in death, the Keeper looked younger than she did. Helena closed her eyes, swallowing back the tears that threatened to spill over.

"Mother, welcome your daughter with open arms," she whispered, before standing and facing the others.

"This ends now."

ROWENA PACED beside her new husband, her hands twitching with agitation. That little upstart had tricked her. A full-fledged war was currently underway in her courtyard. That was unacceptable.

"I thought your warriors were supposed to be unstoppable!" she snapped.

"Flesh is not immune to fire, My Queen. The Talyrians were an unexpected obstacle."

"They are no less immune to your blades. Perhaps you should try using them."

Kai-Soren's lips folded in a flat line, displeasure barely concealed in his golden eyes.

"I see just as many Chosen corpses," he pointed out.

Rowena's eyes narrowed, her eyes blazing with blue fire. "I lost another General tonight. No amount of lives will justify that death."

"You have four others in your service."

She opened her mouth to point out the obvious and stopped herself. The less he knew, the better.

"There's one now," Kai-Soren said, gesturing toward the courtyard. Her General was blinking around, setting off dust storms that were clearing the battlefield of fighting men, if not of their resulting corpses.

A small smile reached her lips. At least someone was finding success this night. The fewer people left to fight for her enemy, the better.

"You would do well to release the others. They will finish this."

"And risk losing all of them?"

"They are your most powerful weapon, My Queen. They should be fighting."

Rowena weighed the risk against her desire to win. "Perhaps just one more," she decided, signaling for the General she referred to as Pestilence to come over. He reached her side, bringing with him the scent of decayed earth.

"Slaughter them," she ordered.

The man dipped his head and moved to join the battle. His gait was slow and measured, the vegetation beneath his feet withering with each step. Her General opened his mouth, preparing to blow into the faces of nearby Chosen.

A blur of red streaked across the sky, another Talyrian whelp shooting a stream of fire from its snout. He was heading straight for Pestilence.

"No!" Rowena cried, calling on her power. A jet of purple light burst from her fingers, hitting the Talyrian in its side and throwing it off course before its fire could reach her General.

There was a surge of euphoria as the Talyrian's power began to fill her. Rowena's lips curved in a sexual smile, and she fed more of her power into the transfer she'd unknowingly established. As creatures of Spirit, the connection was ten times stronger than what she experienced when creating her Shadows.

The Talyrian's blue eyes began to glow with lavender fire before black lines began to snake across their luminous surface.

Another burst of color came barreling toward her, a Talyrian trying to protect its pride mate. Rowena lifted her other hand, a twin jet of purple power colliding with the newcomer until its eyes also began to change.

"You are mine!" Rowena shouted, draining them both until the change was complete. The flow of power ceased, and Rowena was just about to send her newest pets back into the sky to fight their kin when an invisible blow struck her in the chest.

The breath left her lungs, and she stumbled with a low moan. Suddenly weak, Rowena struggled to stand. She called on her reserve of power, shock quickly replaced by fury to find it almost empty. A loss of power at that scale could mean only one thing. Another of her Generals was gone.

Rowena's head snapped up, her skin colorless and clammy. "It's time to go."

"But, My Queen—"

"Now."

Kai-Soren looked like he wanted to argue further, but he kept silent, moving instead to help her stand. It was a testament to how weak she felt that she allowed it. They needed to get away and regroup. There was no victory to be found here.

It pained her to walk away from her home, but by morning, Greyspire would be a ruin. There was nothing left for her here. There was a hidden network of caves not too far away. Rowena would take what was left of her people and go to ground. She looked over her shoulder, the smoldering flames glittering in her Talyrians' eyes.

A secret smile curved her lips. Perhaps today hadn't been a complete loss after all.

CHAPTER 13

"*I* swear I saw some of the Shadows running away!" Serena insisted.

"They were probably chasing after their puppet master," Kragen said.

Serena refused to be dismissed. "No, you aren't hearing me. They were attacking some of the Storm Forged, and then they just stopped. They've never fled from a fight before."

The group around her fell silent as they digested the news and what the change of behavior could mean. Helena listened with only half an ear, more interested in watching Greyspire burn. By anyone's standard, the attack had been a success. Anyone's standard but hers. They had few casualties, had taken out two of the enemy's biggest weapons, and crippled her to the point that she fled. But it still wasn't enough. She was still alive.

Joquil broke the silence first, his amber eyes glowing with interest, "Helena's hunch was right. Rowena's power *is* tied to her Generals. She must be using their power to bolster her own."

"And when you removed two of them, she suffered a major loss of power," Von continued, picking up the thread of his thought.

"Don't you see what this means?" Nial asked with excitement. "She can be beat, Helena. If we take out the rest of her Generals before she has a chance to make any more, she will be defenseless against you."

"I don't know about defenseless," Joquil cautioned. "She was still a Damaskiri in her own right, which does require significant power."

"All that means is that she can access Spirit," Serena interjected. "Helena is a master of all five Branches. Rowena doesn't stand a chance against her."

Helena knew they wanted her to be excited by the news, but she couldn't muster the energy. Because of her obsession with breaking Helena's Circle, she'd had a feeling that Rowena would fall without her Generals. Their entire plan had been based upon that premise. The problem was they'd had their chance and failed.

Realizing that she wasn't as thrilled by their discovery as they were, the group fell quiet again.

"Kiri?"

Helena turned her attention back to them. Despite the obvious signs of battle, most were bright-eyed and energized from what they had deemed a victory. At the moment, all Helena felt was bone-deep weariness. She was too drained from the excessive use of power to feel anything else. Timmins was the only other person present who seemed withdrawn. Helena knew that he was struggling to process Miranda's death. It couldn't be easy watching someone you cared about murdered in front of your eyes while you were helpless to stop it.

Von moved closer to her, sensing that she needed the support, both physically and emotionally.

"Thank you."

His fingers wove through hers in response.

"So, what now?" Nial asked, wrapping his arm around his mate.

Helena's mind went blank. She had no clue what to do now. All she had planned for was getting into the castle and launching the surprise assault on Greyspire. She hadn't anticipated an after. Where did they even start when they didn't know where Rowena had gone?

"We should go after her and press our advantage," Serena said.

"Where would we go?" Helena asked.

Serena shifted her weight, at a loss. Her point made, Helena sighed.

"We regroup and get ready for the next battle," Von spoke up, answering the question for her.

Ronan nodded. "Our people have earned a warm meal and rest, at the very least."

"We also need to bury our dead," Timmins said, his voice rusty. Helena did not know if it was from disuse or from the screaming.

A weight settled over them as they thought about the lost Keeper.

"Where is Effie?" Helena asked, voicing the question that was on each of their minds.

"She is still with the others," Ronan answered. "Shall I bring her to you?"

She closed her eyes and nodded, not relishing the task of having to let Effie know about her grandmother. Even that small physical act was a chore. She needed to sleep, but the chance of that happening anytime soon was highly unlikely.

After that, there didn't seem to be much left to say. The battle was over, at least for now. Their enemy had escaped, leaving no trace of her whereabouts behind. There was nothing left for them here.

Even though the future was unclear, the next step seemed fairly obvious.

"Let's go home."

To say that she was angry would have been the understatement of the century. The numbness she'd felt immediately preceding the battle had long since passed and the truth had set in, sending Helena into a full-blown rage.

Rowena had gotten away. Again. The pale-faced harpy slunk away in the middle of battle rather than face her directly. Helena choked on her fury, the weight of it in her chest threatening to consume her.

Her hands were clenched into fists, the tips of her black talons sliding out to bite into the tender skin of her palms. It was hard to maintain control with her emotions at war within her. The others declared their mission a victory, their enemy forced to retreat. Helena couldn't quite see it that way. They'd only eliminated two of their five primary targets. The others were still out there, and now they'd lost the element of surprise, which had been their only true advantage.

Helena had never admitted it out loud, but she'd secretly been hoping that last night would be the end of it. Her plan may not have been fool-proof, but it had been sound. If they had only found the Generals before Rowena caught on to them. *If only...*

The words echoed through her mind, ruthless with their taunting promise. She had been so close, and her victory had been stolen from her. All because Rowena had found a way to escape while she had been distracted by saving her people. Now they were back to square one, with absolutely no idea where the harlot had slipped off to.

She sighed. Presented with the same set of options, Helena would have made the same decisions. Every. Single. Time. Ronan and her Circle's lives would always come before going after Rowena. Perhaps that made her weak and predictable, but she would never sacrifice one for the other.

A frisson of awareness brushed against her senses, alerting her to her Mate's presence long before she acknowledged him. Von's hands settled on her shoulders, the warmth of his touch doing little to ease the turmoil inside of her.

"You have to be kinder to yourself, *Mira*."

"She got away."

"But not without sustaining a major blow. She would not have felt the need to run if she hadn't been scared, Helena."

Helena's jaw flexed, her next words gritted out between clenched teeth. "They got Miranda." She felt the loss of the Keeper deeply. The woman's wisdom and guidance had been invaluable. More than that, she had genuinely liked her. They had not been close, not like she and Darrin, but there had been true kinship there. Miranda had been her friend.

"We all know the risk of battle, Helena. And if anyone can know the time and place of their death, the Keeper was certainly among them."

"How is Effie?" she asked, changing the subject.

Von let out a long breath. "She is... unwell."

Helena's eyes fell closed, the guilt of inflicting more pain on the poor woman because of this war was yet another burden she would carry with her. "I should go see her."

Von's fingers dug into her shoulders. "I would advise against that. At least for the moment."

"Why? What's wrong?" Helena asked, twisting out of his grasp to face him.

He weighed his words carefully before speaking. "She has no one left; it is a hard reality to face."

"She has us," Helena snapped. "Perhaps she needs to be reminded that she is not alone."

"Ronan tried..."

"And?"

"Effie attacked him."

Helena's brows lifted. "Oh."

Von shrugged before stating matter-of-factly, "She is not ready for comfort. She needs to work through the pain before she can start to heal."

"Then let me provide a target."

"Helena," he protested as she moved past him.

"It might as well be me, Von. It is no less than I deserve. She cannot do or say any worse than I am already doing to myself."

His eyes were sad as they met hers. "You are too hard on yourself, my love."

His words were meant to soothe and yet they only enraged her further. He couldn't possibly understand the extent of what she was feeling right now. Helena swallowed back her emotions, trying to explain. "It is my plan that led to her death. If anyone deserves that girl's anger, it is I."

"You did not kill her!" Von swore, slamming his fist into the table, causing it to topple over and crash to the floor.

"Not directly, but my choices did!" Helena raged, flinging the door open.

"When are you going to learn what it means to lead?" he snarled.

The words hurt. Helena looked back over her shoulder, the fingers that held onto the door turning white from the force with which she held it. "When did you stop caring about other people's lives?"

Von's eyes went wide, his mouth falling open. She did not wait for him to speak, not trusting either of them to refrain from saying something that would only cause more damage. They had never fought before, not like this. She knew that it was only love and concern for her that had him speaking as he did. But he did not truly understand what it was like for her. He was able to separate his emotions from battle, she could not. To her, each life was a splinter shoved deep into her heart. Each and every one a scratch that drew blood until she felt like she was slowly bleeding to death.

She stormed through the halls, her temper fueling her momentum. It did not take long to locate Effie; the sounds of furniture being thrown against the wall more than enough of an indication that she was heading in the right direction.

Helena didn't bother knocking before opening the door and walking into the room. Her eyes performed a cursory inspection, noting the shards of wood with interest. The amount of destruction present was impressive for such a small woman. She had even managed to overturn the bed.

"Stupid. Mindless. Waste!" Effie screamed, each word punctuated by a picture being slammed against the side of an armoire that had seen better days.

"Is that how you greet all of your friends, or am I special?" Helena asked in a deceptively neutral tone.

Effie looked up, startled to find she was no longer alone. Her eyes were red-rimmed, deep purple circles beneath them. She had clearly not slept. Or bathed. Her long blonde curls hung in limp and dirty clumps about her shoulders. Her skin streaked with dirt and what looked like blood. All the joy and quiet peace that Helena had begun to associate with Effie was gone; snuffed out like a candle that had reached the end of its wick.

"Kiri," she said formally, her voice hoarse. Effie dropped the picture, the crash sounding too loud in the now painfully quiet room.

Her chin dipped, her hands fluttering to her sides where they continued to twitch restlessly.

"When did I stop being Helena?"

Effie looked up, her blue eyes shining brightly. "I apologize, Kiri. I do not think I am fit for company."

Helena gave the room a pointed glance. "I see that, and yet here I am."

"What do you want?" the girl snapped, before slapping a hand over her mouth. "Apologies, Kiri. I did warn you—"

Helena waved away the apology. "There's no need, I understand."

Effie pressed her lips together, looking like she wanted to argue the point.

Helena's answering laugh was entirely without humor. "You don't think I understand what it's like to lose the final member of one's family? Is your memory that short?"

Tears filled Effie's eyes, the fight leaving her in one watery breath. "Darrin was hard enough, but now I-I have n-nothing left," she whispered brokenly.

Helena moved closer to the grieving girl, her own heart breaking at the sight. This was her fault. "That's not true," Helena murmured, fighting her own tears as she wrapped her arms around Effie's trembling body.

Effie sobbed into Helena's chest, her stream of words entirely unintelligible. Each wave of grief struck Helena like a blow. She had done this, and there was nothing she could do to fix it. It was a long while before Effie's tears abated. She was still shaking as she pushed out of Helena's embrace.

"If I find her before you do, I'm going to kill her myself!" Effie vowed, her low voice no less menacing despite its lack of volume.

"I think you've earned that right," Helena said, as Effie stepped back, wiping at her eyes. "I just wish we knew where to look."

As if the words were a trigger, Effie's body went rigid, her eyes rolling back into her head. Effie's body began to spasm, the tremors so violent that Helena feared for the woman's safety.

"Effie!" Helena shouted, jumping forward to grab her before she hurt herself. "Help!" Helena screamed, sending the plea down the bond and out loud for any that would hear her.

The shaking continued for what felt like hours but may have only been a minute. Effie groaned, her knees sagging. Helena caught her weight and eased her to the ground mere seconds before Effie began to vomit. Helena held the dirty strands of hair out of her face and rubbed her heaving back soothingly.

"What happened?" Von demanded, his weapon drawn and ready for battle. Seeing Effie cradled in Helena's arms as she continued to empty the contents of her stomach, he dropped his weapon and moved inside the room. "Is she okay?"

Helena shrugged, too shocked to reply. One moment they'd been talking; the next Effie had fallen into a seizure the likes of which she'd never seen.

"I saw her," Effie gasped.

"Saw who?" Helena asked in confusion, looking around the room as Effie sat up.

"Rowena."

"What! Where?" Von demanded, just as Ronan and Joquil reached the door.

"Is she hurt?" Ronan demanded, eyeing the trembling Effie.

Von silenced him with a look.

"No, Helena." Effie licked her lips and grimaced. "I *Saw* her."

Understanding dawned and Helena's eyes went wide. She shot a startled look to her Mate, whose own expression was a mix of shock and awe. Apparently, Miranda's legacy hadn't ended with her death after all.

Effie was a Keeper.

CHAPTER 14

*T*he low murmur of voices continued as Helena helped Effie into a chair. The rest of the Circle had been summoned so that they could be present when Effie described her vision.

"Are we sure she's a Keeper? Miranda never did *that* when she had a vision," Kragen asked in a low voice.

"Did you ever see Miranda while she was in the throes of a vision?" Joquil asked, just as quietly.

"Well, no, but don't you think she would have said something?"

"Why? What reason would she have to share that with us?"

Kragen shrugged, his dark eyes considering as they moved back to Effie.

For her part, Effie hadn't spoken further since delivering the news that had shocked them all. At the moment, she was staring at a fixed point on the table, not meeting any of their eyes. Her body was curled in on itself as if she was trying to become as small as possible.

"Effie," Helena said in a soft voice. "Can you tell us what you Saw?"

"I—" she paused to lick her lips. "I'll try."

"Take your time," Ronan said, placing his hand on her shoulder. She flinched, the contact too much for her battered senses. Ronan dropped his hand with a muffled apology.

Effie's eyes lifted, scanning the room before settling on Timmins. His face was pale and drawn, but he gave her an encouraging nod. She took a deep breath and gave a jerky nod of her own. "I was in a dungeon, I think."

"What makes you think it was a dungeon?" Von asked. His voice was calm and measured, the question a prompt not a means of interrogation.

"There were bars," Effie said, her eyes taking a faraway cast.

"What else do you see?"

"A man," she replied in a dreamlike tone.

"What is he wearing?" Helena asked.

"Black with…" her brow furrowed as she searched for the word, "straps?"

"Sounds like an Endoshan," Ronan said softly. The others murmured their agreement.

"Where is Rowena in your vision?" Von asked, trying to direct her focus.

Effie whimpered. "She's mad at the man. She has him gripped by the throat and is saying something. She's so angry."

"Is there anyone else there?" Von asked.

Effie was silent for a few beats. "Yes."

"Do you recognize them?"

She shook her head.

"Can you describe them?"

"Children," she whispered, her body trembling with the word. Whatever she was seeing terrified her.

Helena's eyes shot to Kragen. "She's draining more of them."

Kragen's face was grim. "That's what it sounds like."

Renewed anger surged through Helena at the thought. Now Effie wasn't the only one who was shaking, although it was outrage and not fear that had Helena on edge.

"Is there anything else?" Von asked.

Effie shook her head.

"Thank you, Effie."

She slumped in her chair, completely worn out from the events of the afternoon.

"Perhaps you should lie down and rest for a while," Helena suggested. "Would you like that?"

Effie nodded.

"She can use my room. It's closest," Timmins offered, stepping forward to assist Effie.

She gave him what barely passed for a smile, leaning on him heavily as they left the room.

"So, what does it mean?" Ronan asked once they were alone.

Kragen was the first to speak. "They are in Endoshan, clearly."

"You think?" Helena asked, not certain it was that obvious.

It was Von who answered. "They are allies, it's a logical step."

"But an obvious one," she pointed out.

"It may be obvious, but it does not make it untrue," Joquil said. "Let's think about this logically. You said that Effie entered into the vision *after* you mentioned needing to know where Rowena was located." Joquil waited for her confirmation before he continued, "The first thing she saw was an Endoshan man. That answers the question, doesn't it?"

Helena frowned. That seemed far too simple an explanation. "I don't think that's how visions work. Miranda mentioned more than once that visions aren't straightforward."

Von lifted his hands and shrugged. "It gives us a direction at least, which is more than we have now."

"How do we even know what she saw is occurring now? Maybe it's where Rowena is *going* to be? Or if it is where she is now, how do we know she'll still be there by the time we arrive?" Helena felt like she was the only one not ready to spring into action.

"We don't," Joquil said, "but I can't help but refer back to the sequence of events. It was your words that triggered the vision. One can only assume the vision was an answer to a question."

"But I didn't ask a question," Helena pointed out.

Joquil gave her a look, clearly not appreciating her distinction. "A need then. The vision responded to your need to know where she was. You did not say where she is *going* to be, you said where she *is*."

Helena frowned, still not totally convinced. She looked around the room at their faces. *Why are they all so determined to believe this is the answer?*

Kragen spoke up next. "Rowena was severely weakened during the attack. It makes sense that she would need to go somewhere relatively close to seek out a new source of energy. Endoshan fits that description."

Helena sighed and nodded. That much at least was true.

"We need to find her before she has time to recover fully," Von said.

Helena nodded again. "I know."

"This is our best option," he said.

"This is our only option," Ronan countered.

That's when the answer to her earlier question came to her. Her men needed a purpose. They could not stand sitting still spinning their wheels while their enemy was still out there. Like Von had said, if nothing else, this at least gave them something to do. Worst case scenario she wasn't there, and they were back where they started. But if she was... they could strike while she was still weak.

"Even if she's not there, Kiri," Kragen said, "those children might be. We have to save them."

That sealed it for her. Fruitless endeavor or not, Kragen was right. For the children alone, the trip would be worth it. "Fine," Helena said on a sigh. "Endoshan it is."

"When do you want to be ready to leave?" Ronan asked, already standing.

"Soon," Helena said wearily. "Before nightfall."

They had barely been back in Tigaera for a day, and already they were talking about leaving again. Many of them hadn't even had a chance to sleep since their return, herself included, and she was feeling the strain.

"I'll make sure the others are ready," Ronan promised before leaving. Joquil and Kragen followed him, leaving Von and Helena alone.

He stood next to her, just out of reach, and suddenly the distance felt entirely too far.

"Can you just hold me, and we'll pretend neither of us said anything heinous?"

"There's no need to pretend, *Mira*. You may have had a point."

Helena shook her head. "I was wrong, and you didn't deserve that. Least of all from me."

"You won't even accept my letting you off the hook without putting up a fight," he muttered. His lips quirked up as he reached for her, wrapping his arms around her and kissing the top of her head.

Helena let out a watery laugh.

Von's voice grew serious. "I'm sorry if my words were insensitive or callous."

"Me too. I didn't mean it when I said that you didn't care about others." She wrapped her arms around his waist and held him tight, burying her face in his neck and breathing in the spicy scent of him.

He tilted her chin up so that her eyes met his. "If I was hard on you, it was only because it hurts me to watch you beat yourself up. I can protect you from any enemy except yourself."

"I know," she whispered, her lower lip trembling.

He kissed her then, his lips sealing over hers, taking away the pain, anger, and grief that had been spiraling within her and making her feel off balance.

"I love you, Mira. Always."

"I love you, too."

They pulled apart, Helena feeling steady for the first time since leaving Greyspire.

"What can I do to help ease the burden?" he asked, brushing a stray curl from her cheek.

"You already did it."

He brushed his lips against hers again before looking down to ask, "This is probably a bad time to yell at you for putting yourself at risk, isn't it?"

Helena let out a snort of laughter. "Probably."

He sighed. "I thought so. As long as you know that we will talk about it." For all that his voice was light, she knew he was serious.

Helena nodded. She had made a mistake allowing herself to drain her power so completely at the ball. To be caught damn near defenseless when in the den of her enemy was a rookie mistake. One that she was lucky to have survived.

"Can we get through all of this first? Then I promise I will let you snarl at me as much as you want, and I won't complain once."

Von threw his head back and laughed.

She shoved at his chest playfully. "I know that I scared you. I'm sorry for that. I will try to be more careful."

The smile fell from his lips and his eyes went molten. "Don't you understand? It's self-preservation that makes me want to tuck you away and fight your battles for you. You are more precious to me than anything in this world, Helena. When I say that you are Mine, I do not simply mean my mate. You are my purpose. Without you, I am lost."

"Von," she whispered, the floor feeling like it just dropped from under her. But she did understand, because it was the same for her. She had already had to live in a world without him, and she'd be damned if she ever had to suffer it again.

The need to be close overwhelmed them, and he swept her up in his arms, her legs wrapping around his waist. Everything else could wait, for now the only thing that mattered was the man that held her heart in the palm of his hand.

THERE WAS a light knock on the door.

"Come in!" Helena called, hurriedly folding a few additional shirts to stuff into her pack.

"Is this a bad time?" Effie asked, her voice much more controlled than the last time they'd spoken.

Helena looked up with a frazzled smile. "Not if you don't mind talking while I pack."

"Do you want some help?"

"No, I think I've got it. How are you feeling?"

"Better." Effie searched the room for a seat, but there were clothes scattered about everywhere. "Where's Alina?"

"I gave her the night off. Packing is keeping my hands busy, which is a welcome thing at the moment."

Effie nodded her understanding. "I always thought chores were an excellent distraction."

Helena made a face that had the other woman laughing.

"I didn't say I enjoyed them."

"Fair enough," Helena said, watching as Effie finally decided to perch on the edge of her bed. She looked like she would flee at the first loud noise, she was also entirely dwarfed by the massive bed; her feet not even able to touch the ground.

Effie was looking much better than earlier, although the bath probably had a lot to do with it. Color had returned to her skin, and her hair no longer looked or smelled like the contents of a rubbish bin.

Helena dropped her pack so that she could give her full attention to her friend. "Have there been any other side effects?"

Effie shook her head, her eyes focused on her feet, which were swinging back and forth.

Despite her silence, Helena could tell something was definitely weighing on her. "Do you want to talk about it?"

When she spoke, she floored Helena with her words. "I don't know how to be special."

"Effie—" she protested, but the other woman shook her head and kept talking.

"No, it's okay. I was raised ungifted, I knew that it made me different, and after a while, I came to terms with the fact that I would never have any magic of my own. But now..." Effie's big eyes lifted and met hers. Helena was overcome by the sense of utter helplessness she found there. "I don't even know who I am anymore. Everything I thought I knew... everything that was true... it's gone."

"I know what that feels like."

Effie tilted her head, looking very much like an inquisitive bird. "With all due respect, Kiri. I don't think you do."

Helena's eyes searched hers, wanting to argue, but biting back the words.

"You thought that you were ungifted, but you were never surrounded by those that had magic. You were loved and cared for your whole life. All I ever wanted was to be special enough that my parents would love me. Or to have enough magic that I could live with my grandmother. I was obsessed with it for years before I finally came to terms with the fact that I could never be more than I was."

She didn't look angry as she spoke, only resigned. Helena wasn't sure which was worse.

"You have to understand, Helena. I was nothing. Worse than nothing, for even the servants usually had some ounce of magic, and there wasn't even a single drop in me. I had to fight every day to prove that I wasn't a worthless piece of shit."

Helena flinched. She'd never heard such harsh words from Effie.

"I had to learn how to be invisible, how to do what so many others could do without trying. And now..." she lifted her hands in a helpless shrug, "now I have this gift that I don't understand and I don't want. I would give anything to give it back if it meant she could return." Tears filled Effie's eyes, and she blinked furiously, trying to force them away.

"I'm so sorry, Effie," Helena whispered, knowing the words were useless. They wouldn't make anything better.

Effie wiped away a few stray tears. "It's okay."

"Is there anything I can do to help?"

"I want to come with you."

Helena froze, the words catching her off guard. "Are you sure?"

Effie's jaw clenched, and her hands curled into fists. "I have every right to be there."

"Of course you do. It's just... if you need time—"

"No. Not more crying. Tears don't change anything, only actions do. I want to act."

Helena found herself nodding in agreement. She knew exactly how Effie felt.

"It was my vision that helped you make this decision; I want to see it through."

"Okay."

"Good." Effie let out a breath then, her shoulders sagging. She had been prepared to fight the issue.

"Effie?"

"Yes?"

"For what it's worth, you've never been anything less than amazing to me."

Effie's lower lip trembled. "No one has ever said anything like that to me before."

"I have always admired your quiet strength. In fact, I was jealous of just how sure of yourself you were. I haven't felt that confident or capable a day in my life, and certainly not once since I found out I was Kiri."

Effie gaped at her in surprise.

Helena shrugged. "We all carry our scars, Effie. Just because you can't see them, doesn't mean they aren't there."

"I'll try to remember that."

"It will get easier as you learn how to use your new gifts. Try to remember that it's not something that you have to do on your own. We are all here to help you adjust, however we can."

"Thank you, Helena."

They shared a smile, Effie pushing herself off of the bed and back to her feet. "I guess I should go repack as well. Thanks for letting me come with you, and for listening."

"Anytime."

Effie was almost out the door when she stopped and looked back. "I guess you do understand, after all." With a final shy smile, Effie shut the door behind her.

Helena stared at the closed door for a long time without moving. There was a lot hidden in the words that Effie hadn't said. Secret pains and doubts that still haunted her. Helena would never have guessed that there was so much hidden beneath the surface; Effie hid her past well.

If Helena had learned anything leading up to her trial, it was that one's unspoken fears were the biggest obstacles. There was nothing harder to face than your own demons forged from self-doubt. She just hoped that Effie would remember what she said, and not suffer in silence.

"Mother, stay close to her," Helena whispered, turning back to her clothes. "She is going to need you in the days to come."

CHAPTER 15

*E*ndoshan was not what Helena expected. After her brief visit to Etillion, and knowing that at one time it had been the sister city to Endoshan, she'd expected it to be nearly the same. To an extent perhaps it was, but the differences far outweighed the similarities. Instead of Etillion's rolling green hills, there were wide stretches of dark, swampy water, and there were lush trees with thick ropey vines that hung between them. The heat was oppressive. The air like a living thing around them; a thick barrier that made each movement sluggish.

Even though it bordered Vyruul, it may as well be across the entire realm. There was not a speck of ice in sight. Helena doubted snow was something few, if any, Endoshans had experienced until they'd arrived at Vyruul the first time.

There was a low buzzing and then a loud crack as Ronan slapped his neck. He moved his hand away and inspected it with a grimace. "Bugs should not be allowed to be as big as one's hand. It's disgusting." He shook his hand to fling away the offending insect.

"Gross," Serena muttered, jumping out of the way.

Helena was inclined to agree. Endoshan had the distinct aura of a predator. Something that was hiding in the distance, tracking your movement and preparing to strike. She shuddered. Generally, she was a fan of wildlife, but these were no snuggly creatures. The wildlife here was like nothing she'd experienced growing up in Tigaera. Sure, they had bugs and even a wild wolf or two, but their insects were little harmless ones. Nothing on the scale of the massive buzzing creatures they'd discovered upon their arrival. She was stepping carefully, not wanting to be surprised with a stinger in the eye.

"Are you certain we're in the right place?" she asked Amara. The Etillions were the only ones who had been to Endoshan before, although not since the wall had been erected and Endoshan had effectively closed its borders against them.

Amara nodded. "It's been a few years since our last scouting mission, but the keep should be just around the next bend."

A light breeze stirred the branches of the trees and the resulting whisper of the leaves made the hair along her arms stand on end. Helena risked a glance over her shoulder, more certain than ever that their movements were being tracked.

Helena clutched the small bag of Kaelpas stones tighter in her hand. Never had she had this kind of reaction to a place before. A sense of danger lingered in the air, not like the taint they'd found in the Forest of Whispers, but a wrongness nonetheless. She wanted to go home. They could track Rowena a different way.

Von reached for her hand, squeezing it reassuringly. "You all right, *Mira?*"

She went to nod and stopped herself. The truth was, she wasn't. She just didn't understand what her instinct was trying to tell her. "Stay on guard," she answered instead.

Von studied her face before giving a slow nod. He made a low whistling sound that drew Ronan and Serena up short, along with the Daejarans standing nearest to them. Ronan met Von's eyes and gave a short nod of his own. The sound had been a warning, some signal they had set up long ago so that they could communicate efficiently and without giving anything away.

Von kept his fingers threaded through hers, and Helena was grateful for the contact. No one else seemed to be having the same kind of reaction that she was having, other than mild discomfort because of the heat or a general dislike of the bugs. Whatever she sensed was affecting her alone. *Lovely.*

Helena drew on her power to amplify her senses, realizing the only way she was going to figure out what she was sensing, without it sneaking up and catching them off guard, was to actively search for it. She cast her awareness out, using her magically enhanced eyes to study the world around her. The trees and creatures of the swamp came into sharper focus, the colors of their life essence creating a vivid rainbow that would have been beautiful, if the feeling of otherness wasn't also more apparent.

The trees glowed a deep earthy green, while the bugs appeared as floating specks of lavender, and there, beneath the surface of the water, something was a deep, pulsing red. Despite the size of the shape beneath the surface, Helena sensed nothing that had triggered alarm bells. She continued to search around her, seeing the warm glow of her comrades, especially the beautiful strands that linked her to her Circle.

Her brow furrowed, nothing so far felt out of place. It was not until her final sweep that she finally noticed something amiss. Amongst all of the color, there was a yawning chasm of empty black. Helena stumbled, the void causing her body to break out into a cold sweat. *What was it?*

Even as everything inside of her urged her to stay away, Helena forced herself to start moving toward it.

Worried voices called after her, surprised to see her break rank without so much as a word.

"Helena?"

"Kiri?"

She didn't know how to explain what was happening, so she didn't even try.

And then the one voice she could never ignore called to her. *"Mira?"*

"I need to see this."

"See what?"

"I don't know."

"You aren't going anywhere alone, Helena. We don't know what's out there."

She knew better than to argue after what happened in Greyspire, and truth be told, she didn't want to face this on her own. She just knew that whatever it was, she was going to wish she had never found it. She already wished she had never stepped foot in this Mother-forsaken realm.

Von said something to the others, but she barely heard him. She was wholly focused on the void. Reaching it was going to require crossing the swamp, and she was not equipped with anything other than her power to reach the other side. Not wanting to waste time trying to find a vessel that they could commandeer, Helena used the trick she had learned while visiting the Storm Forged and urged the water to part for her.

There were a few startled gasps behind her as the army witnessed the act. The water was nowhere near as deep as the ocean, and it did not take long for two walls of water to form on either side of her, both towering high over her head. From the corner of her eye, she could see glowing blue orbs that must have been fish playfully swimming in the still churning water.

Helena took the first tentative step, her heart somewhere in the vicinity of her throat. There was a squelching sound as the thick mud clung to her boot. It took more effort than she would have thought to cross the distance, the mud trying to suck her down into its depths. Despite the slow crossing, Von remained right beside her.

Soon, all she could hear was the sound of her racing heart as they finally reached the other side of the water and the raised bit of land where the source of the void seemed to reside. With each step that carried her to the edge of the darkness, she could feel a quiet voice whimpering in the recesses of her mind. *No. I don't want to do this. Please, don't make me do this.*

She was less than two steps away from the void when she saw something that would have had her falling to her knees if Von hadn't been there to catch her. Bones. Thousands of small, child-sized bones.

There were no words. Helena gaped at Von, who was staring at the mass grave in disgust, his jaw continuously clenching and unclenching.

Rowena had done a number of terrible things, but this might have been the worst, if for no other reason than the sheer number of innocent children that she would have had to murder to leave behind that many bones. This was clearly what she had been busy doing with the children of Endoshan. What wasn't clear was whether her new husband knew about it. The remote nature of the mass grave gave the impression that it was a secret, but given the sheer number of bones, someone had to have helped her. It was the only plausible way to cover up a genocide of this magnitude.

"Can you at least put their souls to rest?" Von asked.

The words caught Helena off guard, forcing her to a truth she had not had time to fully process. It was a sense of emptiness that had led her to this place, and a void by its very nature was an absence. It was difficult, but Helena forced herself to discount the piles of bones that were visible as far as she could see. She tried to focus instead on what else might be hidden beyond normal sight.

Helena sucked in a breath as realization dawned. "There are no souls here," she murmured.

Von looked at her sharply. "In the Forest, even when Rowena had destroyed the Night Stalker village, the souls of those that were slain were still present. Why would it be different here?"

"Because of how she murdered them." Helena's voice was hollow.

Von turned to fully face her. "What do you mean?"

Helena swallowed, letting the hold of her power drop, not wanting to feel any more than she absolutely had to. She felt raw and battered, each new revelation bringing with it a surge of powerful emotions that were slowly destroying her. It was like she was under attack from the inside out, and she was entirely incapable of protecting herself from further assault. There was only one defense against the kind of atrocity she was facing, and it was something that the Mother's Vessel would never know: an utter lack of empathy. Only someone truly soulless would be immune.

Soulless.

Helena's eyes moved to Von. "She did not simply kill them. She stole their lives."

Von's eyes narrowed, not understanding the distinction.

"We have always known that Rowena twisted her power, using her Spirit magic to steal the wills and bodies of those that serve her. What we had not allowed ourselves to consider, was that it was more than just their wills she was stealing. Rowena creates her Shadows by taking control of their souls. It is how she gained so much power."

Von looked pale. "I don't... I'm not sure I understand."

Helena didn't blame him. It was too horrific a thought. "You have witnessed Rowena try to transform one into a Shadow."

He nodded, having nearly been a victim himself.

"When she makes that connection, she is taking a part of their essence into herself, creating her own twisted bond. It is what allows her to assert her will over them. They are her puppets, because they are quite literally tied to her. She does not drain them completely, since the body cannot survive without its soul. She needs them to stay alive just enough that they can serve her."

She could tell by the glint in his eye that Von was starting to understand. "Children cannot fight, so they have no use to her."

Helena nodded. "And so she consumes every drop."

"This..." Von started, his voice breaking, "this is the source of her power?"

She desperately wished that she could deny it, but the proof was literally at their feet. "Whatever she has done to so pervert her magic, has allowed her to eat the souls of her victims. That kind of life force must be potent. It has exponentially strengthened whatever gifts she was born with."

"So why isn't she affected when the Shadows die the same way she is when the Generals do?"

It was a good question, and one she already guessed the answer to. "She has taken all but a drop of what remains in her Shadows. They are already a part of her; their loss is no more than a snip of hair falling to the ground. It is a different relationship with the Generals."

"You've lost me again," Von admitted, looking frustrated that he was slower to make the connections that she had.

Helena grew thoughtful, trying to think of an easier way to explain. "The Vessel required a Mate, one strong enough to help her withstand the strength of her power so that it did not consume her."

Von nodded.

"Rowena stole power. More power than she was ever supposed to have. She is not strong enough to contain it on her own, and she does not have a Mate to help her carry the burden."

"So she uses her Generals as a way to keep and control the power," Von stated.

"Exactly. It is why they are so strong."

"When she loses a General, she loses a significant amount of the power she amassed from the Shadows," Von finished, finally understanding.

Helena nodded, looking back out over the scattered bones. "And it is why she was in such a hurry to recoup it."

Von fell silent.

The kind of selfishness that would allow someone to kill without mercy was almost beyond comprehension. These were children. Hundreds and possibly thousands of lives filled with potential that would never be fulfilled. *How could the Mother let this happen? Where is the justice?*

Helena realized she must have asked the questions out loud when Von responded.

"You are the Mother's justice. Let's find her, Helena. Let's find her and make her pay for what she has done."

Helena turned her back on the bones, not wanting to watch as they slowly sank down into the black earth. There was no life left here. Whatever Rowena had done had caused the earth itself to recoil from the taint. Helena pumped her magic back into the land, even as she began to walk away. It sucked greedily, using her power to repair the damage. By the time they had returned to their friends, the water had reclaimed the path, and Helena knew without looking that the void was gone.

It was going to take a lot more than that for her to say the same. The proof of what they were facing, the level to which Rowena would stoop to win, could no longer be ignored. There was only one way this war would end, and it was the same way it started.

Death.

CHAPTER 16

*A*lthough they had reunited with the others, Helena remained apart from the group, not ready to relive what she had seen just yet. She left it up to Von to fill them in on the discovery, and to answer the questions such a revelation would necessitate. Knowing that the images would haunt both her waking and nighttime hours was bad enough, but the thought of having to say it aloud and bring those images to life made her want to vomit.

"Are you all right, Kiri?" Reyna asked.

Helena jumped, not having heard her approach. It was a good reminder that she could not afford to become lost in her thoughts right now. She considered lying, but after eyeing the Night Stalker's leader, she decided to go with the truth. "No." She sighed. "Not even a little bit."

"It sounds horrible. So many…" Reyna trailed off, the swirls of paint doing little to hide her pained expression.

Helena's eyes fell closed, and she swallowed, taking a few seconds to let her stomach settle before she responded. "You would think, with as much death as I've seen in the last few months, that it wouldn't affect me like this. But they were only children, Reyna. They didn't deserve this; hell, not even the worst kind of criminal deserves it. Especially not what she's done to them," Helena paused, her shaking hand reaching out and grasping Reyna's. "There won't even be any peace for them. She didn't just take their futures, Reyna. She stole their afterlife. Without souls, they can never return to the Mother."

Reyna's dark green eyes shuttered, but she returned Helena's squeeze with one of her own.

The raw emotions were making her vulnerable, leading Helena to a confession she would not have otherwise made to any but her Mate. "I don't know how to set my emotions aside and lead them right now," she whispered, referring to the army at her back. "All I want to do is curl up and cry over the waste she's made of those lives." Helena's voice was ragged by the time she was done speaking. She sucked in a quick breath and turned to face Reyna directly. "How do you deal with it?"

Reyna's brows shot up in surprised. "You think that it's a lack of emotion that helps me lead?"

Helena nodded. "In order to make rational decisions you have to set them aside, don't you?"

"That sounds like something a man told you."

The memories of Timmins and Joquil helping her prepare for her trial came to mind, and Helena almost smiled at how accurate an assessment it was. In her case, it had been two men.

Reyna laughed bitterly. "Maybe that is true for some rulers, but I would argue the opposite. It is the things we have the strongest reactions to that shows us what our path must be."

Some of the tension in Helena's chest loosened. Learning that a ruler as strong as Reyna let her emotions influence her decisions was a relief. Moreover, there was comfort, and a sense of solidarity, in knowing that she was not the only one who did so. Helena squeezed Reyna's hand once more, this time as a silent thank you, before letting it go. She finally felt steady enough to continue the journey without borrowing someone else's strength.

The Endoshan Keep came into view a couple of seconds later. It looked abandoned, but not because it was in ruins. This was no crumbling castle. Everything still looked pristine, as if everyone finished with their chores and simply got up and left. It was also entirely too quiet, the usual noises of people going about their day absent.

"You don't think we'll find her there, do you?" Reyna asked, watching Helena's face as she took in their surroundings.

Helena shook her head, her eyes not straying from the keep. "No, I don't."

"And yet, you brought your army here anyway." It wasn't a question, but it sounded like one.

"In the end, it matters not if she is here. The choice led us to something we needed to see. If that is all we get from the excursion, it was still an important piece of the puzzle to collect."

Reyna nodded her agreement. "The girl's vision led you here for a reason. Perhaps it just wasn't the one you had thought."

The two women walked in silence a bit longer before coming to a full stop. The rest of the Circle caught up to them a few moments later, their collective faces grim as they studied the keep.

"It's too quiet for an army to be housed within," Kragen said, echoing Helena's earlier assessment.

"That doesn't mean someone isn't tucked away inside," Ronan pointed out.

"It would have to be a fairly small group," Helena mused.

"You think we will find more than one person inside?" Von asked.

Helena shrugged. "Rowena would never go somewhere alone. Especially now. At the very least, she is going to keep her Generals close." She shot Reyna a look.

The Night Stalker looked amused watching Helena carefully walk the line between her beliefs and her Circle's expectations regarding what they would find inside. Studied more carefully, Helena had not actually answered Von's question. She supplied a truth, yes, but it was one that allowed the others to hear what they wanted. Reyna winked at Helena before schooling her face back into a neutral mask.

"What do you want to do, Kiri?" Joquil asked, putting the decision in her hands.

"We're already here. We may as well go inside and see what there is to find."

Von and Ronan split up the troops, selecting a small contingent of men to come inside with them. If Rowena was inside, they didn't want to be caught off-guard. Although, had Helena really believed the Corruptor was here, she would have stormed the damn keep with her whole army, not a mere handful of men. No matter how talented they were.

Effie forced her way forward, her eyes leveled on Helena. "I'm coming with you."

Timmins opened his mouth to protest, but Helena silenced him with a look. "As you wish, Effie. Just stay close."

Without further ceremony, Helena and the others made their way to the door.

SHE COULD HEAR the sound of their footsteps as their boots scratched against the stone floors. There was no other noise to counteract the rustling echo off of the walls. Endoshan Keep was utterly empty. At least, so far.

"Effie, does this look familiar?" Von asked.

The blonde shook her head, her curls swinging wildly. "No. Everything was darker in my vision, and I don't remember seeing any windows. I was underground, perhaps?"

The group looked around the expansive first floor for some sign of a stairwell.

"Over here!" Joquil called.

Helena and the others spun in a circle trying to find him.

"Where are you?" she shouted.

Joquil's head popped out from behind what looked like the center of a stone wall.

Effie screamed, her hand over her heart as if she was trying to keep it from flying out of her chest. "Mother's tits!"

"That shouldn't be possible, right?" Ronan asked in a low voice.

"Definitely not," Kragen replied.

Joquil shifted and suddenly his body was in full view. He was grinning. "Apologies, there's a hidden walkway here. Just walk straight toward me and then look to your left, you'll see what I mean."

There were some dubious eyebrows, but the group took a few tentative steps toward him.

"Oh, this is fun!" Kragen said, seeing what Joquil had meant. "Helena, we definitely need one of these at the Palace."

A few paces behind the others, it took her a bit longer to understand what they were talking about. Once she did, she certainly understood the appeal.

From a distance, Joquil appeared to be standing in front of a solid stone wall. Once you were standing next to him, however, it was clearly an optical illusion. There was another, identical, half-wall directly in front of the other. This allowed for a hidden hallway to be put in plain view. A great place to hide and eavesdrop if nothing else. Helena wondered how many other secret passageways existed in the keep, and if there were, in fact, some in the Palace.

The passage was only large enough for them to walk single file, so Joquil took the lead while one of the Daejarans took the rear. Von insisted on walking in front of Helena, which she couldn't say she overly minded. It gave her a nice view.

Ever since they completed the bond, it had become easier to catch snippets of her Mate's thoughts. Von had clearly just picked up on hers because he asked, *"Like what you see, Mira?"*

"Always."

"Aren't you the one always reminding me we have to stay focused?"

"We could die in the next twenty seconds. If I'm about to return to the Mother, I want to know I spent my last few moments on Her earth wisely."

She could see his shoulders shaking with laughter. *"Fair point well made, as always. Ogle away."*

"As if I needed your permission."

"I'm going to remember you said that."

The distraction was a welcome reprieve from the darkness that surrounded them. Every little sliver of light was the difference between holding on to hope or falling into despair. Helena would selfishly take what happiness she could, for as long as she could. Rowena didn't get to steal that from her, like she had with so much else. The day that they stopped holding on to hope, to the light, was the day that Rowena won. Helena would rather die than let that happen. These stolen moments were the proof that it wasn't over yet.

The hallway dipped, bringing them down a moldy smelling ramp and into a smaller chamber. They filtered into the room, one by one, each of them spreading out to allow the others to step inside. There was little light here, and what small bit was available was from a few flickering candles that were suspended from the walls.

Effie's gasp was the only confirmation Helena needed that this was the place from her vision. The room was long but narrow, a row of cages along the back half of the room. Cages that were occupied. There were about ten children chained in half as many cages. They seemed to be drugged, their small heads dangling down to their chests, and none of them reacting to the appearance of the others in the room.

Helena's rage was swift and absolute. Not waiting for anyone else, she pushed ahead, her hand already outstretched with the intention of breaking open each of the cages.

"Helena, wait," Timmins cautioned softly.

She spun around, her teeth bared in a snarl. "You dare stop me, Advisor?" She had made the transition from Helena to Vessel so quickly, the sound of her harmonious voice surprised even her. It was low and throaty, and there was no mistaking the threat beneath her question.

Timmins held his hands up. "I mean no offense, Kiri. It's just, the children appear to be in stasis. There might be some kind of alarm you could trigger if you touch them."

"Good," she growled, her teeth feeling too large for her mouth. "Let them know I am here. Let them face me." She could feel the black claws pushing their way out of her hands, the predator inside her primed to fight.

Timmins nodded, backing slowly away from her.

Helena reached the first cage, her magic-enhanced claws tearing the door from the cage with a loud crash.

"Who needs an alarm?" Ronan asked.

She was careful to sheath the claws as she reached to brush limp brown hair off the child's face. It was a little girl, her features pinched with fear, even in her unconscious state. There were deep shadows beneath her eyes, and her skin looked waxy. She was clearly unwell. Helena eyed the chains, trying to determine the best way to release the girl, without her getting hurt.

There was an audible click and a hidden door opened, an Endoshan man Helena recognized storming into the room.

Effie whimpered, her skin bone-white. "It's happening," she whispered.

The Chosen went on high alert, knowing that Rowena had been in Effie's vision.

"What do you think you're—" the man's eyes went wide, recognition cutting his tirade short. "Kiri?"

Helena's iridescent eyes were narrowed into twin slits as she stalked toward him. "Where is your queen?" she demanded.

"I don't know, Kiri."

"Liar!" she screamed, throwing her arm up as a bolt of purple power blasted from her palm and into his chest. The Endoshan went flying back into the wall, crumpling to the floor.

"I-I swear, Kiri. I have not seen her since Kai left with her."

"Get up!"

The man struggled to push himself back into a standing position.

"We know about your little boneyard," Helena said, her voice low and menacing.

He gulped audibly. "I tried to reason with him, but he said it was the only way to ensure Endoshan's future."

Helena closed the distance between them, her steps slow and measured. "Is your future more meaningful than theirs?" she asked once they were almost nose to nose, gesturing toward the children in the cages.

"N-no, Kiri."

"So why do you get to live when you've sentenced them to death?"

"I-I haven't, Kiri." The man was crying now, tears falling freely from his golden eyes.

"How do we release them?" she asked, giving him a final opportunity to save himself.

"I don't know," he moaned. "Please, believe me."

"If you do not want to answer for her crimes, it would serve you well to tell me what you know."

"N-nothing, I swear!"

Her power was already coiled and ready to strike. Helena saw nothing but the man's eyes as she warned him, "I will give you until the count of three."

"K-Kiri," he begged.

"One."

"I don't know!"

"Two."

Whatever he saw in her face had him trying to run. Helena's hand snapped out, closing around his throat and holding him in place. His fate was sealed.

"Three," she whispered.

Helena unleashed her power, the full force of it moving through her arm and slamming into his body where they were connected. He gasped, his eyes bulging. One second, he was there; the next, he was gone. It was over as quickly as it began.

She stepped back, looking at her now empty hand. It was coated in a fine red dust. All that remained of him was the dust, which now covered everything between her and the wall she'd held him against. Her power had completely vaporized him. The bloodlust was beginning to fade, and what she'd just done was starting to seep into her awareness.

Helena turned toward the others, her breaths coming in shallow pants. They stared at her in stunned silence, Effie's hand pressed to her mouth. The fact that they didn't know how to approach her right now only increased the sense of alienation she was feeling. *What have I done?*

Reyna was the first to speak, not having the same sense of hesitation as the others. "Are you all right, Kiri?"

She wordlessly shook her head. Helena honestly didn't know what she was. She had never killed another person unprovoked before. She had fought during battles, protecting those she loved and destroying Rowena's Shadows without a second thought, but this had been different. There was no conscious thought, no decision to act. She just did.

Von approached her slowly. *"Mira, look at me."*

She lifted her eyes to his.

"You were well within your right to enact justice for those children."

She sucked in another breath, feeling lightheaded.

"Just focus on me."

Helena nodded to indicate she was trying.

"You did nothing wrong."

"I killed him." Even her psychic voice was trembling.

"You are the Mother's justice. Your actions are her own."

"I am the Mother's justice," she repeated slowly, her voice hollow.

"She was displeased, and She acted through Her Vessel," Timmins chimed in, his voice measured.

The rest of her Circle nodded their agreement, none of them looking at her with anything close to judgment. It was concern for her that had stayed their action, not disgust at what she had done. Their acceptance did more than anything else could.

Helena nodded, her breathing starting to slow. She looked down, shuddering as she realized she was still coated in what was left of the Endoshan.

"Let me help," Joquil murmured, stepping toward her. He waited for Helena's nod before saying, "Close your eyes."

She obeyed, and he moved his open palm over her, a gentle breeze stirring up the strands of hair that had escaped from her braid.

"You can open them," he murmured.

When Helena looked down, she was clean again. All trace of the red dust was gone.

"Thank you," she breathed.

"Of course, Kiri." Joquil stepped back, and Helena turned toward the cages.

The rage that had settled with the Endoshan's death lifted its head again at the sight of the children. Helena forced herself to breathe, pushing the anger down. It had no place here since it would not help the children be any less caged.

Helena walked back toward them, focusing on a sense of icy calm rather than fiery rage. She ran her fingers along the cool steel bars, walking the length of the cage doors that remained. The bars froze beneath the contact. Once she reached the end, she turned and released a breath, the bars snapping and falling to the ground.

Without being asked, the rest of the Chosen moved forward, using their various powers or simply their brute strength to snap the chains that held the children. The small bodies sagged, but the Chosen caught them before they fell, carefully lifting them and carrying them out. From there the children were gently laid out on the floor until each one looked like they might only be sleeping.

"Can you wake them?" Reyna asked.

"Of course she can," Ronan said, winking at Helena.

She gave him a small smile, appreciating the show of support. "It really depends what she's done to them," Helena admitted.

"A bigger concern is what we're going to do with them once they are awake," Timmins said.

He had a point. They couldn't very well take the children with them.

"We'll send them to the Palace," Helena decided on the spot. "We will raise them in Tigaera. If the Endoshans did not think they were worth keeping, they do not deserve to have them back."

There were murmurs of approval.

One of Ronan's men stepped forward. "If you will lend me a stone, Kiri, I can make sure they arrive safely and are well cared for."

"Thank you, Geralt."

The dark-haired man nodded. "It is the least we can do for them."

That much settled, Helena knelt next to the nearest child. It was the same one she'd first discovered. Helena placed her hand gently on the girl's forehead, her eyes fluttering closed as she used her power to seek out the source of the unnatural sleep.

Helena half expected that Rowena had kept the children drugged with *Bella Morte* as she had with Von, but there wasn't a trace of the hallucinogen in her body. *Thank the Mother for small miracles.*

Losing track of time and awareness of her physical body, Helena sent her power out, searching for any sign of interference. It took a couple of passes until she realized it was not a physical issue.

Her eyes opened and she sighed. It was deceptively simple, but no less evil for its simplicity. Rowena had used some of her Spirit to force the children into this state. All it took was a compulsion telling the children to go to sleep, and they had been helpless to fight the urge. Without Rowena here to remove the order, they could not wake on their own.

Not wanting the poor things to be terrified upon waking, Helena crafted her own finely woven compulsion. Bright purple tendrils began to flow out of Helena and wrap themselves around each of the sleeping bodies. She reinforced each tendril with some of her healing magic so that they would wake feeling rested and without any lingering side effects of the obvious drain Rowena had already performed.

Once she was certain the magic had taken hold, Helena said, "You are safe. It's time to wake up now."

The glowing tendrils, which had formed a tightly woven net around each of them, sank into the children until the strands disappeared entirely.

With a rather undignified yawn, the little girl beside Helena stretched and opened her eyes. "Is it time for breakfast?" she asked with a sweet lisp.

"Just about, dear one," Helena replied, brushing the soft hair off her forehead.

The girl scrunched her upturned nose. "Why are you crying? Did something bad happen?"

Helena brushed at her eyes. "It's nothing you need to worry about right now, darling."

Around her, the others began to wake up, the children curiously, but fearlessly, inspecting the grown-ups around them. Helena knew, had it not been for her magic, they would be much more suspicious of the strangers, especially had they remembered what had happened to them.

Von helped her stand, and Helena hid her face in his neck. At least this time her tears were from relief.

She'd finally arrived in time to save someone.

CHAPTER 17

"*A*re we returning to Tigaera as well?"

The children had been sent to the Palace almost immediately. Without having searched the rest of the keep, no one felt comfortable with the idea of letting them remain there any longer than strictly necessary.

After a thorough search, they were able to determine that the rest of the keep was, in fact, abandoned. The man Helena had killed, the one whose name she didn't even know, had been the only one that remained. Probably to keep an eye on Rowena's pets.

Not sure of their next steps, the Circle gathered in the kitchen. The others, minus Effie who stayed behind, had been sent back to fill in the rest of the army on what had transpired.

"Without a clear destination, where else would we go?" Helena asked, in reply to Kragen's question.

"We could see if asking about Rowena triggers another vision," Ronan said, his eyes shooting over to Effie apologetically.

Effie licked her lips, her eyes darting between Helena and Ronan. "But I was wrong before. I don't know what I'm doing."

"No one blames you, Effie. Look at what we were able to accomplish today because your vision led us here," Ronan said.

"But I was wrong," she insisted.

Timmins was studying Effie carefully. "Your vision is simply a series of images that require your interpretation to decipher their message. Without training, it's understandable that you might infer the wrong meaning."

"It's a shitty time to try to learn," Effie huffed.

Helena's lips twitched up; she liked this side of her. Their sweet flower had grown thorns.

The ghost of a smile made a brief appearance on Timmins' face. "We just need to learn what the images mean to you. Perhaps there were subtle details you missed because you didn't know to look for them."

"What do you mean?" Effie asked, her brows lowering in confusion.

"Well," Timmins paused, choosing his words with care. "Your vision was triggered by a question. The series of images chosen to answer the question are unique to you. They could only be things that held some sort of personal significance or meaning since you cannot See what you do not already know. There'd be no way for you to accurately explain or discern its significance. So, therefore the images must be intimately tied to you and your understanding of them."

Helena could see where he was coming from, but she didn't fully agree with his assessment. "Miranda told me that visions are never straightforward. I doubt we can take them at face value."

"How would we explain that Effie knew to come to Endoshan then?" Von asked.

"Maybe it's not just the images themselves, but their relationship to each other?" Joquil asked.

"Technically Effie didn't know. You were the ones that made the connection to the man she described and Endoshan," Helena reminded them.

The others fell silent. It was hard to solve a puzzle when you couldn't see the pieces.

"Effie, I want you to try something for me, if you wouldn't mind," Von said.

She nodded, biting down on her bottom lip hard enough Helena was worried she might draw blood.

"Close your eyes and try to picture what you Saw."

Effie's eyes widened, but she nodded again and followed his direction.

"Can you see it?"

"Yes," she whispered.

"What are you looking at?"

"The man."

"Had you seen him before?"

"I'm not sure."

"What is it about him that stands out?"

"His leathers. I recognized them." Her eyes popped open. "Joquil was right, it must be association."

"That's great, Effie," Von smiled warmly. "Try again, and this time I want you to focus on the moment when Rowena appears."

Effie swallowed and closed her eyes. After a moment she whispered, "Okay."

"Why do you think the vision is showing you Rowena?"

Her brows furrowed, not understanding the question. "Because it *is* Rowena."

"Is it?"

"It's her," Effie said emphatically.

"Describe her to me."

Effie sighed. "Blonde hair, cold blue eyes, her hand is wrapped around the man's throat as she yells at him."

Helena shivered, not liking how close the description was to her own actions.

"What else?" Von prompted.

"She has a crown..."

"What kind of crown?"

Effie's eyes scrunched in confusion. "Light? No, that's not right. It looks like it's glowing. It's casting light... it's fire?" Effie opened her eyes, looking at the others. "Why would Rowena be wearing a crown like that? Helena is the one who's supposed to wear the Crown of Embers."

Helena flinched at the words, every eye in the room focusing on her.

"She wants the crown?" Kragen offered.

Timmins shook his head. "It's not just the crown she wants. She wants Helena's power."

The others continued to throw out suggestions, but Helena had her own suspicion. "Effie?"

Wide cornflower blue eyes met hers. "Yes?"

"Was there," Helena swallowed, "was there a mirror in your vision?"

"A mirror?"

Helena nodded.

Effie closed her eyes, going silent for a few seconds before she responded. "Yes." She opened her eyes. "What does that mean?"

Helena's shoulders dropped. "It means that it was never Rowena that you Saw. It was always me."

Quiet filled the room as her words sunk in.

"But why? That would mean the vision wasn't triggered by your question at all."

Helena shrugged. "It was stranger that we thought it had been. Miranda never mentioned any of her visions working that way. I think it was purely coincidence that you happened to inherit your power in that moment."

Effie frowned.

"I am the mirror," Helena said matter-of-factly. "You saw my crown on her head, because it was a warning of what would happen when we got here. Of who I would become. She brings out the worst in me, the parts of me that are most like her. It's what she's always wanted."

"No, that's not possible. You are the Vessel."

"And she is the Corruptor. Every move she's made has been with the hope of making me snap. It's why she went after my Mate." Helena shuddered. "She has no idea how close she was to succeeding."

"Helena," Von started, his eyes turning gold.

She stopped him with the lift of her hand. "When Darrin first told me who I was, he reminded me that like calls to like, of what it would mean if I became corrupted. If Rowena is successful, think of what she could accomplish with me on her side."

"But you'd never join her," Effie protested.

"Not unless pushed past all reason," Von said.

"Fuck me," Ronan whispered. "This has all been a trap. Everything."

Helena nodded. "She's been a step ahead of us this whole time."

"She is toying with you," Kragen growled.

"She wants to break me so that I will destroy the Chosen."

"What sense does that make? Who would be left to rule?" Effie asked.

Dread pooled in Helena's stomach as she replied, "Those that she's already corrupted. It would be the start of the Shadow Years. Literally. And I would be the ultimate puppet."

Von moved into her line of sight, forcing her to meet his gaze. "That is *never* going to happen."

"Of course it fucking isn't!" Ronan shouted. "Helena, you can't possibly think she's going to win."

"Look at what happened today," she whispered. "She got to me."

"Who wouldn't be affected by what she had done to those children?" Ronan asked.

Helena shrugged helplessly. "Who else could have done what I did, because of their reaction?"

There was no answer to that, because there was no one else. Only Helena, in her capacity as the Vessel, could have mete out that kind of punishment.

"But it was the Mother's justice," Timmins insisted.

"Unless it wasn't."

Helena felt like her mind was spinning in a million different directions. There was still something they were missing. A piece of the puzzle that they didn't have that was keeping them from being able to see a truth just out of their reach.

Von grasped her face in his hands. "There is nothing, *nothing*," he repeated, "that could ever bring you to the darkness."

"You're wrong."

"You are nothing but light, Helena. You are *my* light."

Tears started to fill her eyes at the certainty in his voice. She may be confused, but there was not a trace of doubt in her Mate.

"Do you hear me?" he asked, his forehead dropping to hers.

"Yes," she said for his ears alone.

"I will keep reminding you until you believe in yourself as much as I do."

"I do not deserve your faith in me. I do not deserve you."

"Yes, you do. Otherwise the Mother would have never brought us together."

"Perhaps this is the game," Ronan said thoughtfully, breaking her from the spell Von had wrapped around her. "Maybe she wants you to be crippled by doubt so that you are too afraid to do what must be done."

Helena could neither agree nor disagree with his assessment. They had grossly underestimated the woman.

The simple fact was, when it came to Rowena, anything was possible.

HELENA PACED, her earlier revelations keeping her from being able to find any solace in sleep. All of it was a terrifying montage that haunted her waking hours. Who needed nightmares when their reality was one already?

She had come to her garden to walk amongst the simplest form of beauty, needing to see something pure and untainted. Especially now when she could hardly stand to look upon her own reflection. The truth was, she felt unclean. Rowena may not have actually corrupted her, but it felt like it.

When they'd gotten home, Helena had scrubbed her skin until she felt raw, and still it had done nothing to remove the sense of vile filth that surrounded her. This was not a superficial grime that could be removed with ease. It was a dirty smear that defiled her very soul. She may never feel clean again.

"What are you doing out here alone?" Von asked, stepping away from the tree she had once caused to burst with life. It had been in a state of eternal bloom ever since. The memory felt like it belonged to someone else. Helena wished that her foibles were still only minor inconveniences. Mistakes now could lead, and quite frankly had already led, to innocent people being killed.

Helena shrugged, not having a simple answer for her Mate.

He walked toward her, his eyes glittering in the pale moonlight. His fingers brushed against her flowers, until he grasped one and plucked it from its bush. He offered it to her silently.

She accepted his gift, holding the blossom up to her nose to sniff its heady fragrance.

"Beautiful," she sighed, returning her attention to him.

"Yes, you are," Von agreed, brushing his thumb along her jaw and leaning down to kiss her.

"You have a habit of giving me flowers," she murmured once he pulled away.

"They make you smile."

"Mother knows I could certainly use something to smile about right about now." Von gestured toward the flower, making her laugh. "Touché."

"That's better."

Helena rested her head against his shoulder, curling into his body and welcoming the warmth that surrounded her as he held her close. "I'm scared," she whispered.

"I know."

Of course he did. Given their bond, he likely felt her emotions as if they were his own. "I'm trying to be strong."

He tipped her chin up. "You are strong."

"I don't feel like it. How did she weave that web so carefully? How did she know I'd go there?"

Von loosed a breath and looked over her head and into the night as he contemplated her question. "From a tactical standpoint, it makes sense that you would go to investigate Endoshan after learning of their betrayal. She had to assume at some point you would find your way there, and so she left a surprise for you to stumble across along your way. I wouldn't be surprised if there were a few other similar presents scattered along Elysia for you to discover. Even if you don't find them all, you'd be certain to come across at least one of them."

Helena nodded thoughtfully. "I just hate that she was right. She seems to know me better than I know her."

"She sees your compassion as a weakness to exploit. What she doesn't understand is that she's wrong."

"Is she? It worked, didn't it?"

"You lose sight of your wins so easily."

Helena lifted her shoulder in a shrug. "It was a draw at best. She still proved her point."

"So did you."

She tilted her head to stare up at him. "How can your belief in me be so unwavering?"

"I know your soul," Von said simply, holding his hand just above her heart. "If our situations were reversed, would you doubt me?"

"Not for a second."

"There you go."

"But—"

He placed a finger against her lips. "Maybe the question you should be asking is why are you so quick to question yourself? We are the same, you and I; two halves of a whole. If you would not doubt me, there's no reason you should doubt yourself."

She smiled under his finger before nipping at it.

"Light always shines brightest in the dark," he said before claiming her mouth in a heated kiss.

Helena melted into him, loving the way they fit together in every sense of the word.

"Your pep talks have gotten better," she teased.

"I've had a great mentor."

She chuckled. "I love you."

"And I you."

Snuggling back into him, she asked, "So what should I do now, Oh Wise One?"

"You seek out the darkness and you shine."

"When you put it that way, it sounds so easy."

Von's laughter rumbled beneath her, and as always, Helena found peace in the arms of the man who could see her even when she lost sight of herself.

CHAPTER 18

*I*t had been three days, and Helena was no closer to figuring out where to go next. The more time they gave Rowena to scheme, the worse it was going to be once they found her. They needed to act. Now.

"I don't see any way around it," Helena said on a defeated sigh, "we need to go to Bael and seek out the Triumvirate."

Ronan let out a low growl, and Helena peered up at him with tired eyes. Her Shield had not forgotten what happened the last time they had come face-to-face with the powerful trio. Even Von, who had only heard about it after the fact, looked darkly unhappy.

"Look, I don't like it any more than you do. But we're lost here, and I don't see any of you coming up with better ideas. Best case scenario, they point us in the right direction. Worst case, we're in the exact same position we are now."

"It might be good for Effie to meet some of the other Keepers. She could probably use some of their guidance right about now," Timmins said thoughtfully.

Helena clung to the words. "See, exactly! Even more of a reason to go to the Keepers."

"What does Effie have to say about this?" Kragen asked.

"I haven't exactly mentioned it to her yet," Helena admitted. "If she'd rather not come, I'm not going to force her to. It's got to be her choice."

The others nodded their agreement.

"So it's settled."

"Helena," Joquil interjected.

She turned toward her Master. "Yes?"

"Do you know where exactly to find the Keepers?"

Helena's face fell. She did not. There was only one among them who did, and she was dead. "Mother's tits, I can't catch a break," she swore, drawing some amused looks from her Circle.

"I might have an idea," Ronan said.

She turned to him hopefully.

"The Forest of Whispers borders Bael, perhaps Reyna and the Night Stalkers know where to start."

"Good call. I much prefer that option to the one I had."

"Which was?" he asked, his lips already curling up in a smirk.

"Wandering around Bael aimlessly until we found them."

"I should have known," Ronan replied. "You always do seem to prefer the direct approach."

Helena rolled her eyes. He was really starting to turn into the older brother she never wanted. Never wanted, but dearly loved.

There were a few chuckles as the others began to stand, sensing that the meeting was coming to a close.

"It's more likely that they would have found us," Timmins muttered as he pushed his chair in, the heavy wood scraping across the stone floor.

Helena was inclined to agree, especially given their history of sneaking up on her. "Well, either way."

He gave her a small smile and made his way toward the door. "I'll go find Effie and let her know what we are planning."

"Thank you."

The men filtered out until only Von was left. He tugged on her braid, leaning over to kiss her once before heading out. "I think a couple of the Talyrians should come with us."

That reminded her of something she'd been meaning to ask him.

"Speaking of Talyrians... does Starshine seem to be acting strange to you?"

Von stopped and lifted a brow. "You mean more than usual?"

Helena bit her lip. "I don't know what it is, but she seems more... restless? Agitated? I'm not sure, just more something since we've returned from Vyruul."

"Perhaps having her pride in that kind of danger upset her."

"Mmm, perhaps," she murmured.

"You think it's something else?"

Helena shrugged. "The pride has been in hiding. No one has been allowed to see them, not even me. Starshine actually growled at me when I tried to visit them yesterday."

Von tried not to laugh at the childlike offense his Mate had clearly taken to the rebuff.

"Do you think one of the pride has been injured and that's why she doesn't want anyone around? She's protecting them?"

It was Von's turn to shrug. "She's a Queen, it seems like something she would do. Hell, it's something that *you* would do. Perhaps you should try again. If one of them is harmed, Starshine may not want to leave them."

Helena frowned. The thought of something happening to one of those beautiful creatures had her stomach churning. She should have paid closer attention, but she'd been distracted by Miranda's death and then Effie's vision. There hadn't been any free time to spend with the Talyrian Queen, which was why she hadn't had a chance to go see her before yesterday. Helena intended to remedy that oversight and try again with a bit more insistence today.

"Good idea, I'll go down there now."

"Want me to come with you?" he offered.

"No, I don't think so. I want to give them as few reasons as possible to turn me away. Another human might tip the scales against me."

He nodded. "Let me know if you need me."

"I always need you." She smiled.

His eyes glowed with silver fire. "Likewise, my love."

With a wink, he was gone, and Helena went to make good on her promise.

LEAVES CRACKLED underneath her boots as Helena made her way into the series of caves the Talyrians had claimed as their own. It was only a short hike away from the Palace, the main entry just off a bubbling brook that wound its way through her gardens and into a small knot of trees. Prior to her travels, Helena would have considered the trees a forest in their own right, but after experiencing the Forest of Whispers, and even Bael, she knew the description did not ring true.

She purposely made as much noise as possible, not wanting the Talyrians to feel as though she was sneaking up on them. Given that their hearing was likely far superior to her own, she did not think it was necessary, but she didn't want to take any chances.

From the moody swipe of Starshine's tail when Helena approached the cave entrance, it would seem she had made the right decision.

"Hello, my beautiful girl."

Starshine snorted, plumes of smoke rising from her snout.

"Is that any way to greet your friend?" Helena asked, keeping her voice light. She held up her empty hands to signal her intention.

Starshine's turquoise eyes tracked the movement. The only sign of the creature's unease was the nervous flick of her tail.

Helena noted the twitch, but carried on anyway. She took two tentative steps forward, her back stiffening as Starshine bared her teeth and began to growl low in her throat. Knowing she was treading on dangerous ground, Helena stopped entirely.

"Is it all humans that you are mad at, or is it just me?"

Starshine whined and pawed the air, her massive claws sheathed but still deadly.

Helena wasn't sure how to interpret that answer.

"Did something happen to one of the pride?" she asked in a soft voice.

From the drop of Starshine's head at the question, Helena could only infer that she was correct.

"Are they injured? Would you like me to help?"

Starshine huffed, a low angry sound.

Helena swallowed. The Talyrian had never done anything to threaten her before, and while the actions Starshine made were mildly aggressive, Helena did not think they were aimed at her specifically.

"Did... did someone not survive the attack?" she asked in a horrified whisper, for it was the only thing she could think of that would provoke this kind of hostility.

Starshine opened her mouth and roared. Heat blasted against Helena as Starshine's breath rushed over her, causing her cloak and hair to fly back.

Helena's hands were shaking as she held them up again. "I'm so sorry," she whispered brokenly, closing the distance between them and wrapping her arms around Starshine's neck.

The Talyrian tolerated the embrace, but her velvety body was practically vibrating with tension.

"I didn't know. I'm so sorry, girl."

Starshine let out another huff that sounded more like a whimper.

"We will make her pay for this, you have my promise."

At her words, Starshine seemed to relax, finally pressing some of her weight against Helena's body.

Helena pulled away slightly, wanting to be able to look into the Talyrian's eyes as she spoke. "That is part of why I came to visit. We are trying to track that evil bitch and her minions down. I know that you are in mourning, but I would like for you to come with us."

There was nothing to signal what Starshine thought of her words until the massive head dipped in what would have passed for a nod on a human.

Relief filled her, and Helena allowed herself a sharp smile. "I cannot promise you that I will let you repay her kindness in kind."

Starshine's eyes narrowed and she snarled softly.

"You can have anyone else, my beautiful girl. But Rowena's death belongs to me."

The words were infused with her power, her body making the small transformations that tied her so closely to the creature beside her.

Starshine inspected Helena, appreciating the signs of the predator she saw before her.

There was another huff, and Helena knew that the Talyrian had agreed. With that settled, all they needed now was to find her.

Then they could both take their revenge.

CHAPTER 19

"I'm sorry that this was the best we were able to do, Kiri," Reyna said as they ducked beneath a low vine.

Helena laughed. "There's no reason to apologize, Reyna. This is still better than what I would have been able to accomplish."

The Night Stalkers had been familiar with Bael, but only to a certain extent. Large parts of the jungle were off limits to them, keeping them out with very powerful magical barriers. They knew only of the Keeper's Catacombs in theory, having a rough idea of where they might be located given the presence of the barriers. Even still, their guess was a better starting point than what Helena would have been able to offer as it got them straight into the heart of the jungle, thereby saving days of travel on foot.

If the others were tired of bouncing around Elysia in search of Rowena, they gave no indication. If anything, her army seemed more determined than ever.

Ronan moved into place beside her, his handsome face grim as he studied their surroundings.

"Need something?" she asked.

Ronan's eyes cut to hers. "Not specifically, but being here again has me on edge."

Helena couldn't help but notice that Reyna was staring resolutely ahead, completely ignoring the exchange.

"Did I miss something?" Helena asked Von.

"You didn't hear?" Von asked in surprise.

"Considering my question, I think you can safely surmise the answer."

She felt his chuckle as if he was standing right behind her. *"When Reyna learned what happened with the Air General, she ran up to him and slapped him across the face."*

"Wait... what?" Helena stopped dead in her place, her mouth hanging open in shock. *"How in the Mother's name did I miss that?"*

"It happened while you were dealing with other things. I just thought you knew."

"Why did she slap him?"

Von sounded darkly amused as he replied, *"I think her words were something to the effect of 'I didn't risk my life saving you once so that you could go ahead and hand it over at the next opportunity.'"*

"That sounds reasonable," Helena said, her lips turning up in a smile. *"I wish I could have been there to see it."*

"It was fairly memorable, to say the least. I don't think anyone has ever dared to put Ronan in his place like that before."

"What did Ronan have to say about it?"

"Well, at first he sort of glared at her—"

"As Ronan is prone to do."

Von laughed, and the feeling of his mirth filled her with warmth. *"Exactly. But instead of laying into her, as he would have anyone else, he just apologized and watched her storm off."*

"How very interesting."

"Don't you go and start meddling. Those two need to work out whatever is between them on their own."

"I never meddle."

Von's silence was as damning as anything he could have possibly said.

"I don't!" she insisted.

Realizing that Ronan and Reyna had stopped a few feet away while waiting for her to catch up, she rushed forward. "Sorry, distracted."

"Clearly," Ronan said, his jaw clenched. "Do try to pay more attention, Helena. Need I remind you what happened last time you went for a walk here?"

"I don't like your tone," she informed him primly, not appreciating his insinuation on top of the one Von had just given her.

"I don't care."

Helena huffed, ready to remind him who served who when Reyna spun toward her Shield.

"Don't you have something better to do?" she snapped, her eyes like glittering emeralds.

"Something more important than keeping my Kiri safe? No, I don't. I'm the Shield, that's literally my number one priority."

Reyna let out a cold laugh. "Oh, is that what you were doing? It sounded more like you were trying to bully her."

Ronan's blue eyes went wide. "What the hell would you know about it, Night Stalker?"

"As the only other one of us that rules, I would assume a hell of a lot more than you."

"Keep your eyes open," Ronan snapped, his jaw clenched as he turned and walked back to the others.

There was a long moment of silence until Helena finally broke it by asking, "So, you and Ronan, huh?"

Reyna shot wide eyes at Helena before wisps of shadow began to roll up her neck, almost like she was trying to conceal herself behind them. It was an interesting way to blush.

"Listen, you two are adults. I'm less concerned about what you do together and more worried about how it affects him. Ronan is one of the most selflessly loyal men I have ever known. If all you are interested in is toying with him, then you should leave it alone."

"Toying with him?" Reyna repeated. "Not that it's any of your business—"

"He's my Shield, his well-being is very much my business. As much as I like you Night Stalker, if you hurt him, you will have to answer to me."

Reyna's mouth was still open like she wanted to say something, but she closed it when she realized Helena's eyes had turned into sparkling iridescence.

"Fair enough."

Helena nodded, and the two continued to walk in silence.

"You wouldn't call that meddling?" Von asked.

"It was a warning."

"Ronan is perfectly capable of taking care of himself."

"I just watched him piece himself together after the last woman broke his heart. I'm not going to stand idly by and watch it happen again."

"I don't think Reyna's the type of woman who would be that careless, knowing who he belongs to."

"Nor do I, but sometimes a reminder can be useful in resetting one's priorities."

She could hear Von's laugh from somewhere behind her. *"So was it a warning or a reminder?"*

"Why can't it be both?"

"Ronan is lucky to have such a fierce protector."

"He would do the same for me."

"Given that I am the one who would be on the other side of the threats, I am not entirely sure how to feel about that."

Helena smirked. *"You planning on doing something that requires threats?"*

"Not at the moment, but you never know. Forever is a long time; I'm bound to do something stupid eventually."

"Noted. I'll ask Ronan to keep his eyes peeled, just in case he sees an opportunity to give you a good reminder."

"Mother save me. Knowing Ronan, he's going to start coming up with reasons to crawl up my ass and then use protecting you as an excuse to get away with it."

They were both snickering when they came upon a wide clearing that was surrounded on three sides by a burbling stream. Helena glanced toward the sky, or what little of it she could see.

"We should probably set up camp here for the night. We'll send scouts ahead to see if they can find the first of the barriers so we know how close we are come morning."

There were a few shouts of agreement as others set to work.

DINNER HAD BEEN A QUIET AFFAIR. A large part of it probably had to do with their diminished size, but Helena knew it also had something to do with the fact that they were all on high alert. Once again, she was traveling with only a select few of her guard plus a small retinue of Reyna's Night Stalkers. Anduin and the Storm Forged had remained behind with the rest of the army at the Palace, ready to call them back if Rowena struck there, or to join Helena if she called for him.

The entire group was scattered around a fire, having just finished off a rabbit and vegetable stew that Effie had prepared for them. How she'd managed to make something so delicious with limited resources was beyond impressive.

"It was amazing, Effie!" Helena said, using a bit of magic to clean the dish before returning the bowl and spoon to her pack.

The rest of them gave satisfied murmurs of agreement.

"Thank you," she beamed. "It was nice to have a familiar task to focus on for a while."

Effie was just settling into place beside Helena when a startled shout had everyone jumping up.

"Sorry everyone! False alarm," a red-faced Daejaran said. "It was just a spider. Caught the little fucker climbing up my neck and I over reacted. You can all stand down."

Helena let out a relieved laugh, glad that she hadn't been the one to have an eight-legged friend crawling all over her. Turning to Effie, to see if she shared in the amusement, Helena let out a startled cry of her own.

Effie's blue eyes had rolled back into her head, and she had already started convulsing.

Helena rolled her onto her side and did what she could to keep her from hurting herself.

"What should we do?" Reyna asked.

"I don't think there's anything we can do," Helena murmured, wincing in sympathy as her friend was lost to her vision.

"She just has to ride it out," Timmins added.

Helena discretely wiped away the drool that had started to run from Effie's mouth, her skin feeling like ice beneath her fingers. She had no idea how long the vision lasted, it felt like hours as her friend's body spasmed although it was probably less than a minute in total.

Once she began to still, and it was just small twinges in her arms and legs, Effie's eyes fluttered open. The whites of her eyes were bloodshot, and a small trail of blood was dripping out of her mouth from where she must have bit down on her cheek.

"Do you think you can sit up?" Helena asked in a low voice.

Effie groaned.

"It's okay; take all the time you need. There's no rush."

Effie's pupils were fully dilated, only the barest trace of blue ringing around the swollen black pupils. She still didn't seem to be entirely present.

Looking at her with a healer's curiosity, Helena pressed the palm of her hand into Effie's forehead. Perhaps she could help speed up her friend's recovery by easing the pain the vision had caused.

Helena closed her eyes and pushed a small tendril of power into the newest Keeper.

"Helena, wait!"

She wasn't sure whose voice it was, perhaps it was many, but it didn't matter. As soon as Helena's power flowed into Effie's body, the damage was already done.

Instead of Helena being able to seek out and sever the final ties of the vision, the vision sank its claws into her, sucking her down into its final haunting scenes.

At first, Helena wasn't sure what was happening. The world had become entirely muted, everything cast in shades of gray. It wasn't until she realized that she was no longer kneeling in the clearing that she understood where she was.

"Effie?" she called, but no noise left her mouth. It seemed that she could only bear witness to the events unfolding before her, not interact with them.

Helena looked around, trying to make sense of what was happening. There was nothing she immediately recognized about her surroundings. It looked like she was sitting in the center of a massive web, each shimmering tendril trembling as if caught in the middle of a storm. She could not see far enough to determine what had anchored the web, it seemed to span out as far as she could see in every direction.

An ice-blue spider appeared and began to make its way carefully across the shaking web. It chittered, seeming excited by what it had trapped. Nervous, Helena tried to move out of the center of the web, not wanting to be there when the spider inevitably reached the center.

The more she tried to free herself from the sticky strings, the more hopelessly entangled she became, until eventually, she was fully encased in the silky strands. It wasn't until the ghostly twilight of the world went dark and she was completely encased in darkness that Helena began to scream.

IT WAS the sound of her screams the sent him running, his pants only hastily half-laced. Von had stepped away to water some plants, certain that the others could keep his Mate safe in the handful of seconds he would be out of sight. He was already plotting Ronan's murder for allowing whatever it was to put that level of fear in her voice.

"You have one fucking job, you bastard," he muttered darkly. Logically, he knew Ronan was not to blame for whatever was happening, but having a target to direct his anger toward was infinitely better than the alternative.

He blinked his way back, not paying attention to anything other than where the trees were, since he didn't think it would feel too good randomly appearing right in the middle of one. It took him all of three seconds to make the journey back to their camp, his heart somewhere in the vicinity of his throat the entire time.

When he burst through the last of the vines, he saw Effie curled into the fetal position, Timmins whispering in her ear, and Helena curled into Ronan's arms, her entire body shaking.

"Somebody tell me what the fuck is going on, right the fuck now," he ordered, his voice filled with deadly menace. Anyone that knew him, knew better than to ignore the threat barely concealed within the words. He was on the edge of reason, a heartbeat away from grabbing his weapon and asking questions later.

Surprisingly, it was Reyna who answered.

"Helena was trying to help Effie. Another of her visions was triggered, and it looked like she was finally past the worst of it when Helena touched her. The vision must have pulled your Mate in, one second she was in control of her body, the next she was slumped over the Keeper."

Von's eyes narrowed, not liking that his enemy was something he could not battle. He moved through the others to Helena, carefully pulling her from Ronan's grasp and lifting her in his arms. Her scream had terrified him more than he'd like to admit, and right now, feeling her against him was as much for him as it was for her.

"I'm right here, Mira," he told her. *"You're safe."*

Her tremors began to subside almost immediately. She pulled away, looking sheepish. "I'm not entirely certain what happened."

"It looks like you were drawn into Effie's vision," Ronan said, his voice even although his eyes were wild.

"That's what it felt like," she agreed, her voice not quite steady.

"Is that normal?" Von asked, seeking out Timmins, who usually had the answers for this kind of thing.

Timmins shrugged. "When it comes to the Keepers, there's very little that is known."

Von frowned. "Are you all right?" he asked Helena, who still seemed paler than he would have liked.

She nodded. "I think so. I couldn't even tell you what it was that had me so scared. I just knew that if I stayed there one more second it would have been the end of me." She shuddered, her tongue darting out to lick her lips.

"I felt it too," Effie croaked. Their heads all turned toward her.

"Did you See what I did?" Helena asked.

Effie shrugged. "I wasn't aware of you at all, so I don't know."

"Can you tell the rest of us what you Saw?" Timmins asked.

Effie swayed where she sat. "I can try."

"If you need awhile to recover..." Helena started.

She shook her head. "It's all right. I'd rather get this over with."

"Was it like before?" Kragen asked.

At the same time, Ronan asked, "Did you see Rowena again?"

Effie shook her head. "No. It wasn't like before. I didn't See any people this time."

"If you didn't See people, then what did you See?" Helena asked.

Effie's eyes narrowed as she searched for the words to describe her vision. "It felt more abstract this time. It wasn't as if I was watching a scene as it was happening, like with Rowena and the Endoshan. This time, it was like the images were all a metaphor." She stopped, looking confused. "I'm sorry, I'm not sure how to explain it."

"It's okay, dear. Why don't you just start by telling us what the images were," Timmins said with a kind smile.

Effie nodded, still looking the worse for wear. "At first there was smoke, the kind that you see just after a fire goes out. It was thick and gray; everything was gray."

Von found his eyes moving to Helena, who was silently nodding along with Effie's words.

"After the smoke cleared, all I could see was a web. It was beautiful and so elaborate. Each strand was unique, both in color and in its substance. I found myself wanting to pluck one, knowing that it would show me who or what the strand represented, but I couldn't. At first each strand twinkled with its own separate life, but then the longer I stared, the more they blended until I could no longer tell where one began and another ended." The words were coming out in a rush, and Effie had to pause to catch her breath.

Helena moved out of his arms and sat beside Effie, her hand reaching out to hold the other woman's in a show of solidarity.

Effie smiled at her gratefully before continuing. "Something changed then. It felt like the air contracted, becoming almost heavier. There was chanting, but I couldn't tell if it was one voice or many. The words were coming too fast for me to be able to make any sense of them. That was when I noticed that something was trapped in the center of the web. It thrashed wildly, trying to escape, but only managed to get itself more helplessly tangled in the strands."

Helena let out a gasp. "It was me."

All eyes turned toward her. Helena put her hand up to her mouth and shook her head. "I'm sorry, Effie. Please continue."

Effie blinked, seeming confused by the interruption, but she nodded after a moment and finished her recounting. "Once the victim was fully cocooned in the strands, a spider appeared. It was the palest blue, almost the color of snow, and it had odd markings along its head and body. It was excited by its catch and was eagerly making its way to the middle of the web to see what it had caught. That's where it ended."

Some of the color was starting to return to Effie's face now that she had completed her tale, but while she was looking more normal, Helena was deathly white.

"What did you mean 'It was me'?" Von asked, his arms crossed over his chest.

Helena looked up at him with worried aqua eyes. "When I tried to heal Effie, my power must have latched onto hers. I saw the last moments of the vision, but from a different vantage. I," Helena faltered, taking a shaky breath. Effie squeezed her hand, her eyes shining with understanding. Helena's words sounded forced as she continued, "I was in the center of the web. I tried to break free, but I couldn't. Then I saw the spider, it was beautiful and deadly. I knew if it reached me, I was dead. I started struggling harder, and all of a sudden the world went completely dark. That's when... that's when I started screaming."

Von felt icy fingers move along his spine. He did not pretend to understand he knew what the vision was supposed to represent, but it was clear that Helena and Rowena both played a part. And based on the two retellings of the vision, it certainly did not appear that things were about to go in their favor.

"What do you think it means?" Joquil asked, flames dancing in his eyes as he stared at the women from across the fire.

Helena and Effie shared a glance. Helena shrugged, and Effie opened her mouth to answer. "I think the web represents a trap, one that it takes many people to create."

"The trap must be for me," Helena said.

"Given that you were in the center of it, I'm inclined to agree," Timmins murmured.

"Isn't that too obvious?" Von protested, desperate to find a different explanation.

"What would you say that means?" Kragen asked, and not unkindly.

Von shrugged. "I don't know, maybe Helena is at the center because she is the one who sets the trap."

Ronan's worried eyes found his. "Why then is she the one that was caught in it? And why would someone else be the spider?"

"The spider was Rowena," Helena said, her voice stronger and more sure than it had been until now.

Von thought so too. The coloring the two women described sounded very much like the cold eyes that had found him in most of his nightmares.

The group fell silent, no one sure what to think.

"Do you think it was a warning?" Effie asked hopefully. "Something sent to me now so we could be on guard and avoid it?"

"Aren't we on guard already?" Helena asked with a humorless laugh.

"If the vision is of the future, then the events have not yet passed and can therefore be changed," Timmins said.

Helena looked up at him. "So you're an expert on prophecy now?"

Timmins's cheeks went pink, but he did not respond.

Helena groaned. "I'm sorry. I do not mean to be so surly, it's just… if the vision is the future, then that means I'm destined to be caught in that web. Which feels like it means I'm destined to fail."

"There is always more than one way to interpret a vision, Kiri."

The spectral voice spoke in his mind and had his hand reaching for his weapon. The sound of surprised gasps and weapons being drawn met his ears as Von looked for the source of the voice that had spoken in his mind.

"I told you our new daughter would come to us."

"Her power is strong and yet still untested."

"She needs to learn how to properly harness her gift."

"It will come with time."

As the voices continued to speak, three robed figures entered the clearing. Von would like to say it was a relief to see them, but he'd be lying. On the bright side, they no longer had to spend the next few days wandering around aimlessly because their mission had just been accomplished. At least, in a manner of speaking.

They may not have found the Keepers, but the Keepers had just found them.

*H*er Circle remained on guard as Helena pushed herself up to stand on shaky legs. "Good evening, Triumvirate. To what do we owe this unexpected visit?" she asked, erring on the side of formality.

"You were the one that sought us out, were you not?"

"Why then the surprise when you found us?"

As always, Helena could not tell which of the three figures were speaking to her. Thankfully, their hoods remained firmly in place, and she did not have to worry about staring into their sightless eyes. Or rather, the place where their eyes had once been.

"Well, to be frank. Technically we did not find you. Therein lies the element of surprise."

There were a few snickers of amusement, but the others soon lapsed back to silence.

Helena sighed, realizing she would not get very far with sarcasm and these men. "We were seeking your aid, yes."

"And here we are."

"You seem troubled, Kiri."

"I am," Helena admitted. "The events of the last few weeks are weighing on me heavily."

"You speak of our daughter's death."

Helena nodded. "In part." She couldn't help wondering if they used the term daughter literally, although given that they had already used the label twice referring to two different individuals, she thought it unlikely.

"It was foretold."

"No one can escape the hour of their passing."

"It is as much a part of life as breathing."

"Even so, it was a devastating loss."

"To return to the Mother is a blessing, Kiri."

"You of all people should know that."

Helena bristled. "Death is never easy on those that are left behind."

"Perhaps."

It was disorienting trying to have a conversation with three separate entities that spoke as though they were one. The voices filled her mind with absolutely no indication of where they were coming from. Helena did her best to look at and speak to all of them, although perhaps focusing on the center figure would have been enough. He did seem to be their leader.

Effie rose to stand at her side. "Are you here for me?" she demanded. Her chin was tilted up, an act that portrayed defiant strength, although her small frame continued to tremble.

The three heads swiveled in perfect synchronicity to look at her. *"One could argue daughter, that you are here for us."*

"Stop calling me that," Effie said through gritted teeth. "The only parents I had are long dead."

Helena placed a hand on Effie's arm. The movement was a reminder of support, not a call to be silent. Effie censored herself anyway, taking a deep breath.

"Can you help us?" Helena asked, pulling their unnerving attention back to her.

"It is not our place to interfere, only to act as witnesses."

"And guides," Helena reminded them.

The central figure shrugged. *"When it suits us."*

"And staving off the potential genocide of the Chosen doesn't suit you?" Helena's eyes were narrowed in dangerous slits.

"You misunderstand, Kiri. We see many paths, all of which hang off a number of various choices to be made by many individuals."

"To tip the balance could disrupt everything and cause the worst possible outcome."

"We cannot *interfere."*

Helena huffed. It was sound logic, but it didn't make her feel any better at the moment.

"So how do you know when to step in?" Effie asked, her head tilted like a curious cat.

"When it is the only option."

"And now?" Von asked. "Is it the only option now?"

There was a subtle shake of their heads. *"No."*

"There are still choices that must be made."

"But what of my visions?" Effie asked. "Do they not show us what will come to pass?"

"Our gifts are not always supposed to be shared, daughter."

"The misinterpretation of a single one could be treacherous."

"It takes years before one knows how to interpret them with any measure of accuracy."

Helena watched Effie's back straighten at their words, her spine going rigid and her shoulders lifting until they were up around her ears. She was clearly worried about damage she may have caused bringing them to Endoshan.

"I didn't know," she whispered mournfully.

That is enough of that, Helena thought, having no desire for the woman to beat herself up over something that was hardly her fault. "Well, the fact of the matter is that the vision was not just shared, it was also experienced by another. Namely, me. You might as well lend your insights before I make a categorically terrible decision based off what was Seen. You know what my failure means."

Without being able to see their expressions, Helena could not truly know what reaction her words had caused, but there was an unmistakable aura of annoyance rolling off of the trio.

"Very well, Kiri."

"It seems that you leave us with no choice."

Helena could feel Von's mirth, and she shot him a startled glance. *"What is there to possibly be laughing at right now?"* she asked through their bond.

"It seems you found the answer on how to force their hand."

"I did?"

Von's eyes glowed with his amusement. *"Unintentional meddling."*

Helena scowled, rolling her eyes and dismissing him.

"Come here, daughter."

Effie's trembling increased, and she clasped her hands in front of her to try to disguise her nerves.

"You have nothing to fear from us."

"To begin, we must See what you Saw."

"I could just tell you," she offered. "You know, from here."

Ronan placed his hand on her shoulder. Effie looked up at him with scared blue eyes.

"Your retelling will be inaccurate."

"No detail is too small."

"The only way to truly Know is to experience."

Helena could feel the 'I told you so' ready to spring from Timmins lips even from where she was standing.

"It's all right, Effie. We're all right here. We won't let anything bad happen to you," Helena promised.

Ronan reinforced her words with a nod of his own. Ever since Darrin's death, Effie had found comfort in her Shield's imposing presence. It was likely a side effect of what they'd experienced together on the battlefield when Darrin died before their eyes. Either way, Helena couldn't fault her. She knew all too well how important it was to have a safe harbor when one felt like they were drowning. Ronan had been that for her as well while Von had been imprisoned.

Effie swallowed and walked over to the hooded figures. Helena knew it was one of the hardest things she'd had to do. Nothing about the trio was particularly reassuring.

"What do I need to do?" she asked.

"Just close your eyes."

Helena was grateful that the Triumvirate was still choosing to speak in a manner that allowed them all to listen. She was intimately aware of the fact that they could be selective about who they allowed to hear their psychic voices.

Helena could feel the tension emanating from her Circle, without needing to access their strengthened connection through her Jaka. She could feel it, because it was an extension of her own.

The figure in the middle lifted his arm, his tattooed hand with its shifting blue markings revealed as the long sleeves of his robe fell back. He placed his hand on the center of Effie's forehead, very similar to what Helena had done when she'd intended to heal her.

Effie inhaled audibly, and then her head fell back. Her arms dangled uselessly at her sides and her knees buckled, but she did not fall. For all that he was only touching her head, the Keeper seemed to have a firm grasp on her.

There were several tense heartbeats as the Triumvirate did whatever it was they needed to do. Helena knew it was over when Effie sucked in a deep breath, sounding like it was the first she'd had since they'd started. The Keeper released her, and she stumbled forward. He caught her by the shoulders before she could knock him over, setting her unceremoniously back on her feet.

"Was that it?" Effie rasped, eager to move back to the others.

The Triumvirate nodded, and she did nothing to disguise her hurried retreat to the safety of her friends.

"So what does it mean?" Helena asked, bracing herself for the blow.

"Why ask when you already know, Kiri?"

Of all the things for them to say, that was not what she was expecting. True, she had a feeling she knew, but she was desperately hoping she'd been wrong.

"But I don't know. Not for sure. Miranda always warned me visions were never straightforward." Helena was starting to feel like that was her new mantra, she was holding on to the belief that the words were true.

"They rarely are, but that does not mean that you do not already have everything you need to guide you to the correct answer."

"I need you!" she shouted, her annoyance at their intentional opaqueness and the strain of everything else coming to a head.

"Look within yourself for the answer, Kiri."

"We can offer no further help here."

"Mother's tits!" Helena shouted, throwing her hands into the air. Someone had better start giving her a straight answer soon or she was going to start flinging fireballs and to the hell with them all.

"Helena might have what she needs, but I don't," Effie said, her voice no less strong for its softness.

The Triumvirate were silent as they contemplated her words.

"We cannot risk revealing our secrets to you while you remain with them."

"What the hell is that supposed to mean?" Helena raged.

"It is as we already said."

"We cannot interfere."

"Our daughter's ties to you are too strong."

"She would not be able to resist sharing what she learned."

"And in doing so, she could do more harm than good."

"I can keep a fucking secret!" Effie blurted out, surprising them all with her vehemence. "It was my thrice-damned vision, I deserve to know what it means."

"And you will."

"Should you come with us."

That stopped them all short.

"Come with you?" Effie repeated dumbstruck. She looked around at the others, her face draining of color.

"It's the only way for you to learn, daughter."

"You know we speak the truth."

Helena swallowed back her protests, knowing that this was a choice Effie needed to make for herself. As much as she desired answers, she would not get in the way of her friend's destiny.

"But I…" Effie started. "What about the war?"

Helena took Effie's hand, pulling her attention. "There are many ways to fight. Not all of them involve a battlefield."

"If I'm gone, I cannot help you. I won't be able to avenge them," she whispered, her voice wavering with unshed tears.

"Who's to say that's not exactly where you're supposed to be? The Mother has plans for us all, Effie. Maybe that is where you have to go to finish the fight."

Effie wanted to protest, but she could not deny the ring of truth in Helena's words. "Is that what you would choose, Helena?"

Helena shook her head, not wanting to sway her in either direction.

"Please," Effie begged.

"Isn't that the choice I already made? It wasn't long ago someone came to fetch me."

The reference to Darrin seemed to bring a sense of peace. All trace of sadness and doubt vanished, and Effie nodded resolutely. "You're right. If this is the path set before me, I should follow it. I do not want to risk your lives with my ignorance. We've already had a taste of what that is like."

"Effie," Helena said, shaking her head.

"No, it's all right." She turned toward the Triumvirate. "I will go with you. But I would like to spend the night with my friends to say goodbye, if that's all right. Can you come for me in the morning?"

"Yes."

"We could see her off," Helena offered. "If you tell us where to bring her."

"The Catacombs are not for your eyes, Kiri."

"They are the sacred place of the Keepers."

"Only those with the gift have ever stepped foot within."

Helena wanted to throw her title in their faces and demand that they let her go, but she knew it was futile. Her fight was elsewhere.

"Can we not visit?" Ronan asked.

"This goodbye will not be forever."

"Our daughter will let you know when she is ready to see you again."

"Your messages will always find their way to her."

Feeling somewhat better at the news, Helena loosed a shaky breath.

"Until tomorrow then," Effie said, surprising the rest of them with her dismissal.

The Triumvirate did not respond, they merely turned and disappeared back into the forest from whence they'd came.

CHAPTER 21

"*W*ell, shit," Ronan said.

"I think that sums it up nicely," Von said dryly.

"What the fuck are we supposed to do with that? Not only are they refusing to explain what the vision means, they're also taking away the source of the vision, so we have absolutely no fucking idea what lies ahead," Ronan sputtered.

"How's that any different from where we were before?" Helena asked, amused at her Shield's unexpected rant. She knew why she was upset, but she hadn't expected him to feel the same.

"Well, it's not, but... they were supposed to help us, damn it!" Ronan was fuming.

Helena couldn't help herself, her shoulders began to shake with barely suppressed laughter.

"You're laughing?" he asked as the rest of the group joined in. "How can you laugh at a time like this?" Seeing that they had no intention of stopping any time soon, he threw his hands up in the air. "This is a load of steaming wolf shit and you know it!"

"I'm sorry," Helena hiccupped, wiping a tear from her eye. "It's not that I disagree, it's just this is all par for the course, wouldn't you say? Of course the people that can decipher the vision refuse to tell us what it means. These are the same men," Helena paused, wondering for the first time if the Triumvirate were in fact all male. That was a mystery for another day. Waving away the thought, she continued, "That like to give me warnings by terrorizing me."

"I'm sorry, Kiri. I had hoped given what's at stake that they would be more forthcoming," Timmins said on a sigh.

"It's not your fault," she said.

During all of this, Effie remained quiet.

"I'm sorry," Helena said, instantly sobering. "It's not too late to change your mind. If you'd rather not go with them—"

"No. They're right. I'm no use to anybody until I learn how to understand these visions. Besides, it can't possibly be normal for them to affect me as they do. Perhaps they can help me fight the side effects."

Helena pressed her lips together. "You have a home with us any time you desire. You might be a Keeper, Effie, but you will always be one of us."

Effie's lower lip quavered but she fought back her tears. "Thank you, Helena. I will hold you to that."

That much settled, Kragen directed them back to the matter at hand. "So what do you think they meant, you 'have everything you need to guide you to the correct answer'?"

"Precisely that, I'd gather," Timmins said, rubbing his eyes.

Kragen rolled his. "Thanks for that illuminating contribution, Advisor. As always, your insights prove invaluable."

Timmins shrugged. "Not every nugget is going to be perfection. Sometimes one can only work with what's in front of them."

Helena groaned. "They clearly believe that I do not require any outside input to arrive at the correct conclusion. That means that I just need to decipher the clues based on what I already know to be true."

"So how long do you think this is going to take? Ten, twenty minutes?" Ronan drawled, his lips curling into a sarcastic smile.

If only she felt that confident in her ability to rationalize everything out. The only reason she'd been able to connect the dots on Effie's previous vision is because it'd come to pass first, and they'd been able to work backwards. There was no way that particular approach was going to help them again this time.

"At least," Helena replied, wrinkling her nose at him. "Prick."

Ronan gave her a mocking bow. "I live to serve, Kiri."

Helena snorted. "A little more serving and a little less sarcasm, if you will."

Her Shield winked. "What reason could you possibly have to keep me around if I turned so predictable? It's not like you require a second Advisor!"

The other Circle members laughed as Timmins began to clap in long, drawn-out movements. "Your wit sir, is legendary."

The conversation was rapidly devolving, and Helena knew that if she didn't step in fast, they'd lose the thread entirely. "All right, all right. You can tease Timmins later. Right now we have a vision to interpret."

Effie shuffled forward, her hands nervously playing with the front of her dress. "Perhaps I should go pack my things. From what they said, I don't want to unduly influence your assessment."

Helena frowned. "Don't you think that they would have insisted on your going with them immediately, if they were truly worried about it?"

The blonde woman's face brightened considerably. "You're right! Carry on then."

One by one the group settled into place around the campfire. In another time or place, Helena could have simply been regaling them with ghost stories. She yearned for such a day and such simple pleasures.

Von sat directly across from her, his blade brother on one side and his blood brother on the other. Serena sat on the floor between Nial's legs, while Reyna and Ryder chose spots next to Ronan, who lifted a brow at the choice but provided no further comment. Kragen, Timmins, and Joquil took the spots beside Nial, filling in that side of the semi-circle and leaving the rest of the group to sit beside the Night Stalkers. Starshine, who had been off hunting for her dinner, chose that moment to stalk quietly into their camp and take a seat behind her Mate.

Von lifted a hand to rub her in greeting, but she bared her fangs at him. "Or not," he muttered, his hand falling back to his side.

Some things never change. Even in times of chaos, people were just people. It was an uplifting thought. Helena's eyes moved over the group, her heart feeling full. They were faced with the biggest threat the Chosen had to deal with, and yet they still found a way to hold on to their humanity. Her eyes fell on Ronan; they teased. On Reyna; they flirted. On the newly mated Nial and Serena; they loved. The Mother's Chosen were not as fragile as they appeared. For all that their lives could be taken in less time than it took to draw a full breath, so too could they live. It was a beautiful thing, this ability to adapt and endure.

Feeling inspired, Helena turned to Effie, who was standing beside her. "Shall we try this again?"

"What would you like me to do?"

"Well let's talk it out, starting with what we think we know."

"The spider obviously represents Rowena," Von said, not wasting any time.

Helena nodded. "I'm inclined to agree. It's my feeling that the color of spider matched the same cold color of her eyes. And only Rowena would get that much pleasure out of trapping someone."

"That was my thought as well," Effie said.

"Very well, I think we can accept that as fact and move forward."

Unfortunately, that was the first and only fact on which they agreed. The group talked well into the night, each minute detail of the vision hashed out with no further understanding of what it represented.

"But the web is clearly a trap left by the spider, who in this case we all agree is Rowena!" Joquil shouted in exasperation.

"If each strand is a separate individual, those must indicate the Chosen. Rowena's followers lack that kind of diversity," Timmins said as he paced around the fire.

"The Chosen would never agree to be part of such a scheme!" Effie insisted.

"Who says they have a choice? Rowena is a gifted manipulator," Von said.

On and on it went, until she couldn't take it anymore. The longer Helena listened to the other's talk, the more certain she became that she alone would find the answer. For all that her friends were her resources, the truth of the vision lied within her.

"Enough," Helena said wearily. "We've come up with several possible solutions, none of which feel quite right. I'm sure we're on to something, but we may as well get some sleep and try again with fresh perspectives in the morning."

Her words had a sobering effect as the group remembered what the morning would bring.

"She's right," Von said, pushing himself to a standing position. "We aren't getting anywhere; we might as well call it a night."

There were a few murmurs of agreement as people began to make their way to their tents. Effie remained behind.

"I'll wait for you inside," Von said, gesturing to the tent they would share.

"I'll be right there," Helena said with a thankful smile.

"I'm sorry I couldn't be more helpful, Helena. I really wanted to be the one that gave you what you needed to defeat that evil bitch." For all her venom, Effie still reminded Helena of a kitten that had just discovered its claws. The thought made her smile.

"Who's to say that you haven't? Just because you couldn't solve the riddle doesn't mean that you haven't given me the answer."

Effie looked down as she considered the words. "I hope so."

"One way or another, I will find my answer, and I hope," Helena said, her hand reaching out to touch Effie's arm, "that you find yours as well."

One side of Effie's mouth lifted in a wry smile. "Who can say? With the way those three communicate, you never know what you're going to end up with."

Helena laughed. "How very, very true."

When Helena had fallen silent, Effie met her eyes head on and said, "I guess this is it then."

"We will have time in the morning—"

"You and I both know that they will arrive for me long before you wake. They gave me tonight, but they did not promise me the morning," Effie said, cutting her off.

She was right. Helena sighed. "Did you not want to say goodbye to the others?"

Effie shook her head. "I've said enough goodbyes for now. I have no intention of saying it again anytime soon."

Helena tilted her head. "It isn't really goodbye, you know. We'll see each other again."

Effie nodded, her eyes already starting to take on some of the ancient wisdom that her grandmother's had held. "Eventually."

"You take care of yourself, Effie. If you have need of anything, all you have to do is call." Helena held out one of her last fully charged Kaelpas stones. "You will always have a place in my court."

Effie took the stone, clasping it to her chest. "Thank you for being my friend, Helena. You were the first I ever really had."

The words struck her like a blow, and she reached out, pulling Effie in for a hug. "I'm going to miss you."

"And I you."

"Farewell, Effie."

"Send her straight to hell," Effie replied, stepping out of her arms.

Helena nodded, her expression serious. "I intend to."

Effie stared at her a moment longer before turning and walking into the tent she was sharing with Reyna.

When the morning came, she was gone.

CHAPTER 22

*R*owena stood looking out over what should by rights be her Queendom. The harsh winds of Vyruul were whipping her hair out of its binding, but it was the only part of her that reacted to the extreme cold of her surroundings. The heat of her rage had long since cooled. Now it was as if she was forged from the ice itself. There was little that would cause her pristine façade to crack.

"My Queen?" Kai-Soren called.

"What do you want?" Rowena asked without turning to face him. They'd been married less than a week and already he'd disappointed her.

"The men are growing restless. When can we return home?"

"Home?" she scoffed. "What home? Greyspire is in ruins, no thanks to you and your 'men,' or did you already forget?"

Kai-Soren waited a moment before replying. "There's still the keep at Endoshan—"

"The Mother will strike me dead before I go crawling into that pile of stones you call a keep."

She could feel his wounded pride from where she stood. Men were so easily broken.

"Well perhaps the men could return so that they at least have a roof over their heads and warmth instead of freezing to death in this cave."

"You seek out comfort over the safety of your Queen? You'd leave me here unprotected?" Her voice grew colder with each word she spoke until the wind soon seemed balmy by comparison.

"Rowena, I—"

"How dare you address me so informally," she snapped, finally spinning around. The full power of her ire was unleashed on him, and for the first time since she'd known him, he looked truly unnerved.

His golden eyes were wide, the whites clearly visible on both top and bottom. He caught himself and quickly schooled his face into an impassive mask. "Apologies, My Queen. It will not happen again."

Rowena sighed, wishing she could use a small bit of compulsion magic to make him less insufferable. Alas, she could not give up the charade entirely. Not yet, but as soon as she could... Rowena's eyes narrowed in malicious glee. Her darling husband Kai-Soren was living on borrowed time, and it tickled her to no end that he was completely clueless.

"You know that we must remain here until I find acceptable replacements for the two that were lost. I cannot let that sniveling impostor discover me until then."

"How do you expect to find anyone while we hide in a cave?" he asked, causing her to grit her teeth.

"I'm working on it."

His eyes shuttered; his faith in her ability to lead was dwindling more each day. He thought her weak for hiding, but she was not sitting idle. As always, she was thinking four and five steps ahead of everyone. How else would she have been able to fool so many into believing she was dead? Things were set in motion long before she ever knew she'd end up here. It was only a matter of time.

Rowena turned back toward Elysia, dismissing him without a word. She was the rightful ruler of the Chosen. One way or another, she'd reclaim her throne.

There was never any doubt about how this was going to end.

SHE WALKED AMONGST THE TWILIGHT, *the stars illuminating the path before her with their brilliance. On either side, trees stretched up into the sky, obscuring what lay beyond them. All she could see was the path before her and the stars in the sky watching over her, lighting her way.*

She walked alone, but felt no sense of fear. It was safe here; there was nothing but peace in the starlight. She continued to wander until the road began to curve, opening up on the shore of a beach. The stars continued to shine down, the water reflecting their light back up at them. Everything was awash in shades of blue, giving the secluded beach an air of ethereality.

Seeing nothing else, she walked across the powder soft sand toward the shore. Once she reached the edge, she let her bare toes dip into the water, not caring that the bottom of her gown grew wet. She tilted her head up toward the sky, feeling her hair brush against her back. It tickled, causing her to smile and close her eyes, wanting to memorize the feeling of total peace.

She had no idea how she got here, no clue where she was, and yet she did not want to leave.

"To remain means you must also leave behind. Could you really do that?"

Opening her eyes, she saw the figure of a woman take shape beside her.

"Miranda?" she asked. It was not surprise she felt at seeing the Keeper, merely wonder.

"Hello, Kiri."

Helena smiled. There was no accurate way to describe her joy at finding the friend she thought she had lost.

"Is this where you live now?" Helena asked, looking around for some sign of a dwelling.

Miranda's answering smile was kind. "No. I am just visiting, as are you."

A breeze picked up, causing her to shiver for the first time. Helena cast a glance up at the sky, feeling like some of the stars were starting to dim. The first tendril of concern snaked up her spine.

Miranda held out a hand. "Walk with me a ways."

Helena took her hand and the two women began to walk along the shore.

"Your mind is heavy," Miranda said.

The thoughts and worries that she had forgotten while admiring the stars started to come back, reminding her of what waited. "Yes," she sighed. "I don't know what to do, or how I am supposed to defeat her."

"Yes you do."

Helena frowned.

"Look," Miranda whispered, her arms lifting until they were fully extended on either side of her. Helena let out a startled gasp. The beach had disappeared, giving way to a meadow. The sun was shining overhead and flowers were dancing in the breeze. She blinked, but the image remained intact.

"How did you do that?" Helena asked.

Miranda smiled. "You do not need to look far for your answer, Helena."

Helena opened her mouth, questions ready to fall from her lips, but Miranda stopped her. "The Mother has given you everything you need."

With that, the Keeper lifted a hand and ran it along her cheek and the meadow disappeared.

Helena bolted upright, her heart still thundering as she pulled her consciousness from the grips of the dream. It took her a moment to remember where she was. Seeing the familiar purple of her bed, she let out a deep breath. She was home. She was safe.

Von grunted and rolled toward her, his arms trying to pull her closer, but Helena disentangled herself and pushed out of the bed to pad across the cool floor.

Why did I dream about Miranda? Is she trying to tell me something? For all that she was awake, Helena still felt like her brain was a bit foggy from sleep. Before Darrin had come to her and told her of her destiny, Helena had never put much stock into dreams having any sort of relevance. After all, they were just the images one's mind assigned to things that they had experienced during the day and were remembering on some unconscious level. Weren't they?

Now that she had firsthand knowledge of visions and prophecy, Helena wasn't so sure. Miranda's presence in her dreams had to mean something. It couldn't just be coincidence, not with everything else that had been going on recently.

Helena was absently aware that she had started pacing. Her mind was trying to tell her something. Something that had to do with Miranda. If only she could figure out what.

Frustrated, she sighed, stopping in her tracks. She wasn't getting anywhere, and the longer she was awake, the faster she lost the threads of her dream, which meant if there were clues hidden there, she was quickly losing access to them.

"Oh blast it!" she cursed under her breath, grabbing a lilac robe from the chair where she'd discarded it earlier. She belted the robe loosely and headed for the door. There was no way she was going to fall back asleep now, so she might as well try to get some work done.

If she couldn't recall the specifics of the dream, maybe going to the last place she'd spent time with Miranda might trigger something. It was as good a plan as any this early in the morning. Especially since she couldn't exactly run the idea by others since the rest of her Circle were still abed. She might as well make use of the quiet time to see if she couldn't get any farther deciphering that vision.

Helena moved quickly through the halls of the Palace, not stopping to appreciate any of the small touches that usually captivated her attention. It was completely quiet, something that rarely happened given the number of people running around at any given minute, but for once, it was calm. Dim lights danced in their orbs to light the way for anyone that might need to move around while it was still dark out. It was just enough to see by, and she made her way to the library in record time.

She pushed open the heavy door and stepped into the dark room. There was no natural light in here, so the room was pitch black except for where a sliver of light fell in from the doorway. Helena used her power to softly illuminate the room and then closed the door behind her. The table she'd spent so much time at when trying to find a spell to fool Rowena sat untouched. Helena smiled, Alina must have refused to let anyone put the books away in case Helena had need of them.

Looking down, her eyes ran over the titles while her fingers brushed against the leather-bound tomes. There was something lovely about all the scrolling text and faded colors. So much knowledge hidden within the dusty pages, painstakingly preserved by one who thought it important enough to pass on. If only answers were that easy to find. Helena wished there was a way for her to simply ask her question aloud and have the exact book she needed be pulled out and opened to the page where the answer lay. How easy that would make things.

She lowered herself into the comfortable armchair and pulled her robe more tightly around her. She let her head fall back against its cushioned surface while her mind returned to the last time she was here.

What was it Miranda had told her? Something about trying to think about the problem from a different angle. All right, fine. All this time they'd assumed that the web was Rowena's given that she was the spider. *But what if it wasn't? Whose else could it be? What else could it represent?*

Helena lost track of time as she contemplated the answers to these questions.

According to Effie, the strands of the web had all been different. It reminded Helena a bit of the time she'd been in Bael, her power making her see the colorful strands of power within each of her Circle.

"Maybe the web is a trap created by many," Helena mused, following that train of thought. "Or one so elaborate that it requires significant power to complete it."

Helena's fingers brushed against one of the books, the glittering gold of its title barely visible in the soft light. *The Power of Illusions.* Her finger traced the gilded letters. It wasn't until she was on the second looping o that something snapped into place. Helena sat up.

"Illusions."

That last time she'd been in here, she'd been trying to discover how

184

to create an illusion powerful enough to hide the Night Stalkers in plain sight.

"Is that what you were trying to help me remember?" she asked, not sure who she was talking to. Helena began talking her way through possible answers. "The illusion of a web. No, it's not that literal. Okay... so something that makes it look like I am trapped. Something big enough and believable enough that Rowena buys it."

Excitement had her jumping from the chair. She knew that she was on the right track now. After a few more minutes of mulling over the details, she actually laughed out loud; the answer was so obvious. "The trap is not for me! It's for Rowena! Something to draw her out so that this final battle can be on our terms!"

Helena could feel the truth in her words, and relief filled her. That was what the vision had been showing them. Finally, they had an answer about what to do, but as quickly as her excitement came, it fled.

Helena slumped back into the chair. She'd managed to solve the puzzle, but now she had a bigger problem. What illusion could she possibly cast that would be enticing enough for Rowena to crawl out of hiding?

"You want to do what?" Ronan asked incredulously.

"I want to lay a trap."

"Right, I heard that part," Ronan said. "Where you lost me is the bit about how you are planning to use yourself as bait."

Helena folded her arms. "What part about it are you struggling with?"

"The part where your life is in danger!" he snapped, looking at Von. "Are you just going to sit there or are you going to help me talk some sense into your Mate?"

Von did not look much happier than Ronan, although he'd already resigned himself to her decision. After all, he could appreciate the brilliance of the strategy, even as he hated what it would require.

"You cannot ask us to stand aside while you practically hand yourself over to that she-bitch."

Helena knew that it was fear that made him speak to her like she was incapable of protecting herself, but even still, the insinuation stung. "You don't actually get a say in this, you do realize that, don't you?"

Ronan glowered at her.

Turning to address the others Helena added, "None of you have to help me, but this is what I need to do. Every time we've fought her until now it's been on her terms. That has to stop. We cannot possibly win while Rowena has the upper hand. This is our only way to change that."

None of her men looked happy, but they could not disagree with the assessment.

"How do you plan to lure her?" Joquil asked.

Helena pressed her lips together. This is where things got a little murky. She had the rough sketch of a plan, but not a fully realized idea. She was hoping that they would help fill in those gaps, but given their state of mind, they might be more inclined to use the holes to argue against her.

"I want to create an illusion."

Timmins frowned. "How do you plan on casting an illusion grand enough to reach her where she is?"

"Well, I want it to be big enough that news reaches her wherever she is hiding."

"So this is not just an illusion for Rowena, this is something that will affect anyone who sees it?" Von clarified.

Helena nodded. "I think that's the only way it will work."

"Something on that scale is going to require substantial power, perhaps even more than you are capable of accessing alone," Joquil said, his brows low over his worried amber eyes.

"I think it's safe to say it definitely will require more power than I possess."

"Even with our bond?" Von asked, his eyes darkening.

Helena nodded.

"So you use the Jaka and pull from the rest of the Circle," Kragen said with a shrug.

"It won't be enough."

The silence spoke volumes. They were finally starting to realize the scope of what she was talking about.

"So where do you plan on getting access to that kind of power?"

"I'm not entirely sure yet, but I know that there is a way."

"All right," Ronan interjected, "so let's say you get the power source figured out. What kind of illusion are you talking about?"

Helena took a deep breath, shifting uncomfortably in her chair. "Rowena's gift in Endoshan was meant to be a trigger. She doesn't know yet that we've already found it, so I want her to think it worked. The one thing we have always been able to count on with Rowena is her pride. She thinks that she is infallible. If she believes that I fell for her trap and turned, she will come running to collect her prize."

While she'd been speaking, Helena had been staring resolutely down at the table, but once she was done, she looked back up. Von's eyes were the first to find hers.

"You're going to pretend that you have turned." His voice was quiet thunder.

Helena nodded slowly.

"And you plan on being convincing enough that Rowena isn't the only one that falls for it?"

"Yes."

"What kind of destruction are you talking?" Kragen asked, his face serious.

Helena lifted her eyes to him. "Absolute."

"Mother's tits," Ronan swore. "Can you actually do that?"

"I think so. I've already been shown what my corruption looks like," Helena paused to let out a humorless laugh. "Trust me, it's not a sight you easily forget."

"Your trial," Timmins whispered, remembering her description of what had transpired there.

"What happens when she comes for you?" Von asked. He was no

longer sitting at the table but had stood and was holding himself stiffly. He looked like he had a very loose grasp on his control.

Helena forced herself to stand.

"Helena, what happens when she comes for you?" he repeated, his voice deadly soft. He'd never spoken to her that way before, it was a tone he reserved exclusively for those he had at the tip of his sword.

She pushed her shoulders back and tilted her chin up, refusing to be intimidated.

"Answer the question," he growled.

"She takes me."

The room erupted. Before she could move, Von had blinked and had destroyed the table by landing on top of it. Splinters were still falling around them. The others had barely pushed out of their chairs in time, but even they had rounded on her.

"Absolutely not," Von snarled, his nose pressed against hers.

"She has to believe she's won."

"No. Fucking. Way." He enunciated each word slowly, his eyes pure gold.

"She has—"

"No!" he shouted. "You want to do this fine, but she does not lay a hand on you."

Helena forced herself to breathe and not react to his temper. Von was terrified. She could feel the tidal wave of emotion surging through her. He had been Rowena's prisoner once, and the thought of Helena being put in a similar situation was causing him to unravel. The only way to defuse him was to help him calm down.

"We will not give her time to actually harm me," Helena insisted, forcing her voice to stay steady as she mentally added *or not very much*. This wouldn't work without proof. Rowena would need to be certain of her victory before letting her guard down long enough for them to strike.

Von tilted his head, looking like an inquisitive Talyrian. "Explain."

"While Rowena is distracted by me, the rest of you will attack. We need to finish off the Generals so that while Rowena and I are alone, I can finally end her."

Von's eyes searched hers and he started to shake his head. "I don't like it. There's something you aren't saying."

She could feel him probing at her mind, and so she reinforced every mental barrier she had. It was the first time she'd ever actively tried to keep him out. From the wounded look in his eyes, Von knew what she was doing.

"This is the only way."

Her Circle was silent, the five men each processing her words.

"Are you sure?" Kragen asked.

"As sure as I can be."

"How much can we tell the others?" Joquil asked.

"As little as possible," Helena said with a wince. Sometimes to save a friend, you have to play the enemy. In her case, it might not be enough to simply play. Helena shut down that line of thinking, not ready to contemplate all of the ways this could go wrong.

Timmins' brows pulled together in a frown. "It will not be easy to keep this from everyone."

"They can know we set a trap, but not what it is. I think it's safer for everyone that way."

"I will start working with Kragen and the others on a strategy," Ronan said. It was as close as she was going to get at a peace offering right now.

Helena nodded.

"Joquil and I will see what we can find about helping you acquire the additional power that you will need," Timmins offered.

"Thank you."

The four of them left, leaving Von and her alone.

"You're really going to do this?" he asked.

"I have to."

"This will not be an easy part for you to play," he said levelly.

"I know."

"There are some who will never fully trust you again."

"I know," she said again, her voice trembling slightly.

Von let out a deep breath, his shoulders falling. Running a hand through his hair, he shook his head. "She'll never believe you've turned if I'm still unharmed."

Helena swallowed. She hadn't considered that.

"You're going to have to use me."

Helena began to shake her head. "No. I don't want you anywhere near this."

Von shrugged. "We all have our parts to play. You committed us to this path, and according to you, there's no other way but through. So we will walk down it. Together."

"Von," she whispered, knowing he was right and hating what it meant.

"It will be the thing that convinces the others." He gave her a grim but determined smile. "In this case, *Mira*. I think you have to ask yourself, what would Rowena do?"

Helena frowned. The kind of game he was talking about was a dangerous one indeed. "With as much power as I think will be running through me, there's no guarantee..." she trailed off, not able to say the words out loud. *"The damage could be permanent. You could be seriously hurt."*

Von closed the distance between them, pulling her into his arms and resting his head on top of hers. "So could you, *Mira*. It is the risk we take whenever we step onto the battlefield."

The adrenaline that had been running through her ever since she woke up that morning had finally started to ebb, leaving her exhausted. She knew this plan was risky, but she also knew it was their only option. She had been okay with the idea of getting hurt herself if it meant saving the others, but the thought of Von suffering at her hands made her ill.

"I don't know if I can do it," she said into his chest. "The chance of losing control..."

Von pressed a finger to her lips, his eyes so filled with love that her heart ached. "I've told you before, I trust you with my life, Helena. Now's my chance to prove it."

CHAPTER 23

*V*on watched Helena retreat further into herself. Her aqua eyes stared unseeing out the window and her arms were wrapped protectively around her middle. As the days passed and they struggled to find the answers she needed, she grew more despondent and withdrawn. He knew that the thought of having to deceive the people she loved was weighing on her, and the longer she had to put it off, the more time she had to think about all of the things that could go wrong.

He was in awe of her power. The fact that she had the capability of creating an illusion on that grand a scale was hard for him to comprehend. He recalled the nightmarish day when they'd received Rowena's box, and the rush of power he'd experienced as Helena channeled her resulting rage through him to siphon it off. At the time, he'd thought she must have finally reached the limit of what she could control.

Von shook his head at his foolishness. He now realized that was only a teardrop in the ocean compared to the amount she would have to manipulate and maintain for what she was about to attempt.

He'd tried to talk her through it, but words were empty. It wasn't like he had any sort of firsthand knowledge about what she was going through. Hand him a sword and point him in the right direction and he'd figure it out as he went, but this... this was a whole different battlefield.

Von sighed, his lips drawn in a flat line. All he knew for sure was that watching her go through this, and being helpless to do anything, was driving him mad. He'd already worn out three training dummies and four new recruits trying to find an outlet for the pent-up frustration. Ronan had banned him from the practice ring after he'd knocked a Daejaran trainee unconscious with a single blow, which meant that now, even that small bit of relief had been taken from him.

He let his eyes trail along his Mate, noting the pensive crease between her arched brows and the way her lips tilted in a frown. Even now, she still managed to take his breath away.

There was a mistaken belief amongst the Chosen that the Mother's Vessel was perfect. Those were the ones that did not truly see her; the ones that did not understand her. For Von, it was obvious, but then, she was his other half. Helena's true power stemmed from her flaws. She may not be perfect in the general sense of the term, but he wouldn't have wanted her if she had been. How could someone who had never truly experienced life and all of its messiness ever fully understand one such as him? But Helena did, and it was because she was no stranger to grief, or humility, or anger. Things someone can only ever learn by experiencing firsthand the pain of mistakes and heartache. She was wholly alive, and she had been made for him; a gift he still thanked the Mother for daily, even though he still didn't quite believe he deserved it. And because she was his, he would do anything to save her. Even if it meant sacrificing himself.

What good was life when your reason for living was gone?

Von pushed off of the wall and started to walk toward her, wanting to smooth away the worried crease between her eyes. Before he could reach her, a knock sounded on the door, drawing everyone's attention as it opened without waiting for permission.

His brother tipped his dark head inside.

"Nial?" Von asked, concern already coloring his voice and making it come out sharper than usual. Something must have happened if his brother risked interrupting their meeting. Not that anything much had been happening, but Nial didn't know that. "What's going on?"

"Sorry for the intrusion." Nial was vibrating with tension. It was as if his body was simultaneously trying to come closer and run away, and as a result, he was locked in a perpetual sway as his muscles tried to handle the conflicting orders.

"There's no need to apologize," Helena said, hiding her worried thoughts behind a mask of polite formality. She was getting very skilled at playing the diplomat.

Feeling his eyes on her, Helena looked over and gave him a small smile.

Nial stepped further into the room, his scholar robes rumpled and stained. It would seem they were not the only ones that had been pouring through the archives.

"Did you find something?" he asked his brother, recognizing the excitement shining in his eyes.

Nial nodded. "I think so. It's just a hunch, mind you, but I think it could work."

"Spit it out," Ronan growled, crossing his arms and bringing a booted foot up against the wall.

Timmins gave him a dark look, but didn't waste breath telling him to get his dirty feet off the wall. Poor, proper Timmins. Still offended by the most minor offenses.

"There was something you said that triggered a memory, but I couldn't remember the exact reference out of context, so it took me a few days to locate it." The words poured out of Nial in a rush.

"What did you find, Nial?" Helena asked, her impatience tempered by amusement.

"You mentioned that you needed access to more than just your own power, and I remembered that sometimes for really complex magic, multiple sources are required to anchor it. That's when I remembered the Storm Forged's cyclone."

Von lifted a brow, not sure where his brother was going with this information. "The cyclone is the remnant of the Stormbringer's rise to power. What does that have to do with anchoring a spell?"

Nial shot him an exasperated look. "I'm getting to that."

"Perhaps you should hurry up," Kragen suggested.

"Do you want to hear this or not?" Nial snapped, before realizing who he was speaking to. Color moved up his neck as he dropped his eyes, and his voice. "Apologies, Sword."

"It would seem the only one keeping us from hearing the news is you, boy-o," Joquil commented, his amber eyes glowing with laughter.

Nial sighed. "The Stormbringer's cyclone would die out without constant reinforcement. To channel that much power regularly would drain him almost completely. Yet clearly, that's not the case or he wouldn't be here. The only reason that's possible is because the rest of the Storm Forged help anchor the magic. It is fed by all of them and yet none feel the drain."

"Do we know how it's done?" Helena asked, her aqua eyes bright. Von could feel her hope like a warm blast of sunshine along their bond.

Nial shook his head. "No, but with Anduin here, that's not the issue. If he could talk us through it, I should be able to find a way to replicate it for your use."

"What if he does not want to share Storm Forged secrets?" Timmins asked.

"He won't have a choice," Von said, the hint of a snarl creeping into his voice.

"What are we waiting for?" Helena asked. "Someone go find Anduin."

Kragen jumped up. "On it," he said.

"Thank you, Nial," Helena said, giving Von's brother a tight hug.

"Where's my hug?" Von teased.

"Bring me more information like that and you can have all of them."

Von smirked. *"You never complained about my less-than-scholarly nature before now, Mira."*

Her cheeks heated, and she shook her head at him.

He winked, happy to see her smiling again.

"Good work, brother," Von said, giving Nial a one-armed hug.

Nial glowed at the praise. "As I said, it's just a theory, but—"

"There's no need to be modest. It was a brilliant discovery. One that could very well allow us to seize control of this war. Accept the thanks you're due," Von ordered.

Nial nodded, his quiet pride making his eyes shine.

Von squeezed his shoulder, stepping back to reclaim his place by the hearth. The heavy tension that had been in the room only moments before was gone, replaced by the sweet feeling of relief tinged with hope. His bookish little brother might have just brought them the final piece of this devilish puzzle, and none of them were more thankful than he.

HELENA GOT the feeling that the Storm Forged did not like to be in enclosed spaces for longer than necessary. Anduin had taken the spot closest to the window, and even though he'd only been in the room a handful of minutes at best, he kept casting distracted glances out the window every chance he got.

"Looking for something?" she finally asked.

"I am not usually this far from the sea. I find it unsettling," he admitted, turning his eyes on her.

"For all its beauty, the Palace definitely lacks a view of the ocean," Helena acknowledged.

Anduin smiled, but it did not reach his eyes. "I am surprised that you are seeking out my aid instead of that Night Stalker you so favor."

Helena frowned at the unnecessary vitriol she heard in his voice. There was no need for it when they were all working toward the same goal. "I had not realized you were lacking my attention. I shall endeavor to do better at stroking your ego."

The Stormbringer laughed, the sound reminding her of waves crashing against the sand. "I had not meant offense, only that it is usually her counsel you seek. How may I assist you, Kiri?" The question was directed at her, but his eyes were looking at each of her Circle in kind.

Nial had joined them around the newly repaired table, leaving only

Helena and Anduin standing. Helena could feel their intense focus behind her, but she kept her eyes on the Stormbringer.

"Your cyclone," she stated, causing his brow to lift in surprise. "Can you explain to me how the rest of the Storm Forged help anchor it?"

Anduin studied her, his glowing sapphire eyes searching for something in her expression. "How do you know about that?"

Nial cleared his throat, but Helena spoke before the Stormbringer could look away. "It is common knowledge that the storm would fade without constant tending."

Anduin smiled, but it was a cold, brittle thing. "No, it's not."

Helena rolled her eyes. "It only makes sense that you alone are not responsible for doing so, or you would not be able to stay away from the Ebon Isle for so long. Besides, the drain on you would be considerable. You would be too weak for much more than sitting upon your throne."

His smile fell, and Anduin turned away, his back facing all of them.

"I need to know how the Storm Forged accomplish this, Anduin. It is not a request."

Anduin sighed. "The knowledge of the giving is a sacred thing amongst the Storm Forged. In the wrong hands, it could be perverted... no longer a gift, but a curse."

"All power can be corrupted in the wrong hands," Helena said pointedly.

The Stormbringer nodded, his colorful hair rippling like water. "I will tell you, because I trust you, Helena. You have shown mercy where many others would not."

"Thank you," she said, the relief at his words giving her voice a breathless quality. Entirely too much hinged upon his compliance, and their alliance was still tenuous at best.

Anduin turned back to the room. "Generally, the giving requires a connection, something that links the intention of the one lending their power and the one who will wield it. A joint purpose, if you will. For the Storm Forged, our connection is obvious." Anduin paused, his eyes meeting each of the Circle's, as if trying to convince them of the importance of his words. "It is not enough to trust, the giver's conviction must be absolute, otherwise the power will not be contained once it leaves its source. It will return to the world unrealized."

"Conviction?" Nial asked, looking up from the notes he was furiously scribbling.

"In its purpose. The goal of the magic," Anduin further clarified when he realized the others were not following. "The gift of power must have an end goal; it is what keeps the gift contained."

Helena felt her back stiffen, worry that what she needed would require that she give up the entirety of her plan and thereby condemning it to failure.

"Is it enough that the givers all believed that their gift is going to be used to create a trap? Or would they need to know the specifics of the trap?" Von asked, feeling the tension coiling inside of her. He was careful not to look directly at her, but she could sense his quiet support like a hand brushing down her spine.

Anduin considered the questions. "Knowing the purpose of the trap would be enough. The stronger the belief, the stronger the power. Too many details would muddy the purity of the gift."

"So knowing it was a trap for Rowena that they were helping to build would be ideal?" Helena asked, seeking clarification.

Anduin nodded, and Helena's body relaxed.

"So how does the giving occur?" Nial asked, using Anduin's unfamiliar term.

Anduin closed his eyes, his pulse fluttering wildly in his throat. This was the part that he did not want to reveal, the part that could be twisted and bent until it broke entirely.

"I wouldn't be asking if it wasn't crucial," Helena said softly.

"I know." Anduin opened his eyes. "For us, it is always part of a celebration. We gift our power directly to the Stormbringer, so that it may be gathered and released into the storm itself."

"Forgive my ignorance," Nial interjected, "but how does one gift their power?"

"I am sure there are many ways it could be done, but we use water to aid the transfer." Anduin smiled. "Stick with what you know, right?"

There were a few coughs of laughter, but the room fell silent quickly. "The way I was taught was simple, hold the cup of water in your hands and send your intention into it. When the Stormbringer drinks from the cup, they consume the raw bit of power until they are ready to release it."

"And you're sure this is not simply ceremonial?" Timmins asked, his lips in a dubious frown.

"As one who has partaken of the gifts, I can assure you it is very real," Anduin said, his voice reminding her of the angry churn of the sea.

Helena glanced at the others to see if they had already picked up on their next problem. While Anduin had provided a rather simple answer, it was not going to be as easy as drinking some magically enhanced water. The sheer amount that she needed would preclude it, let alone the fact that she would not be able to contain it long enough to travel far.

"Does it have to be consumed?" Helena asked.

"How else would the power transfer occur?" Anduin asked.

"Would blood work?" Nial asked, surprising them all.

"Blood?" Helena squeaked, the thought of consuming others' blood making her lightheaded.

Nial was biting down on his lip as he sketched something out. He spoke slowly, working his thoughts out on paper before saying them aloud. "If we used blood for the transfer, it could contain and hold the power just as water does. It's a small but potent vessel."

"There can be great power in the blood. It could act as an amplifier," Joquil murmured thoughtfully.

"Uh, guys," Helena said, "I'm not comfortable with the idea of drinking blood."

Nial's eyes widened at the words and he burst out laughing. "Mother no, not drink it. Add yours to it."

Helena took her first full breath since Anduin had joined them.

Joquil and Timmins seemed to understand what Nial was implying, but all Helena understood was that she would not have to drink anyone's blood. She could have wept with her relief.

"Explain," Von said.

"Well, as the Stormbringer stated, the act of tying one's will to the power in order to use it is essential. Rather than having Helena trying to contain that much power inside of her body, she could add a drop of her blood into the rest of gifted drops, and thereby claim them. It would limit the amount of time she had to hold the power so that she could wait until she was ready to release it."

"If it's that easy to take control of the power, what's to stop it from transferring to someone else after they add their blood to the mix?" Ronan asked.

"It goes back to intention," Nial said with a smile.

Ronan looked ready to throttle him. Thankfully, Timmins interjected. "The gift is intended for Helena's use. The power is limited to her and her alone. No one else would be able to lay claim to it."

Nial nodded as if it was obvious.

Helena looked at Anduin. "Do you think it could work?"

"In theory," Anduin shrugged, "I do not see why not. However, it has not been tested. There is always a chance it does not."

Only a chance, but it was the only option available to them. "We will need to make sure that the others understand what we are asking of them. It has to be a choice, freely given." Helena did not want anyone to feel forced to participate.

"Is there anything else we need to know?" Nial asked Anduin, who shook his head. "All right, I will gather what we need. Can the rest of you help collect the," he risked a glance at Helena and chose his words with care, "gifts?"

Her Circle nodded.

"I can help," Helena said, feeling that this was something she should be a part of.

"You have other things to attend to," Von reminded her.

"He's right, Kiri," Joquil added. "You need to be ready to act as soon as we are finished."

Helena sighed. "Fine."

Anduin brushed his hand against her arm. "The Storm Forged will help explain to the rest of the Chosen what to do. When the time comes, we will add our gifts as well."

"Anduin," Helena started, moved that he would offer so freely.

The Stormbringer shrugged. "As you said, we are in this together. Anything we can do to assist, you need only ask." With a small nod, he made his way for the door, the men of her Circle standing to follow.

Von hesitated at the door, looking at her with eyes that saw too much. "It won't be long now," he said.

Helena nodded. "I know."

"You are ready for this, *Mira*."

As always, his faith in her filled her with resolve. "Now to go rid some folks of their blood." Von made a face. "I've been doing it for years and never thought to simply ask for it?"

Helena let out a sharp bark of laughter at the crude joke. He gave her wink, her laughter clearly his intention. He gave her one final roguish grin and walked out, leaving her shaking her head and smiling behind him.

Mother how she loved him.

CHAPTER 24

*I*n less than twenty-four hours, her Circle, along with Anduin's Storm Forged, had managed to collect the blood gifts from the entire Chosen army. Helena had barely been able to contain her tears of astonished gratitude. She had never dared to hope so many would be willing to contribute. Parting with blood was no small ask, and it was rarely required in Chosen spells since their power came from within. However, there were a few records that detailed its powers of amplification as well as its ability to be used as a tracking mechanism. Once acquired, the blood could be used to turn one's power against them. To gift it blindly said much about their trust in her.

Once again, Helena found herself back in the Circle's Chambers. Something about Anduin's reference to a ceremony had stuck with Nial, so Timmins suggested that the Circle, both literal and honorary, wait until the other gifts had been collected before offering their own. This would allow those closest to her to present their offering directly. Helena would be the last to add her blood and would not do so until she was ready to initiate the illusion.

Despite the gravity of their undertaking, the group had worked hard to make this a festive gathering. While it was an unspoken understanding, they knew this might be the last time they were all together, and each of them wanted this memory to hold close in case of the worst.

"There are too many of us crammed in here," Helena laughed, accepting a goblet of wine from Alina.

Alina scanned the crowded room and nodded her agreement. "Indeed, I can hardly hear myself think over the noise. Should I send some people away?" she asked.

Helena shook her head. "No, definitely not. We might just need to move this party outside."

Overhearing her, Ronan shouted his approval. "Mother's tits, yes! It's hot as fucking balls in here."

Helena lifted her brow at the colorful description.

Ronan gave her a one-sided grin and shrugged. "If you had your own set, you'd know what I mean."

Helena took a sip of her wine before giving him a wicked smile. "What makes you think I haven't?"

Her Shield laughed. "Just because you hold your Mate's balls in your knapsack doesn't mean you know what it's like..." Ronan trailed off at her amused expression. "When did you have balls?" he asked, truly astounded.

"When I posed as Micha."

"That's right!" he said, laughing as he shook his head. "I'd forgotten. But still, borrowing a set and actually living with them are two different things."

Helena just laughed at the absurdity of their conversation. "You can keep your knee knockers, Shield. I have no interest in them."

Ronan snorted with laughter, clinking his glass with her own. "Shall we reconvene under the stars then?"

Helena nodded, loving the idea of having the Mother bear witness to their impromptu ceremony.

Ronan let out a long ear-piercing whistle. The room fell silent enough for him to shout, "Outside you scoundrels!" That was all it took for the room to empty and the laughing, tipsy lot to make their way outside.

Helena found herself at the end of the line, smiling softly as she watched them wind their way through the halls. Their laughter bounced off the walls and filled the Palace with easy joy. No one was thinking about what tomorrow would bring. No one except her.

Seeing her lingering behind, Von waited for her to catch up. He didn't have to say anything, she could feel his concern brushing against her and see its echo in his somber gray eyes. The eyes that had always looked straight to the heart of her. Helena never could hide what she was thinking from him.

"I'm fine," she promised, giving him a quick kiss once she reached him at the top of the spiraling stairs. "Just enjoying this while it lasts."

Von rested his arms on the banister beside her. "Aye. It's nice to be home with everyone like this, even if it's temporary."

Home. The word brought a smile to her lips. She had never really thought of the Palace as home. To some extent, that would always be the cottage she had shared with her mother. The Palace was just the place where her things were. For Helena, home was not a building as much as the people that were housed within it. If by home, Von meant spending time with the ones she loved, then she was inclined to agree. It was nice.

On the heels of that thought was a reminder of the people that were missing: Anderson, Darrin, Miranda, and Effie. Those she loved that were no longer able to sit around and drink themselves silly as they toasted to a future they wished would come to be. Her smile turned wistful as she studied her Mate's chiseled profile.

His face was serious despite the smile, as if his thoughts were as heavy as hers. She ran her finger along his nose, causing him to laugh and glance over at her.

She stared at him, her eyes lovingly memorizing every line and angle of his face. The dark slash of his brows, the perfect line of his nose, and sharp edge of his cheekbones. She ran her fingers along the scruff at his jaw, loving the way it scratched her fingers before they made their way into the feather soft strands of his inky black hair.

Von nuzzled into the caress, pressing his lips into the palm of her hand.

"I love you," she whispered when his eyes met hers again.

His eyes darkened, and his hand lifted to brush her cheek. Helena let her eyes fall closed as she leaned into the touch. "I love you, Helena." His voice was deep and warm, wrapping itself around her.

She felt the whisper of a touch on her nose, it was the only warning before his lips dipped down to meet hers. The kiss was achingly gentle, like the sealing of a promise. She pressed against him, eager to deepen it, but he kept it sweet and slow.

"There's no need to rush," he whispered through their bond, his lips continuing to tease her. *"We have our whole lives for this."*

Helena was about to protest, but he stopped her before she could with a hand that tangled in her hair, lightly tugging her back.

"You promised me forever," he said against her lips. Helena's eyes fluttered open to find his tinged with gold and boring into hers. "I refuse to act like tonight will be our last."

Desire and love spiraled through her at the tender rebuke. What had she ever done to be worthy of such a Mate?

Von nipped at her bottom lip before pulling away to gift her one of his most seductive smiles. "I intend to hold you to your promise, Mate."

"As well you should," she whispered, her voice husky. She was leaning forward to claim another kiss when Ronan called loudly from the bottom of the stairs.

"Save that for later, you two. We should probably get on with this before too many of us get too deep in our cups. I can't imagine the alcohol will do much for your magicking."

Helena stepped away with a scowl. She knew he was right, but that didn't make her need any less.

"One day, Ronan," Von called, taking Helena's hand in his as they began their descent, "you're going to find a woman, and I will be able to return the favor with no shortage of enjoyment."

Ronan shrugged, his arms crossed. "Good luck with that, brother."

Once Von was beside him, he leaned close and said in a low growl. "May your balls forever be blue, you smug bastard."

Ronan threw his head back and laughed, the sound rolling through the room and bouncing off the high ceiling.

"What is with you two and your obsession with balls tonight?" Helena asked, shaking her head.

Von raised a brow in confusion. "What do you mean?"

"Ask him, he started it," she said, stepping away from the still laughing Shield and out into the gardens below.

Helena never would have known that the party was unplanned. By the time she reached the garden, tables and chairs were set up with sparkling centerpieces and laden with food. There was also a small platform in the middle of the set-up where Helena assumed she would be standing as people stepped forward with their offering.

Overhead, the sky was filled with stars. She tipped her head back, breathing in the fragrant scent of night-blooming flowers and just basking in the glow of the moonlight. It was a beautiful evening. One made for dancing or sneaking off into the dark corners of the garden with a lover, definitely not one for bloodletting, although that was what it was about to be used for. She sighed and opened her eyes, making her way to the platform. Maybe one night soon she could dance beneath the stars, but tonight was not that night.

Helena took her place, and her friends' animated voices grew quiet as they took note of her. She cleared her throat awkwardly, not sure what to say. She hadn't planned to make a speech tonight, although it was starting to look like it was about to happen anyway.

"I, uh…" she trailed off and shrugged at their polite laughter. "I have no clue what I'm supposed to say right now. Thank you seems too small a phrase to express the depth of my gratitude for your continued sacrifices."

Helena paused to take a breath and settle her nerves, her eyes seeking out each person individually. In the back were her Circle, their strength and combined power making them a considerable force, even at rest. She gave each of them a smile before looking on to Reyna and her favored guards. Next was Anduin and the two women who joined him for most diplomatic events. Then Serena and Nial, representing

Daejara; Alina and her brother, the selected representatives of Tigaera; the Etillions, Amara and Xander; the Caedarans, Tinka and Khouman. It looked like everyone was here. Or maybe not.

With a mighty roar, a bright jet of orange flame, Starshine flew through the sky and landed in the back of the group. The floor rocked with the force of her landing, and a few of the guests stumbled into each other. It would seem that a certain Talyrian had not appreciated being left out of this gathering.

Helena snickered. "Always one for the dramatic entrance," she teased.

Starshine opened her mouth and let out a smoky huff, pale gray smoke twisting up into the sky as her mouth closed. If the sound had a translation, Helena was certain she had just been told to shut up.

Settled once more, the Chosen returned their attention to their Kiri.

"I never wanted this war, but Rowena took that choice away from me when she began slaughtering hundreds of our brothers and sisters. She must be stopped."

There were cheers of approval as her friends lifted their glasses in salute to her words.

"This ends tomorrow. Come dawn I will leave you to set the trap that will bring her straight to me. Your gifts tonight will make that possible."

More raucous cheers rang out at her words. Helena gave them a fierce smile, one filled with bloodlust and promise.

"There is only one way this will end, my friends, and that is with the Corruptor's death. Some sins cannot be forgiven or overlooked. While the Mother is merciful, she will not stand for the slaughter of her Chosen. The time has come for justice."

Starshine tipped her head back and roared into the night sky, the cries of the Chosen deafening as they joined her.

"In the days to come, hold firm to your faith in the Mother, and in me. The only way through this is united. To justice!" Helena shouted, holding up her glass.

"To justice!" they shouted in unison.

Helena drank deep, draining her glass completely. Even without the

Jaka, she could feel the love and approval radiating from those standing before her. More than anything, Helena wanted to be worthy of it, of them. These people were her family, they were her home, and she would die to protect them.

Nial was the first to step forward, an orb of swirling crimson held in his outstretched hand.

He gave her a lopsided grin. "I went ahead and consolidated the other gifts for you. I had the feeling you might appreciate not having to deal with it in its organic form."

Helena grinned. "Whatever gave you that impression?"

He winked. "Call it instinct."

"Thank you, Nial." Her heart clenched at the sweetness of his gesture.

He placed the orb in her hand and she was surprised by its warmth. The orb was smooth, like glass, while the swirls of red rose and crashed like the sea inside.

Nial nodded, holding out his hand as he slashed his palm with a silver dagger she had not noticed until then. He squeezed his fist together, his eyes focusing intently on the orb she now held cupped in her palms. Two drops of blood dripped onto the surface of the orb, which absorbed it instantly, leaving no trace of the dark liquid on its surface.

Helena shivered, the hair on her arms standing on end as the offering merged with its predecessors. This was potent magic indeed. Her eyes lifted, but Nial was already holding out the now clean blade to the next person.

One by one they came to her. First the Chosen delegates, then the Forsaken, with her Circle going last. Just as Kragen was to hand the blade to Ronan, Starshine snarled, stalking her way to Helena's platform.

Ronan raised a brow, unsure of the Talyrian's intent. "Are you next?" he asked.

Starshine huffed and nudged him to the side.

Ronan backed away with wide eyes. "Are you seeing this?" he asked Von in a loud whisper.

Von, who had slightly more experience with the Talyrian Queen than the others, merely chuckled. "Just don't get in her way and you'll be fine," he promised.

The platform gave Helena enough height that she was able to meet Starshine's gaze head on. The Talyrian dipped her head, using a fang to slash at the thick pad of her paw. The blood welled quickly and Helena held out the orb, her heart aching at the beading red that left a trail behind it on the snow-white fur.

Beyond all others, Helena had never anticipated this. "Thank you," she whispered, emotion causing her voice to break.

Starshine huffed again and then held out her paw to Von. It took a moment for clarity, but he finally realized she was demanding that he heal the wound.

"Me?" he asked as he took the paw in his hand.

Starshine bared her teeth like she was just about at her limit of dealing with silly humans when Von held his hand above her paw and closed his eyes. The bright blue of his healing magic moved into Starshine's paw, closing the gash and wiping away all traces of blood.

Von dropped her paw, and Starshine nudged his shoulder with her snout.

Helena snickered. Starshine had practically just called Von a good boy in front of the rest of them.

Ronan was still shaking his head in disbelief as he moved into place. "I don't know how you handle being around more than one of them."

Helena shrugged. "We're kindred."

Ronan's eyes shone bright as he looked into hers. "Yes, we are."

Helena smiled at the way he twisted the words, which allowed her to miss the flash of the blade as he sunk it into his flesh. Even still, she grimaced. She could feel the sting of the cut for each of the men in her Circle, and it resonated a bit more as they went down the line.

"'Tis but a flesh wound," he said with a wink. "I've had worse on the practice field, Hellion. No need to get your panties in a bunch."

"You should go take a long walk off a short cliff," she said with a shit-eating grin of her own.

He reached out with his uninjured hand and gave her arm a squeeze. "A drop of blood is nothing, Helena. If needed, I would lay down my life for you."

Helena swallowed, her laughter dying at the serious blue eyes that stared into hers. "And I for you, Ronan."

"But not today," he said, his teeth flashing in a smile. "Today, we live."

Helena nodded, still blinking back the tears his words had caused. "Today, we live," she agreed.

Ronan stepped away, leaving only her Mate.

Von looked up at her and grinned. "And so we meet again."

"At least no one is booing you this time."

"I'm sure I could remedy that if you'd like to reenact the first time we met?" His words were so earnest that laughter bubbled forth.

"As much as I would love to relive the moment our souls found each other, they just started tolerating you a few weeks ago. No need to get them riled up again."

Von laughed. "Fair enough, *Mira*."

Between one heartbeat and the next, Von had cut his palm and pressed it down into the orb. He closed his hand around it, keeping it cupped in between their hands.

"Von," she warned since he had already given more than just a drop or two.

He did not look away from her. "Everything that I am is yours."

It was a vow he had made to her before, and Helena opened her mouth to reply as lightning flashed in the sky. There were a few shocked gasps as thunder followed, so loud that it sounded like the sky had split in two. Even though she did not look away from her Mate, she could see the rest of the guests look up toward the sky.

"It would seem the Mother has spoken," he said with a wry smile, lifting his hand from the orb.

"Apparently," Helena replied, her body thrumming from the contact with the orb. As his hand lifted, she looked down. The swirls of color were moving so fast they blurred, but that did nothing to hide the effect Von's blood had. After he had added his offering to the mix, the crimson had changed into a bright, luminescent gold.

"You sure know how to give a girl a gift," she murmured, staring at the orb in awe.

"You told me you were tired of flowers," he said.

Helena's eyes cut to his. "Never," she insisted.

He tilted his chin up, and Helena leaned down, meeting him halfway for a soft kiss. His hands went to her waist, and he lifted her off the platform and back onto the ground.

"What are we supposed to do now?" she asked.

Von shrugged, his grin so filled with mischief that her heart began to race with excitement. "Whatever the fuck we want."

"Oh, I'll drink to that," Helena said.

And so they did.

CHAPTER 25

*H*elena woke the next morning with only a small headache from the previous night's festivities. All in all, it could have been much worse. At least she had memories of laughter and dancing—which she was happy to note did occur after all—to offset the minor ache. She rose before the sun, spending those quiet moments brushing the hair from Von's face and kissing him sweetly awake.

"Good morning, handsome."

"Good morning, my love," he grumbled sleepily.

"If we want to leave before the others wake up, we need to get up now," she whispered as she ran her fingers along the curve of his spine.

Von grunted, his word quota for the morning already met. He wrapped his arm around her and pulled her body until it was flush against his.

Helena chuckled, appreciating the sentiment even though she knew she couldn't indulge in it. "I'll leave without you, if you'd rather sleep."

That got his attention. Von opened one bleary eye. "You'll do no such thing."

Helena nodded. "Indeed, I will."

Von sighed and rolled over onto his back with a groan. Helena openly ogled him, appreciating the way the sheet rode low on his hips.

How easy it would be to forget the task at hand and spend the morning in bed with her Mate. Helena forced her eyes away from the chiseled V at his hips. The temptation would be damn near impossible to resist if she didn't try to maintain some semblance of self-control.

"Five more minutes," he pleaded, his arm thrown across his eyes.

She smiled at the petulant cast of his voice and lifted his arm, waiting patiently until he looked at her.

"Now," she said firmly, following the word by sliding out of bed.

"Oh, that's just mean," Von growled as Helena made her way across the room stark naked.

"Consider it an incentive."

Von's eyes were predatory as he sat up, one arm propped behind him. "How so?"

Helena looked over her shoulder, her chestnut curls sliding across her back as she looked up at him through her lashes. "If you catch me before I get dressed, you can have your way with me."

Von was launching himself over the foot of the bed before Helena had finished the sentence, slamming her into the wall with his lips claiming hers in a breathless kiss. He pulled away to look down at her with an unapologetically smug smile. "Challenge accepted."

Helena melted into him, his proximity making her lose track of just exactly what she had been trying to do. There was nothing sweet or gentle about the way his body pressed against her. Von slid his hands down her sides, stopping mid-thigh to grasp her legs and pull them up around his waist.

At Helena's gasp, he pulled back with a chuckle. Nipping her lip before moving his head back toward her ear. "You did promise anything," he growled.

Her head fell back against the wall. "By all means..." her voice trailed off, further coherent words impossible.

He anchored her against the wall with his hips, the throbbing length of him pressed tightly against her aching core while he used his phantom hands to tease her body. "I like this game," he murmured, coming up from another breath-stealing kiss.

Helena's eyelids felt heavy as she forced them open to look at him. "Mmm," she murmured.

"We should play it every morning," he said, sliding his velvety length along her center.

"Oh," she groaned, pressing her hips against him to increase the pressure.

She heard his snicker of approval before his hips swiveled and he drove straight into her.

"Oh!" she gasped again, clenching around every pulsing inch of him.

"Look at me," he demanded as he drove into her.

It was damn near impossible, but she made her eyes focus on his face. There was no need for words. The look in his eyes told her everything he wanted her to know, while the bond reinforced it with its loving heat.

Their frenzied lovemaking was over as quickly as it began, each thrust causing sparks to burst behind her eyelids until she finally lost herself to the ecstasy of his touch. He came with a growl, his teeth biting down into her neck as he spent himself inside her. They stayed there, their hearts thundering in their chests as they held onto each other.

"Now you can go get ready," he told her, letting her body slide down his until her feet touched the floor.

Helena was proud of herself when her knees only buckled once. "I don't know who you think you're giving permission," she informed him primly. "If I hadn't wanted you, I wouldn't have given you the opportunity."

Von's eyes were pure molten silver when he replied, "Oh darling, if you think I was going to let you walk away without reminding you who you belong to, you've forgotten who I am."

Helena turned to face him completely. "Who says *you* were reminding *me*?" With a wink, she spun back around and headed into the bathroom to enjoy the last handful of moments she had left before leaving to face the darkest part of her soul.

LESS THAN AN HOUR LATER, Helena was standing on the top of a hill at the westernmost border of Tigaera. There was nothing particularly special about the area, other than being wedged between the Palace and Endoshan. Helena could have cast her illusion anywhere, the location didn't matter so much as the results, but she felt it would be most believable the closer she was to Rowena's hidden cemetery.

The sun had just started its rise, and the sky was a brilliant wash of red and orange. It looked as if the sky was on fire, and Helena took that as a good sign, considering what she was about to do.

She heard the rustle of Von's clothes as he stepped closer to her, laying each of his hands on her shoulders. Her eyes fell closed, savoring the warmth of his touch. He brushed a kiss to the base of her neck and then, without a word, he walked away to give her the space she needed to concentrate.

There was no more putting it off with strategy meetings, or last-minute ceremonies, or lovemaking. The time had come. Helena pulled the golden orb from the hidden pocket in her cloak, the hair of her arms standing on end at the contact.

The orb pulsed with latent power that called to her, hungry for its release. The pool of her power rippled in response like the flow of the tide feeling the pull of the moon. Helena called on her rage, summoning every pain-filled memory to the front of her mind. She shuddered, her body transforming in response to the swift rise of fury. The tips of her fingers became deadly black claws, and even her teeth felt as though they had lengthened. She didn't give herself time to think before she slashed at her arm with one of the Talyrian claws. Blood rose swiftly, splashing from the gash in her arm and coating the orb.

As soon as her blood made contact, the orb began to glow, shifting from gold to a blinding white. She lifted the orb up, blood still running down her arms and dripping to the ground, before letting go of it entirely. As the orb began to fall, she closed her eyes, shifting her focus as she dove straight into the depths of her power. Helena had never gone that deep that fast, and the rise of power was heady. She could feel her physical body sway, but she did not stop, pushing herself down even deeper.

Distantly, she heard the shattering of glass. That was her cue. Pulling every ounce of power to the surface, Helena opened her eyes and screamed. She screamed for pointless deaths, futures that would never be, and for all the Chosen who had been suffering for so long that their screams had long gone silent with their belief that no one could hear them, or worse, that no one cared. It was the pain of her people that fueled her, and she made herself feel every ugly piece of it.

Birds burst from the trees as thunder began to roll overhead. The sky filled with thick black clouds from which drops of blood began to fall, coating the land in its deep crimson. The earth shook under the assault, the transformation already underway.

Helena did not have to concentrate overly hard on what she wanted. All it took was the echo of three spectral voices in her head for the vision from her trial to bring every gory detail into pristine focus.

'You have a choice before you.'

'See the cost of your choice.'

Blood continued to fall from the sky, while the pieces of ash blowing up from the ground further obscured the air. The trees, once vibrant and alive, were now charred skeletons, many of them still on fire. The unearthly wind continued to whip up piles of ash, flinging them into the air until they fluttered like ghostly butterflies. In the face of such destruction, it was almost impossible to see past her hand, but Helena didn't need to see. She already knew what she would find. The ground was no longer rolling green hills, instead it was endless piles of corpses. She refused to look down, not wanting to be greeted by the faces of the dead. Seeing them once was enough.

She felt his approach before she heard it, and by the time he'd reached her, she was already facing him. Helena watched him fight to keep his face neutral, but she could see her reflection in his eyes. She was a wild thing, more creature than human. Her hair was flying around her while embers flickered at the tips, giving her a fiery halo.

215

Her eyes were not the iridescent color of her power but pits of ebony with shimmering echoes of flame in their depths.

Helena licked her lips, tasting blood and ash. "The eyes can see what the heart knows to be false." She thought she had whispered the words, but they echoed from every direction as if they had been spoken by a legion.

"Then I shall close my eyes, so I see only what is true," Von said.

Helena felt herself waver, and blinked a few times before shoving every emotion besides pain and grief into a deeply recessed part of her heart.

"It is time to break the tether." Again, her words swirled around them while thunder continued to growl in the sky.

Von swallowed but gave no other outward sign of fear. Instead, her beautiful warrior faced her head on and spoke in a controlled voice, "Do your worst and know that I love you."

If she allowed herself to focus on their bond, she might have felt the flutter of panic when she cast the final, darkest part of the spell. As with before, all it took was a memory of voices.

'Without the tether, you will fracture.'

'Eternally lost to the darkness.'

For Rowena to truly fall for Helena's deception, her bond to Von must appear severed. Von had already known what had to happen when he pulled her aside. His strategist's mind had seen the play before she ever did. Mostly because it was not something she would ever willingly consider. Once triggered, it would enable them to each experience the one thing with the potential to destroy them both. There was no telling how they would react.

But this was war, and there was no other choice. Everything about the illusion had to be unfailingly convincing. The Kiri and her Mate must truly believe the bond was gone. That required them to actually *feel* like their bond was gone.

There was no explosion of power this time, just a gasp as Von crumpled to his knees before a loud, keening cry was torn from his throat. "Helena," he rasped, his eyes staring up at her in horror.

She was merciless, focusing only on what she needed the power to do and not the whimpering voice in the back of her mind pleading with her to end this and find another way.

There was no determining how much time had passed when Von finally labored to his feet, his body trembling. When his eyes met hers, they were not the silvery gray that she adored, but a milky white snaking with black.

The illusion had been cast, and the magic was so powerful that by the time Helena was done, even her heart could no longer tell what was true.

CHAPTER 26

*R*onan swore under his breath as he stormed down the stairs and walked out to the armory.

"Rough morning?" Reyna asked in a deceptively sweet voice as he rounded the corner. She began to walk beside him, matching his ground-eating stride with ease.

Ronan scowled at her. "They left without us."

Reyna lifted a brow. "And that surprised you?"

He glared. "Obviously."

Her brows veed over her eyes and she stopped him with a touch. "She gave us a time and a place to meet her. You had to realize Helena was going to go ahead of us."

Ronan bit back a slew of harsh words. He'd been so damn preoccupied he hadn't realized it, and it chafed to no end that Helena and Von had left him behind. He was her Shield damn it. His place was at her side, more so now than ever.

"Whatever," he muttered, slamming into someone rushing the other way. "Get out of my way," Ronan snarled. The poor boy who had been carrying armor whimpered and scurried away.

"You're making children piss themselves now."

"Children, grown men… what's the difference?"

"Really, Ronan?" The disappointment in her voice was undeniable.

Ronan stopped again, running a hand along his face. "I'm just on edge."

"We all are. You're not the only one heading into this battle."

He turned to face her, his eyes blazing with blue fire. "Yes, but there's never been this much at stake before. I've fought for Daejara, I've fought because I've been paid to do it, but never have I been more scared of what happens if I lose."

"It sounds like it's the first time you truly cared about the outcome," Reyna commented softly.

He was about to protest, but she was right. Daejara had been his home, and he'd believed in Von when he'd joined him, but Ronan had never stopped to worry about what tomorrow would bring. If he died in battle, at least he'd go out in a blaze of glory. Now, however, it wasn't even the thought of his death that had his heart filled with dread. Death would be a mercy if they lost.

Determination had him gritting his teeth. He couldn't guarantee that no one would die today, but he'd make damn sure that those corrupted pieces of shit would have to go through him before snuffing out the life of another person that had become his family.

"Chosen!" he shouted, causing everyone in the room to freeze mid-act. "Fall out. We leave in ten to meet your Kiri and join the fight for our way of life!"

The room burst into excited cheers and men and women rushed to finish their preparations.

"Spoken like a man who has something to prove," Reyna said, her eyes looking much softer than they had only moments before.

"Spoken like a man who has something to protect," he corrected. "It is not our lives she wants, it is our souls. Rowena seeks to destroy all that holds any value to the Chosen. Her victory is not simply the end of us, it is the end of everything. Is that not worth fighting against? Mother's tits, Reyna. Is that not worth dying to prevent?"

Reyna was quiet, and Ronan could see the flutter of her pulse at her throat. She was not unaffected by his words, although her face remained impassive.

"Oh the hell with it," she muttered a second before pressing her hands to his cheeks and pulling his face down to hers. When her lips touched his, his heart stuttered. He was frozen for only a heartbeat before his arms slid around her and pulled her lithe body against his.

The kiss was a force of nature, violence and passion colliding as they said with their lips all the things they had not had a chance to express with words.

Reyna pulled back first, panting hard. "You will live today, Shield," she said fiercely, her forest green eyes burning into his. "I'm not done with you yet."

"Yes, ma'am," he whispered, his lips tilting up in a one-sided grin.

Reyna nodded matter-of-factly and disentangled herself from his embrace.

Flickering shadows danced around her body as she walked away, and Ronan found himself staring after her in wonder. Yes, they definitely had some unfinished business.

RONAN STARED at the decimated land before him, his eyes wide with shock.

"Well, it will certainly grab Rowena's attention," Kragen said, his expression a twin of Ronan's.

"That's one way to put it. Have you seen any sign of Helena or Von?"

"Negative," Kragen replied, shifting to face him. "The others are growing restless. They had not anticipated their gifts were going to be used to create... this."

Ronan spared a glance at the people who stood as far from the blood and ash covered land as possible. He didn't blame them. Everything about this place was grating against his senses. The mounds of corpses were especially revolting.

"I almost can't believe Helena was capable of creating this," Kragen muttered.

Ronan had no trouble believing it. He remembered watching her as her power sparked out of control. This was what it looked like when that power was not tempered by her love.

"We should make sure that the Chosen remember this is only a trick meant for Rowena. We cannot afford to have them lose faith in Helena."

Kragen nodded. "It is one thing to be told and another to come face-to-face with the results of said trick. There are likely many that are reconsidering their presence here."

"It was what she intended, since she needs word to get back to Rowena."

Kragen sighed. "I know. I will ensure that the message is reinforced so that it is only a few lost instead of an entire army."

A disturbance in one of the mounds caught his attention, and Ronan squinted, trying to make sense of what he was seeing. One of the corpses was pushing itself up. Wait. That wasn't a corpse. He would have recognized that sword anywhere. He'd helped forge it. That alone was enough for him to recognize the figure that slowly approached them.

"Mother be merciful," Ronan whispered, watching what had once been the brother of his heart take slow shuffling steps toward them. "Helena, what have you done?" Even as he knew this had to be part of the illusion, seeing Von's eyes snaking with the telltale black lines was too much.

Ronan lurched, half running half falling as he raced toward his best friend. "Von!" he shouted, hoping that he would reply and prove that this was only a trick.

The man that had once been Von opened his mouth on an endless scream. That was when Ronan noticed the figure standing in one of the crumbling defense towers in the distance. Her hair billowed around her like she stood at the center of a storm, the ends smoldering embers.

His stomach rolled, and he swallowed hard to avoid being unmanned entirely. It was too much. That couldn't be the woman he'd bound his life to.

Even from this distance, Ronan could tell that soulless black eyes were staring directly at him. He saw her mouth open, although he was too far to hear the words or read her lips. It didn't matter. As soon as Von lunged for him, he knew what she had ordered. It had been one, unmistakable word: attack.

"Let me in on the game, brother," Ronan begged as soon as Von was within hearing distance. "Are we putting on a show for the others?"

Ronan watched in horror as the man who had been more than a brother to him came after him, holding nothing back as he began to fight, not as a warrior but as a Shadow. At first, Ronan clung to the belief that this was all part of the elaborate scheme, and his moves were entirely defensive, but as soon as Von bit into the side of his arm and pulled back with a piece of flesh, Ronan knew they were doomed.

It may have started off as an illusion, but somewhere along the way, Helena had been lost to the darkness. It was the only explanation.

He pushed Von, or what was left of him, away with a snarl and eased himself into a fighting stance. The one thing he still had going for him was that he had fought Von hundreds of times, he knew without conscious thought how and where his friend would strike. For all that Von had lost his mind, his instincts were still intact.

"All right, you bastard. Let's dance."

The next time Von lunged, Ronan pounced, and the two men met in the air before falling to the ground in a tangle of limbs. They fought brutally, holding nothing back as they traded blows. That was nothing new, they'd always pushed each other to the limits, knowing it was necessary to keep them primed for battle. The only difference this time was it wasn't in the name of practice.

This time, the battle was real.

CHAPTER 27

*R*owena stared at the trembling messenger in disbelief. A bubble of something that must be happiness rose in her chest, but the feeling was so foreign, Rowena didn't recognize it. "Say that again," she demanded.

"It is as I said, My Queen. The prophecy has been fulfilled. Even now, the Mother's Vessel is in Endoshan commanding her own army of Shadows into attacking the Chosen army. As one falls, she turns them, using the dead to create a new army."

Rowena fell back in her makeshift throne, her fingers lifting to her lips as a breathless laugh bubbled up. She had won. Her fingers traced her lips, feeling them lift in an unfamiliar smile.

"Bring me my husband," she ordered.

The messenger bowed and swiftly exited the cavern she had claimed as her throne room.

It was done. She had won. Rowena knew it was only a matter of time, but now that it was here… her thoughts continued to chase each other, each one bringing with it a buoyant joy she hadn't experienced since the birth of her twins. Back when the sniveling traitors meant something to her.

"My Queen?" Kai-Soren called as he walked in.

"Have you heard?"

"I have, My Queen." There was a bland sense of disinterest in his voice that confused her, but she was too elated to care.

"Ready the men. We leave for Endoshan before nightfall. It is time to go meet my finest creation."

His dark slash of a brow lifted. "Your creation, My Queen?"

Rowena's smile hung frozen on her lips. "You doubt me?"

"Never, My Queen. I simply do not understand."

That Rowena easily believed. Her smile grew, although now it was tinged with a familiar icy cruelty. "It would seem my pet has discovered my gift. Her acceptance is a most welcome sign."

Kai-Soren shook his head. "I do not follow."

Rowena sighed. He was really taking the fun out of this for her. "You don't need to. All that should matter to you is the Vessel has been shattered. She is ours to use as we please. Don't you know what this means? Elysia and the Chosen are mine."

Her husband looked like he wished to say something more, but apparently he had finally learned his lesson because he simply gave her an empty smile and bowed. "Very good, My Queen. I will make sure the men are ready for our departure."

His lack of excitement didn't matter. He wouldn't be around much longer anyway. Not now that she had what she needed. Once she claimed what was rightfully hers, Kai-Soren would be nothing more than an unpleasant afterthought.

ROWENA HAD to admit she was impressed. She knew that the Vessel would be helpless to resist the pull of her little present, but she hadn't quite expected this. There was no denying that her newest ally was a powerful one, and much more valuable than a full team of Generals. With the kind of power the Vessel was putting off, the need for Generals was obsolete.

Rowena felt a flicker of relief. Considering she had never gotten around to replacing the last two, that was welcome news.

The mounds of corpses made it hard to traverse easily across the land, and the sky continued to rain down blood and ash. The slaughter was absolute. Rowena had thought the messenger said that the Chosen were being turned before they died, but it would appear the Vessel had gotten tired of building her own army. No matter, between the two of them, there were more than enough Shadows already.

She smiled in delight. "If it wasn't already obvious, let us reinforce our victory with a bit more destruction, shall we?" Rowena whistled, calling for the two Talyrians she had managed to turn the last time she had faced off with the Chosen.

Mother of Shadows indeed. Not only did she have the two beasts, she now owned the Vessel as well. The Mother may have spat upon her when she withheld her greatest gift, but it didn't matter anymore because Rowena had fought for, and taken, all that should have belonged to her by right. This victory proved that none were her equal. The Chosen would be obliterated, the entire race replaced by a people of her creation. She would be revered and worshiped for the rest of time.

Rowena could feel the air shift behind her as the wings of the beasts pushed through the blood and ash. Even with the limited light, their bodies cast shadows on the ground below. A figure standing in the middle of the carnage twisted, finally taking notice of Rowena and the army at her back.

Her smile grew as recognition dawned. It was the Mate, or what had once been the Mate. Rowena laughed, it would appear the Vessel had finished what she had started. She still had not seen any sign of her once opponent, but any vestige of doubt that might have remained about the truth of the messenger's words fled at the sight of the twisted figure before her.

She did not require any further proof that Helena's corruption was absolute. That didn't mean she didn't want to drive the point home to completely shatter what was left of the broken army that still hoped to oppose her.

"Destroy him," Rowena commanded, her voice a gleeful purr. Rowena pointed toward Von, and the Shadow Talyrians wasted no time hesitating, purple jets of Shadow Fire spouting from their mouths as they careened toward their target.

Surely no other victory had ever tasted so sweet.

CHAPTER 28

*H*elena's hands were braced on the stone blocks that made up the watchtower. She watched the figures below with no more interest than one gave to an ant. The sense that she was forgetting something important continued to gnaw at her. It had started when the red-headed one grappled with her new pet, but she'd grown tired of watching and had called on her power to encase him in stone.

Her pet had been furious that she'd denied him the kill, but the act had released some of the pressure that had been building in her chest as the fight between them had carried on.

Shortly after, dozens of others had peeled away from the massive crowd gathered at the furthest edge of the field. Her pet had snarled and made like he was going to attack, and soon that nagging feeling rose again until Helena froze those men as well. And then the next. And the next, until finally everyone that remained had been encased in stone. It had taken no more than a thought and each body was a statue, frozen in a moment of time. As coated in blood and ash as they were, it was impossible to tell that they were no longer animated with life.

It didn't matter. Nothing did. All she cared about was that the pressure in her chest eased once they were unable to act further.

Helena had no memory of how she got here or how long she'd been standing as still as one of her statues. She knew not what she waited for, only that she was, in fact, waiting. Time held no meaning. The sky remained a roiling mass of black clouds and lightning as blood fell from the sky. Day or night, it made no difference. The sky cast no true light, only an endless darkness.

She tipped her face back, opening her mouth to gulp the warm liquid, tasting the power and fury that drove the storm, and wanting to claim a part of it for herself. She could feel the magic roll through her, her body warming in response to its call.

A jet of color in the black of the sky caught her eye, and Helena's head twisted toward the movement. Streaks of red and orange were growing larger as they arced through the sky. There was something familiar about the shape of them and the way they moved. Her head tilted as she struggled to remember the name for the flying creatures.

That was when she noticed them swoop low, diving straight for her pet.

The pressure in her chest that had dimmed with the statues, increased until she was gasping for breath. At the same time, she watched the creatures, now shooting purple flames from their mouths, creating a ring of fire her pet could not escape. Helena's fury rose until she could hear her blood roaring in her ears. Two things happened simultaneously, making it impossible to tell which act triggered the other.

The tensioning in her chest broke and a snarling word was torn from her mouth as her body came undone. The word boomed across the sky, wrapping her inside of it as she was remade.

"MINE!"

The figures of stone began to crack, and the black clouds peeled back from the sky, revealing a blood-red moon.

Her body was no longer her own. Helena's back stretched and arched as her battle cry echoed on. Her limbs lengthened, growing thick and corded with muscle until it was too hard to stand on only two feet. She fell forward, noticing the glistening black claws that scratched deep divots into the gray stone, as white fur that sparkled like diamonds began to sprout from her skin.

A weight at her back caused her to shake in an attempt to dislodge it, but as she shook, she felt the weight move with her. Wanting to ease the tension, she rolled her shoulders and saw out of the corner of her eye as she did, a massive golden wing tipped with shiny black talons unfurl.

There was no conscious thought, no sense of self or understanding. Only instinct and one truth that rang louder than everything else.

Mine.

Those foul beasts wanted what was hers, and she wasn't about to let them have it.

Helena roared, pushing herself up until all four of her feet were balanced precariously on the edge of stone. There were shouts below and then the sound of roars filled the sky, filling her chest with the need to answer the call. Tipping her head back she roared, blinding white fire flowing from her mouth to light up the sky.

She was not aware of what happened beneath her, other than the statues were frozen no longer. Now freed, they joined in her cries, adding their voices to the chorus.

She jumped from the ledge, trusting her wings to catch the air. This was no graceful dive, but a mix of physics and haphazard gliding. Her body may know what it wanted to do, but it did not mean she possessed any semblance of talent in this new, powerful form.

Luckily, she did not need to worry about landing. Helena made contact with the larger of the two creatures, her claws sinking into its decaying flesh as easily as parting butter. She held tight as her mouth opened on a furious roar before sinking her teeth into its neck and ripping back. The beast's head was torn from its body and its wings beat once, twice, before stuttering and falling limp. She released her hold on the body as it began to tumble, not ready to go down with it.

Her wings were still outstretched, and she beat them hard to try to regain some height. The other creature turned its lavender eyes toward her, the snaking lines almost hypnotic. *Wrong,* she thought. This beast had once been majestic, but now it was tainted.

It opened its mouth, ready to spew more of its purple fire at her, but she lashed out with a claw, raking it across its eyes. The blow was so strong, it knocked the creature from the sky. She followed it down, not wanting to give her prey a chance to escape.

It tried to correct its descent, its wings pumping furiously, but she caught the sinuous length with her claws and pulled back, hearing a snap and then a furious roar. The wing tore from its body with no more effort than plucking a feather from a bird. It sped toward the ground, tumbling as it fell through the sky.

Helena felt her body stretch as it tried to close the distance between them. There was another roar, and a spout of hot flame before another beast, a white one with black wings and bright turquoise eyes, intercepted the orange body, savagely tearing it apart, flinging the broken pieces away before covering the broken body in cleansing flame.

Helena landed as best she could, her new legs stumbling under the impact. Her fury at the kill being stolen from her was replaced with respect as the other creature calmly stalked toward her. Helena felt the need to curl her tail between her legs. She did not want this one's anger. She feared it but did not understand why.

She held perfectly still as a turquoise eye inspected her, feeling as though she was holding her breath the entire time. The feline was much larger than she was, although Helena knew that she was more than a match for her if it came down to a fight. She could feel the power rippling through her body even in this new form.

But it was not a fight the creature was interested in. After one long sniff, the other cat nuzzled against her and began to lick at her fur, cleaning away the remnants of blood and gore. Helena felt her chest vibrate with pleasure. Where she had once felt only fury and possessive anger, now she felt a tidal wave of love.

The remaining remnants of the illusion fell away, showing the truth that had been concealed by its darkness. What was left of it exploded in a shower of light. The land was green and whole once more, and the only bodies that remained were wholly alive.

Helena blinked, memories returning to her in a rush. She staggered under the weight of what had happened, shocked that she had lost enough of herself to the illusion that she hadn't understood what was happening.

Von, entirely unharmed, ran over to the two Talyrian females, his hands raised.

"Helena?" he asked, his voice rusty. "Are you in there?"

She padded forward, eying her tiny two-legged Mate. Before she could pounce on him and claim him as hers in front of the others, a sharp wail had her hackles rising.

"NO! You stupid bitch, I have already won! You belong to me! You all belong to me!"

Helena snarled at the woman standing on the other side of the hill. *Rowena.*

This was not the time for claiming after all. There was still work to be done. She was the Mother's Vessel; the Mother's vengeance; and now more than ever, the Mother's teeth and claws. It was time to fight.

VON HAD no recollection of what had happened after Helena had cast the final piece of the illusion. He had felt like he was suffocating, the pain of their bond being ripped away more devastatingly painful than he'd ever anticipated. It was like he blacked out, everything about him ceasing to be until just moments ago when he rose from a crouched position on the floor. He'd been surrounded by purple flames, but there had been a gap just large enough for him to launch himself through where the flames had not yet met.

He had seen the glowing iridescent eyes of the second white Talyrian and recognized his Mate instantly. Even in this form, she called to him.

The bond had returned in full force, but the messages it was sending were a chaotic jumble. He wasn't sure if it was Helena's new form, or if it was simply Helena herself. Needing to see for himself that she was okay, he'd ran toward the two Talyrians, slowing down once he was close enough to catch their attention.

Helena's Talyrian gaze zeroed in on him, and he froze in place as a flood of energy zinged through him. He didn't know what had changed, only that she had somehow tapped into even more power than she'd ever held before. Is that what had allowed the change? Or was it merely leftover power from the Chosen's offerings? There were too many questions and no time to get answers.

A woman's angry cry had them looking past Helena's shoulder to the top of a hill. Rowena's fists were clenched in her skirt and her face was twisted in an angry mask. She was furious at their betrayal.

Von smiled, his eyes glittering with malice while his Mate snarled, her Talyrian body posed for attack.

Rowena shouted more orders, but the words were unintelligible from this distance. Three dark figures moved into view, and Von zeroed in on his target. In order to end this once and for all, those three had to go down.

He heard the sound of hundreds of footsteps and glanced over his shoulder to see a confused army come into view. Ronan was at the head, Kragen and Reyna on either side of him. Ronan's blue eyes were troubled and cautious. The others looked equally uncertain.

Helena had warned him that the others might fall victim to the illusion, but he hadn't actually believed her. Since he himself had no recollection of what had happened, he just hoped nothing unforgivable had transpired.

"Von?" Ronan asked.

Von looked around, making sure he was still standing alone. "Who else would I be?"

"Thank the Mother," Ronan said, rushing forward to wrap Von in a bone-crushing hug.

Von grunted but returned the harsh back slaps with a few of his own. "I take it there was some doubt for a while?"

"Just long enough to make me shit myself," Ronan muttered darkly.

Von wanted to laugh, but the fear was still too fresh in his friend's eyes.

"I'm sorry that we scared you. You understand it had to happen, don't you?"

Ronan nodded, but the shadows lingered in his eyes. "Now is not the time for apologies. I'm just glad you are okay."

The Circle fell into place behind him, their eyes rounded as they took in the sight of their Kiri.

"Do you think it's permanent?" Joquil asked in a hushed tone.

"Nothing like this has ever happened before," Timmins replied. "I can only hope for all our sakes that it's not."

"It's not," Von said firmly. There was no doubt in his mind Helena would return to herself once this was over, if not before. There was no telling how long the transformation would last, but he figured it would end once the excess power ran itself out.

There was another cry, and Rowena's Shadows began to swarm the field while her Generals wasted no time wreaking havoc.

Von's brows lowered, and he pulled his sword from its scabbard, running a hand along its length to set it on fire. "Let's finish this," he roared, holding up his sword and rushing head long into the frenzied mob.

The final battle was at hand.

CHAPTER 29

The three Generals split up, one moving straight through the center of the crowd, while the other two moved to each side. It was an unspoken agreement that the Chosen's leaders would divide their main forces to counter the major threats, while the bulk of the army led by Timmins and Joquil would handle the Shadows.

Ronan and Reyna's Night Stalkers peeled toward the left, heading toward a decaying figure that had flies buzzing about him and a trail of dead grass in his wake.

Kragen and the Storm Forged went right, moving to intercept a General that had called forth the water from a nearby stream and was sending wave after wave toward the Chosen gathered nearby.

For his part, Von followed the Talyrians who were chasing down a General whose affinity appeared to be Fire. More of the purple Shadow Fire danced in his hands. The Talyrians could fly far faster than he could run, even while using his power, so Von gave up the chase when he spied Kai-Soren spinning twin daggers in his palms.

Von's mouth stretched into a sinister smile, he would do just as nicely. "Seems you chose the wrong side, Heir."

"I did what was best for my people, Daejaran. Something I think you'd understand."

"Turning on your people to save your own ass? No, I don't think we have anything in common."

Kai-Soren's golden eyes narrowed at the dig. "That only makes this easier." He flung one of the daggers, the silver metal glinting as it spun through the air. Von's blade cut out to his side, knocking the dagger uselessly to the ground. Four more daggers followed in rapid succession, and Von maneuvered his blade just as fast, none of the poisoned daggers meeting their mark.

"That all you got?" Von taunted, pleased to see Kai-Soren's left eye begin to twitch.

"Daejaran scum!" he spat, lunging toward Von.

Anticipating a hidden blade, Von dodged the attack, twirling to the side so that his flaming sword slid across the Endoshan heir's back, the sharp edge of the blade cutting through leather and skin, while Kai-Soren's hair went up in flame. Von smirked, enjoying himself far too much. He'd disliked the heir ever since their first meeting when he'd flung ignorant insult after insult at Von.

For all the prestige laid at the Endoshan warrior's feet, Von was underwhelmed by the skill of their heir. *He probably lets the poison do the work for him.* Von snorted with derision. No true leader should be outmatched by the rest of their people. It's one thing to surround yourself by those strong where you are not, it's another thing entirely to be utterly incompetent. Something wasn't adding up.

Kai-Soren's blows were half-hearted at best, and Von was able to dodge and disarm him easily.

"Stop playing with me and end it," the heir hissed, staring up at Von from where he'd landed on his back after Von had swept his legs out from under him.

Von gave him a long considering look. "Can't stand to deal with the mess you've made of things? Where's that infamous Endoshan honor now?"

Kai-Soren looked away, and it was all the answer Von needed.

"You've failed your people. You are not worthy to lead them."

"End it, Daejaran!"

"With pleasure," Von hissed, using his blade to slit the filthy traitor's throat.

Von was not his Mate. When presented with an opportunity to show mercy, it did not come naturally to him to take that route. Besides, there were less honorable ways to die than on a battlefield during a war. The only mercy Von would show was not telling what was left of his people that their heir had begged for his death like a coward.

It would have to be good enough, and it was still more than he deserved.

HELENA FLEW at the head of the pride, Starshine on her right and Midnight on her left. She could feel the heat of the Talyrian flames as they took out wave after wave of the Shadow army. With each skeletal body that was lost to the flames, she felt an answering call of satisfaction.

She focused solely on the man in black whose hands were playing with purple licks of Fire. If given the chance, he would unleash that corrupted Fire on her people, and it would not stop until it ran out of things to consume. They could not give him that chance.

Starshine roared and the Talyrians broke rank, confusing the Fire General as he could no longer anticipate where the attack would come from. They played with him like a cat with a mouse, one Talyrian swooping in low while another shot off a jet of flame. He dodged the attacks, jumping out of the way of one with barely enough time to dodge the other. He was their puppet on a string.

The General grew tired of the game quickly. He started to lob balls of purple flames up into the sky. For every Talyrian he knocked off course in their attempt to dodge the flame, another one took its place.

Starshine circled the General, swatting at him with extended claws. He raised his arms, trying to protect his face from the deadly tips but was only successful in providing easier access to his skin. Her claws raked against him, thick lines of black ichor beginning to show everywhere Starshine made contact. The General cried out in pain and rage, a ball of Shadow Fire growing in the palm of his hand.

Game time was over.

Helena swooped down, her Talyrian fangs bared as she growled low in her throat. She watched the General's empty eyes staring up at her as her mouth opened and ripped the arm from its socket. Next was Midnight, his teeth raking the flesh clean off the other arm before snapping it in two. With the threat of Shadow Fire neutralized, the General was unable to do more than spin in an impotent circle. Starshine was last, the Talyrian Queen ripping out his throat and completing the kill.

From her place on the hill, Rowena screeched in outrage, more of her power lost. It was nowhere near enough to avenge the unfortunate deaths of the two Talyrians that had fallen to Rowena's twisted power, but it was a damned good start.

The pride flew across the sky, their howls of victory interrupted only by jets of flame as they laid waste to more of the Shadow fiends below.

One down, two to go.

VON SPUN, looking for his next target. Ronan and Reyna looked like they had their hands full with the decaying General, but before he could get to them, a wave knocked him over. His skin stung everywhere the water touched him, and Von hissed in pain. He looked down to see his skin erupt in blisters. Steam rose from the water before it was absorbed back into the earth, which quickly turned to mud.

The decision made for him, Von made his way toward Kragen instead, blinking across the muddy ground instead of fighting against it.

The Water General was keeping the Chosen busy dodging his waves, but the Storm Forged were giving as good as they got. While the Chosen worked on the group of Shadows that were attacking, the Storm Forged worked to take control of the water. Every time it looked like they would be successful, a new wave would appear behind them and break their concentration, causing them to start over.

When it came to controlling Water, there was only one person that outmatched the Stormbringer, and she was currently flying through the sky with the rest of the Talyrians, but at the moment, Anduin seemed anything but in control.

"Stormbringer," Von greeted when he appeared beside him.

Anduin's eyes were pinched and he had broken out into a sweat. "This is the first time water has felt like it was fighting against me. There is something, unclean, about it."

Von nodded, not surprised to hear that the element the General was commanding was tainted. It was the nature of Rowena's Generals.

"What do you need?" Von asked.

"A distraction. Something that will let us take control of the water and cleanse it before returning it to the earth. In its current form, the damage it's doing to the land and its potential to harm those that come into contact with it is…" Anduin shrugged, at a loss for words. "It's bad," he said finally.

Von nodded. A distraction he could do. "Regroup and wait for my signal."

The Stormbringer nodded, looking relieved that someone else was taking control.

Kragen was wiping black ichor from his blade when he looked up at Von. "Slimy little fuckers," he said by way of greeting.

Von laughed and nodded. "That they are, brother."

"I wouldn't mind so much if it wasn't for the smell," Kragen continued conversationally, decapitating another Shadow with his blade as if this was a normal occurrence. Perhaps these days it was.

Seeing as how they did emit the distinct aroma of rotting vegetation and feces, Von wasn't about to disagree.

"Do you remember that one time during training, where the recruit tripped over his own boot and went flying into Ronan?" Von asked.

Kragen gave a snicker of laughter. "I can hardly forget, especially after Ronan bashed the kid upside his head and sent him spinning, but is this really the time to dredge up our fondest memories?" Kragen punctuated the question by driving the tip of his sword into the chest of another Shadow before pulling it out and gutting him.

"We're going to recreate it."

Kragen paused only long enough to look at Von and ask, "You want to trip over your boot and into me? Now?"

"No, dumbass, I want you to launch me into the General so I can knock him over and distract him long enough for Anduin to gain control of the water."

Understanding flickered in Kragen's dark eyes. "You don't want him to see you coming."

"Exactly."

Kragen grinned, his eyes crinkling with unconcealed delight. "Don't take this the wrong way, but I am damned sure I am going to enjoy this far more than you. Brace yourself."

Von was by no means a small man, but Kragen still towered above him. With less effort than he would have liked, Kragen grabbed Von by the back of his shirt and hauled him up into the air. Von could feel the tingle of power as Kragen reinforced his throw with Air. Within seconds, Von was flying, his arms spindling out of control as he flew like an arrow straight toward the General. By the time the bastard noticed him catapulting toward him, the General could do nothing except fall under Von's weight.

There was a loud grunt and crack. After a quick mental check, he was certain that no major injuries were sustained, at least on his part. The General tried to push Von off him, but Von continued to shift and move, keeping the General pinned beneath his weight.

After a moment of the wrestling, Von realized it was absolutely stupid to wait for a distraction when he was in such a prime position. He hoisted himself up just enough to pull one of the daggers he'd knicked from Kai-Soren and drove it into the side of the General's neck. Black ichor spewed from the wound as he drew the blade back out.

"Nighty night," he crooned as the General gasped before wet gurgles of ichor bubbled from his mouth.

Von was enjoying himself entirely too much. Such was the way of the bloodlust.

Kragen stood above him, staring down with such a downcast look that Von was concerned. "What's wrong?"

"Can't you save some for the rest of us?" Kragen winked, and Von shook his head.

"Help me up, Sword, and I'll see what I can do for you."

Kragen grasped Von's forearm and pulled him up with ease. Together the two men turned to face the Storm Forged, who were using the last of the corrupted water to capture and drown the Shadows nearest to them.

"Remind me not to piss that guy off," Kragen said in a low voice.

There was a scream, and the world began to shake.

"Brother," Von said, "the Stormbringer is the least of our worries."

RONAN GRUNTED as the razor-sharp nails of the Shadow scored his skin. They'd been ambushed by the cadavers as soon as they'd gotten within reach of the General.

Reyna took one look at the blight that spread out in a ring wherever he stood and ripped her necklace off. Ronan gave her a baffled look but did not have time to wonder what in the Mother's name she was doing.

A jet of Talyrian fire helped take care of a few Shadows, giving Ronan a chance to breathe and re-center himself. He'd lost track of the battle raging around him, focusing only on the opponents before him and clearing a path to take down another of Rowena's Generals.

Reyna was muttering something under her breath, and Ronan gave her another look.

"What are you doing?"

The Night Stalker blinked up at him. "Summoning the Watchers."

It was Ronan's turn to blink. "I thought that they had fulfilled their promise in the Vale."

Reyna shrugged. "It's all in how you look at it, I suppose. What matters now is that they're here." She gestured toward the horizon where the trees seemed to shift and stretch.

"But—"

She slapped him on the shoulder. "Save your deep thinking for later, Shield. We have enemies to kill."

Ronan shook his head, amazed at how fast the trees had transformed. He recognized the lumbering tree men from the brief time he'd seen them during the Battle of the Vale, but he'd forgotten just how impressive they were. The trees moved slowly, but their massive size more than made up for it by helping them cover the distance quickly; their method of execution by stomping was probably the greatest thing Ronan had ever seen.

Second greatest thing, he corrected instantly, seeing two golden Talyrian wings carry Helena across the sky toward the hill Rowena cowered upon. He still did not understand where the ability to transform had come from, but he was endlessly thankful for it. If Helena was moving toward Rowena, it meant that there must only be one General left.

Ronan sprang back into action, hacking at the Shadows without end. Soon there was nothing between Ronan and the last of the Generals. The man opened his mouth and blew. Ronan watched as a thick green cloud flew from his mouth.

Reyna hissed, moving from somewhere behind Ronan to his side before he could comprehend the movement. She shoved him down, throwing her body on top of his.

"Do you have no regard for your life?" she raged.

"What?"

Reyna scowled, looking as furious as she had when she'd slapped the shit out of him. Once he got over the shock of it, he'd been rather impressed. No one had ever left such a perfect handprint on him for any amount of time, let alone the three hours hers took to even begin to fade.

"He was trying to poison you, or are you too stupid to notice?" Reyna snapped, pulling him back to the present.

Ronan pushed her off, rolling until he was above her. Reyna

squirmed beneath him, and Ronan gave her a look that had her going still.

"Thank you," he said dryly, before looking around to see where the General had moved to.

What he saw next had him jumping to his feet.

In the minute he'd been pushed to the ground, the world had gone to shit. Or part of it had. Everything that had come into contact with the General's plague cloud had withered and died. That included two of the Watchers that had been the closest. The ground was littered with Night Stalkers and Chosen alike, the rotting tree men standing over their bodies like morbid sentinels.

Reyna looked at the bodies of the dead, her own body vibrating with fury until wisps of shadow were floating away from her.

"Reyna," Ronan cautioned, seeing the General turn his attention back to them.

But she was already gone. Shadow-stepping to a place just behind the General, Reyna's daggers flashed as she slid the sharp surface along his neck. She was fast, but so was he. The General had time to puff out one final breath of toxic air. Ronan watched Reyna's eyes go wide, the whites showing as she fought against the General's grasp.

"No!" he roared, fear turning his blood to ice.

Reyna vanished, staggering when she reappeared beside him. Ronan looked at the once flawless face that twisted and sagged on one side, one of her forest green eyes now a milky white.

"Ronan?" she asked, her fear making her voice child-like.

Years of bearing witness to fatal injuries were all that helped him school his face. His expression gave nothing away. Scars meant little to him, he'd had his fair share for years before Helena had taken them away. He ran his hand along the uninjured side of her face, his fingers weaving into her hair to hold her still while he pressed a gentle kiss to the unmarred part of her forehead.

"Ronan?" she asked again, her fingers biting into his arms hard enough to bruise.

Before he could try to murmur nonsensical words of comfort, a scream of inhuman pain filled the air and the ground began to quake.

CHAPTER 30

*H*elena stretched her wings as she glided through the air, loving the feel of her powerful Talyrian form. The battle raged on below, her Chosen laying waste to the Shadow army. She watched from the sky as her friends took out Rowena's Generals, one after the other, and she itched to join them in battle. They were close, so close, to her finally being able to go after Rowena. She felt like a dog on a chain. The beast in her was eager to be unleashed, and the anticipation of being free was causing her blood to roar in her ears. Until the last one fell, she didn't want to risk getting too close. For all of the perks that came with being a Talyrian, she was also a much larger target.

While removed from the bulk of the fighting, Rowena was by no means idle. She was busy shouting orders and trying to replace her fallen Shadows by picking off the Chosen closest to her. A few had fallen from her efforts, but between the Talyrian fire and the speed with which the Generals were being taken out, Rowena could not balance out her losses. It was a fact that brought Helena no end of pleasure. For once they had finally taken, and managed to keep, the upper hand.

After sustaining the loss of two more Generals, the Corruptor was looking decidedly worse for wear. Her hair was falling around her face in limp strands and her pale complexion was a mottled red. She was furious and desperate, a dangerous combination.

Helena knew the moment Rowena decided to change her strategy. She abruptly stopped targeting the Chosen and scrambled her way to the top of another small hill, zeroing in on Helena. Unsure what to expect, Helena swooped down low, which proved to be a costly mistake.

Rowena's mouth fell open in a cruel smile when she saw Helena coming back into range. With a high-pitched scream, she unleashed a jet of corrupted Spirit aimed straight for Helena. Helena was able to easily dodge the first jet, but soon bolt after bolt was being flung her way. She ducked and wove, but it was soon impossible to navigate the sky as it became filled by the evil purple bolts. All Helena could rely on was instinct as she tried to avoid them, but eventually she chose to bank right when she should have dropped down. It was a move that allowed her to avoid one of the glowing jets only to end up flying headfirst into another. Seeing her error, Helena tried to jerk back, using her wings to pull her up, but it was too late.

Searing pain radiated from her chest, and Helena let out a surprised roar as she began to fall from the sky. As she fell, she heard Von echo her cry, his voice a blend of shock and pain as the blow reverberated through their bond. It wasn't just the physical pain they felt, it was the huge drain of power Helena experienced as a result of the leeching shadow bolt. *That thieving bitch just stole my power,* Helena thought with an angry snarl.

Rowena cackled manically, the injection of power more than enough to regenerate her depleted power stores.

Helena tried to beat her wings, but it was as if she'd lost the ability to control them. She continued to tumble through the sky, feeling her body fighting against the transformation back to human as she did. She started to feel true fear as the ground loomed closer. A fall from this height would mean only one thing unless she could find a way to cushion the landing. As she flipped through the air, she caught sight of Von's inky black hair as he raced across the ground.

"Helena!" he roared, his voice frantic.

The feeling of transition was disorientating. She was no longer full Talyrian, but not quite human either. Her golden wings had retracted, and her massive paws were already turning back into pale hands with glinting black claws. Her beautiful fur was gone, replaced by her fighting gear. While in the feline form, some of her senses had sharpened, almost like when she tapped into the sensory enhancement provided by her power, although not quite as potent. Her ability to tap into her rippling pool of power was also impossible in the Talyrian form. As a being made of magic, she supposed it made a certain kind of sense that she couldn't also manipulate it past the abilities already accessible in that form.

In a last-ditch effort, Helena tried to call her power up, but the partial shift was still cutting off her access. She sucked in a breath, at a loss for what to do. For it to end now... like this. The Mother couldn't possibly intend for it to end this way. She opened her mouth to vent her impotent rage the only way she could.

Instead of screaming, she gasped as her body was caught and then... bounced. Stunned, Helena froze, her hands splayed on something malleable and cool. She slowly twisted her neck, looking around her in wonder. A bubble of Air and Water held her suspended in the sky, slowing her descent as she floated the final feet to the ground.

"Mother keep you, Stormbringer," she groaned, dizzy with the relief she felt at Anduin's quick thinking.

She landed, and the bubble burst, releasing some of the wild power that was unique to the Vale. She was back on her feet only a heartbeat before Von reached her. His arms were around her, pulling her trembling, fully human body against him.

"I thought..." he stopped, unable to even utter the words. She didn't need them, the thundering beat of his heart and the icy terror blasting through their bond said more than enough.

"Me too," she whispered.

That was all there was time to say. This was still a battlefield, and Rowena was still very much alive. Fortunately for them all, so was she.

Helena stepped away from her Mate, feeling mostly centered, although a part of her still felt like it was trapped in an endless free fall.

She turned her attention to Rowena, whose malicious smile slipped slightly at the sight of an uninjured Helena.

"Why won't you die?" she screeched, pulling back her arm, ready to release another bolt.

Helena felt a sinister smile of her own stretch across her face. "The feeling is entirely mutual."

The sounds of battle raged on. The earth shook and Rowena doubled over with an inhuman wail. "No!" she cried.

There were only a few feet separating them now, and Helena could read every flicker of emotion that crossed Rowena's face. Helena knew there was only one thing that had the ability to cause the heartless bitch's eyes to widen like that. The last General had fallen. For the first time, Rowena looked truly afraid.

Perfect, the feral part of Helena purred.

Rowena licked her lips, her eyes wide as she cast them about her. "You can't beat me." Helena knew that she meant for the words to sound threatening, but her quavering voice did little to pull it off.

Helena lifted a brow. "Watch me."

WITH THE LAST of the Generals gone, only the Shadows and a handful of the most loyal Endoshans remained. As each General fell, more and more of the Shadows seemed to be breaking free from Rowena's mental hold. The loss of power was affecting her ability to contain them. Even now, more packs of the monsters fled from the battle.

Let them run, Ronan thought with a snarl. He would hunt every last one of them down until Elysia was freed from their taint.

He gently pushed Reyna back, his eyes scanning the field for any sign of his friends. His eyes found Serena's blonde head first. She was hacking away at one of the ambling Shadows, while her mate blasted another beast with Fire. Kragen and the Storm Forged were just past them on the left, using swirling waves of Water to topple Shadows and slowly drown them. Timmins and Joquil were working together to help get the fallen off of the field and out of harm's way. That only left Von and Helena unaccounted for.

The last time he saw her, Helena had been flapping massive golden wings and flying through the air between Starshine and Midnight. He looked toward the sky but did not see her. Ronan frowned.

"What is it?" Reyna asked, her husky voice coming out on a hiss of pain.

Ronan shook his head. It was too soon to say.

A familiar mop of hair caught his eyes at the bottom of a hill. Ronan breathed a sigh of relief. If Von was there, Helena must be nearby. There is no way he'd let her out of his sight once she was grounded.

He lifted his eyes up just in time to watch Helena slap away Rowena's arm.

It felt like the world stopped spinning, the moment suspended in time. At first there was nothing, and then a giant pulse of power knocked him off of his feet. He hit the ground with a grunt, Reyna landing in a sprawl beside him. Ronan shielded his eyes as blinding light shot from Helena's body, making it impossible for him to see what was happening.

"Mother's tits!" he shouted, surprise ripping the words from his chest without conscious thought.

Once the light faded, Ronan pushed himself up, holding out a hand to help pull Reyna back up. The Night Stalker eyed his hand as if debating whether she was going to accept the help.

"Take it," he growled.

For once she didn't argue. Her mismatched eyes blinked up at him, her thick lashes tangling at the tips. "Thank you," she murmured.

"You're welcome," he said more curtly than he intended. Ronan was torn between wanting to pick her up and take her somewhere safe, and wanting to run over to see if Helena was okay.

In the end, the choice was made for him. By the time he pulled his eyes away from Reyna, all that was left to do was watch in awe as one by one Shadows that had been frozen mid attack began to fall. As they hit the floor, their bodies exploded in a shower of dust until nothing but the floating black powder remained.

The Chosen had won.

ROWENA'S glacial blue eyes continued to flicker from side to side, her lips bracketing when she didn't find what she was looking for.

"You have something that belongs to me. I want it back," Helena snarled.

"No," Rowena hissed. "The power is mine. ELYSIA IS MINE!"

Helena borrowed a trick from Von and blinked until she was standing just behind the disheveled blonde. "You'll have to kill me first," she whispered in Rowena's ear.

Rowena's breath hitched, and she spun around, a bolt of power fizzling out as Helena slammed a palm into her arm to knock it away. Rowena's skin began to sizzle where Helena's hand pressed into it, and Rowena began to shriek in rage and pain.

Instinct guiding her, Helena wrapped her hand around the other woman's arm and held tighter. It was the first time they'd ever made any kind of physical contact, and Helena didn't think it was a coincidence. The longer she held on, the more disorientated she became. Rowena struggled against her, but Helena refused to let go even when she felt her own palm begin to blister from the searing heat.

Helena's eyes rolled back in her head, and she let out her own gasp of pain. All she could see was a yawning black chasm. There was nothing but endless darkness; a void that wanted her to sink beneath its weight. It pressed against her, making it hard to breathe. Her chest felt like it was being crushed in a vise, and her lungs were soon starving for air. She sucked in a breath that felt more like swallowing living flame.

Distantly, she thought she heard someone bellow her name, but she was frozen, poised on the edge of a cliff. If she let go, she would fall. Not just down on her knees in the dirt, but down into a never-ending pit. All she could do was hold on, hold tighter, as she clung to life. It was the only way to fight against the feeling of nothingness and despair.

For that's what the darkness was, Helena realized. It was the culmination of every terrible moment of her life played on an eternal loop. This was what it meant to be truly hopeless. It was then that Helena knew she was looking into Rowena's soul. Or rather, her lack of a soul. Whatever twisted things she'd done with her magic had taken the worst kind of toll. No wonder she needed so many Shadows and the Generals to empower her. She had nothing left. She was empty; a husk. There was only a void where what had made her human once resided. It made her more of a monster than her Shadows could ever be.

Helena grit her teeth, unwilling to ever go back to that place. The illusion of corruption had been more than enough for her. She had no intention of ever experiencing that again. Helena focused on Von. It was her love for him that brought her back from the brink once, she knew that he would be the one to help her break the spell again. She couldn't access their bond from this place, but the harder she focused, the easier it was to breathe. Soon she could feel him, like a warm and steady presence that surrounded her. Helena took her first full breath just as a speck of golden light found its way into the darkness.

Rowena continued to scream and thrash as the ground rolled beneath their feet. The sky broke in two as lightning snaked across the sky. A blinding white light burst from Helena as Rowena fell to her knees, her screams of pain drowned out by the roar of thunder.

The golden light grew brighter. The darkness began to roll back, repelled by the light. It slunk away, fading until it was less than the size of a pin, before vanishing completely.

Helena sagged, her hand falling away from Rowena's charred skin.

Rowena was curling into a ball, her body shaking. "What did you do? What did you do to me?" she screamed.

What was left of Rowena was ancient and ghastly. She was utterly ravaged. Her hair had fallen almost completely out, only a few stringy clumps remaining on her bloody scalp. Her body had sunken in on itself, making her look more corpse than living being, and her skin, where it still remained, was oozing. Even her eyes had changed, the colorless orbs crying tears of blood.

"Mother's tits!" The cry sounded behind her, but Helena didn't dare look away from Rowena.

"Nothing less than you deserve." Helena's voice was quiet, but there was no missing the menace in it. There would be no mercy here. The Mother's justice was upon them.

All that was left of the color in Rowena's face drained away. There was no way out of this, and she knew it. Helena didn't let the sight of Rowena's frail and shaking body sway her. She bent down until her nose was a mere breath away from Rowena's.

"This is what happens when you try to take what is mine." The words reverberated with the harmonious voice of her power.

Helena punched her Talyrian claw-tipped hand through Rowena's chest, listening to the wet crunch of her bones with satisfaction. She fisted it around the thumping muscle and jerked back until Rowena's still beating heart was laying in the palm of her hand.

There was a gurgle and bright red blood began to drip from Rowena's mouth.

"Elysia will never be yours," Helena spat, watching the rest of the life drain from Rowena's eyes. Her fist closed around Rowena's heart, crushing it into a fine red dust.

There was a final whistle of breath, but any words she wanted to say died with her.

The Corruptor was dead.

CHAPTER 31

"*L*ong live the Vessel!"

"Mother bless the Kiri!"

Helena smiled as she lifted her chalice to yet another toast. Beneath the table, Von wove his fingers between hers.

"That smile is as fake as the purple flames in the hearth."

Helena shuddered at the reminder. The Chosen had wanted to throw a feast to formally commemorate their victory over the Corruptor. It was a mandatory holiday, all able bodied people joining in the celebration at the Palace or holding their own, smaller parties at home. To that end, the ballroom had been decorated in shades of purple in her honor, but the smoldering purple flames left her tensing in her seat every time they caught her eye. She couldn't help but be reminded of the insidious shadow flames.

She loosed a breath before giving Von a smile that was more a baring of teeth than anything. *"It's not their fault."*

"Eleven hours of celebrating is taxing on the best of us."

Helena smirked. *"You'd never know it by looking at them."*

Von's eyes darkened as his expression grew somber. He brushed his thumb along the back of her hand. *"How are you feeling, Mira?"*

"Do you really need to ask?" Helena asked with a wry lift of her brow.

"You know I don't, but I figured it was politer to let you deny it if you weren't ready to talk."

Helena sighed. It wasn't the time or the place to get into the tangle of emotions she'd been wading through since the battle at Endoshan. *"I will be,"* she answered, negating the need to lie.

It was hard to relax or dance when a part of her was terrified that Rowena would walk through the door at any moment. She'd literally ripped the bitch's heart out, and yet she was afraid it was too good to be true. The woman had haunted her for months, it wasn't something she could let go of easily.

The excited cheers of her people drew her attention back to the dance floor. For the last hour, they'd been competing with demonstrations of their talents, each act a tribute to Helena's first year of reign. Of course, the only moment they seemed to want to recreate was that final bloody battle. It was... too soon.

Helena gripped Von's hand as another shudder wracked her body.

No one knew what Helena had experienced while facing down Rowena's darkness, or even when she came face-to-face with her own during the illusion. Helena didn't have the words to describe it, and the Circle had been too kind to ask more than once. She didn't doubt they had filled in the blanks on their own. That would have to be good enough. No one else needed the nightmares.

Kragen and Joquil were the de facto judges of the competition, Helena adamantly refused to participate, although only the Circle knew that. She watched as the two men crowned the trio who had done an interpretive dance of Helena taking down the Shadow Talyrians. She clapped politely alongside her Mate until the music resumed and the floor filled with dancing bodies.

"Care to dance?"

Helena was about to refuse, but resisted the urge. At least if she was pressed against him, she wouldn't have to be pretending to enjoy herself.

Von stood, pulling her behind him as they joined the others. There were cheers when the Chosen noticed their Kiri dancing alongside them. Von spun her in a slow circle before pulling her body close to his. They swayed slowly, completely ignoring the music's fast-paced tempo. Helena rested her head on Von's shoulder, her mind emptying of everything except the heat of his hands against the small of her back.

"I'm proud of you, Helena."

She pulled her head back to look up at him, her brows scrunching together.

"There are very few people that could face the darkest parts of themselves and walk away whole."

"Who says I did?"

"Me."

The unwavering conviction in his voice did her in. Her lower lip quavered.

Von dipped his head, stealing a kiss and her breath in one fell swoop. *"None of that, beautiful."*

The raucous cheering at their display of affection had Helena pulling back with a laugh, her cheeks tinged pink. Von winked, letting her know that had been his intention. Helena shook her head, before snuggling close once more.

"If I am unscathed, it is only because of you." Helena paused, taking a steadying breath before allowing herself to admit, *"There was a moment on that balcony when I couldn't have cared less what happened below, and then I saw those two Talyrians barreling toward you and it was like I snapped back. Not all of me, not right away, but the pieces that knew you were Mine."*

Von ran a hand along her back, his heart beating steadily beneath her ear. *"It was enough."*

"You were enough. You are what keeps me whole. They might be cheering my name, but none of this would have been possible without you."

Von's eyes glittered suspiciously, and he bent down for another kiss. His teeth grazed her lip as he went to deepen the kiss, but a not-so-discreet cough at her shoulder had them pulling away.

"I believe this dance belongs to me," Ronan said with a smug smile.

Von grunted, his arms tightening around her.

Ronan rolled his eyes. "You have your whole life to fondle my Kiri. Back off and let me dance with her."

Von flashed his teeth in a grin, giving Helena one last kiss before stepping away.

"Are you sure baiting him is a good idea? He's got a lot of free time on his hands these days," Helena asked, stepping into Ronan's arms.

Ronan snickered. "It's how he knows that I love him. Besides, the fucker bit me. He can deal with it."

Helena's head fell back as she laughed, a deep rolling belly laugh. By the time she caught her breath, Ronan was smiling at her.

"It's good to see you laughing again, Hellion."

The nickname had a breath catch in her throat.

"Since he isn't here to tell you, let me say it on his behalf. Your Shield—past, present, and future—are incredibly proud of you."

Helena swallowed back her emotion, opting for a more light-hearted response. "Speaking on behalf of my future Shield as well? Are you planning on being replaced?"

Ronan sputtered. "Replaced? Not even death can rip the title from me, Helena. This life and the next, you're stuck with me."

The tear fell down her cheek before she could try to blink it away. "Well, fuck Ronan. You had to go and make me cry, didn't you?"

Ronan's smile was soft as he pulled her close, shielding her teary eyes from the rest of the room. He dropped his head to whisper in her ear, "It's how you know I love you too."

HELENA STOOD at her window watching the festivities wage on. It had been two weeks since they returned to Tigaera victorious, and the jubilant cries of the Chosen had not stopped since.

Von's arm snaked about her waist, pulling Helena back against his chest.

"What reason could you possibly have to leave our bed?" he asked in a sleepy grumble as he pressed a kiss to her shoulder.

Helena smiled and gestured wordlessly to the dancing bodies below.

"Did they wake you? We can sic Ronan and Kragen on them if you want them to shut up."

Laughter bubbled up at the mental image that caused. "No, no. It's nothing like that." Helena's words faltered, and she shrugged, still smiling as she watched.

The truth was she hadn't been able to sleep for more than an hour or two at a time since they'd come home. Von would keep her awake for hours with his lovemaking until she finally passed out in a sweaty and satiated heap beside him, but inevitably, she would wake up when the same restless energy ate at her.

Von's hand found her hips and tugged her around until she was facing him. Brushing a thick curl from her face, he asked, "What's bothering you, my love?"

Helena shrugged, feeling foolish. Rowena was dead, they were alive. There was simply no explanation for her to feel anything less than ecstatic. But a part of her felt empty. For the first time since her arrival here almost a year ago, there was nothing for her to do.

Even her new friends were returning home when it became clear they could not justify their absences any longer. Anduin and his Storm Forged had left for the Vale a few days ago, with the Daejaran contingent not far behind them. The Caederans and Etillions left yesterday, promising that they would keep in better contact so that nothing like this could ever happen again. Only Reyna and a few of her Night Stalkers remained as guests at the Palace, but Helena thought that had more to do with a certain blue-eyed Daejaran than anything else.

Von laughed, picking up on the nameless emotions. "Can it be that my beautiful Mate is bored?"

She shook her head, intending to disagree but stopped short. Was she? What sense did that make?

In the immediate aftermath of Endoshan, Helena had felt only bone-deep satisfaction. Within a couple of days, the feeling had been replaced with a growing restlessness. She had tried to find an answer about what exactly had transpired when her skin had connected with Rowena's, but the best Timmins had been able to offer was a guess. It was his belief that in Rowena's desperation for power, she sacrificed part of her soul each time she used the corrupted Spirit magic. Eventually, there was nothing left but the void of the corruption within her and when it came into contact with the purity of Helena's completed soul, it shattered. Whether that was true, the Mother only knew, but it was as good an answer as they were going to get.

Either way, the result had been the same. The Shadows fell without Rowena's power to animate them, and without the strength of her Generals to protect her, Rowena was nothing more than a human woman. She was no match at all for the Mother's Vessel. Her death had been swift and total.

Helena frowned. Was that what was bothering her? That it had been over too quickly? After months of build-up, of single-minded focus and purpose, Rowena was dead. What was she supposed to do now?

Von's understanding smile let Helena know that she'd asked the question out loud.

"Whatever the fuck you want," he whispered, pressing a hot kiss to her mouth and making the breath leave her in a whoosh.

She chuckled as he grinned down at her. "Yes, but no one needs me anymore. I've never had a chance to do something just because I've wanted to."

Von frowned, his brows dipping low over his gray eyes. "I need you."

Helena pressed her palm to his scruffy cheek. "I need you too, my love. But that's not what I meant."

She'd grown used to the adventure and its accompanying race of adrenaline through her blood. The thought of only having her days filled with the monotonous tedium of being a political figurehead, even if her nights would be filled by her Mate, left her rather uninspired.

"Darling, no one is saying you have to keep yourself locked away in the Palace."

Interest piqued, she asked in an excited rush, "What are you thinking?"

Von grinned. "You've only seen a sliver of the land that you rule. You have new friends and allies that we can visit or we could go and meet the rest of your people. If that's not to your liking, I'm sure the pride will want to spend time with their newest member."

Helena's smile grew, her heart thumping excitedly at the thought of all the possible adventures that might still be ahead of them.

He ran his nose along hers, pressing a kiss to her cheek before whispering in her ear. "You made me a promise, Mate. Time for just the two of us once the war was over."

Helena's eyes flitted to the unmade bed and then the magically locked door. "What have we been doing these last two weeks?"

"You've been running off to spend time with your friends before they return home, answering Timmins's endless questions so that he could make the appropriate notes for the archives, holding court over your subjects, not to mention the time you spent helping Ronan train the new recruits," Von listed. "By the time I get you to myself, everyone else has all but exhausted you with their demands, but that ends now. You and I are going away."

Her pulse raced at his words. "We are?"

His eyes were molten when they met hers. "We are. Now pack." He slapped her ass once, and Helena's knees locked at the flood of heat that pooled between her legs as a result.

Von's nostrils flared, and his eyes darkened with arousal. "Hold that thought. I want us gone before anyone tries to distract you."

Her smile grew. "We aren't telling them we're leaving?"

Her Mate shook his head. "We'll leave them a note so they don't worry, but for the next few weeks, *Mira*, the only title you'll answer to is Mate, and your only responsibility will be to please me," he whispered, dipping his head for another scorching kiss before stepping away and quickly tossing some clothes in his pack.

Helena licked her lips, her mind going foggy. A different kind of restless heat wound its way through her body. One thing she definitely was not feeling right now was bored.

He lifted a brow when she didn't move. "You coming?"

"Not yet, but I intend to be shortly," she answered in a sexual purr as she slid past him, her pebbled nipples rubbing against his bare chest.

"Fuck it," Von said, grasping her around the legs and tossing her over his shoulder as he carried her back to their bed. "Ten minutes longer won't make a difference."

"Only ten minutes?" she pouted.

He slid his hands up her legs, pulling them wide to make room for him.

"You're insatiable," he murmured, running a calloused finger along her slick fold.

"It's your fault."

Von grinned. "Damn straight."

He slid his body up hers, stopping to kiss and nibble along the way.

"Please," she begged, pressing her hips against his to try to ease the pulsing ache at her center. "I need you."

"I will always need you," he whispered hotly, sliding home in one, hard thrust.

Helena shattered beneath him, wave after wave of her climax flooding through her body, and through their bond.

Von grit his teeth, furiously pumping into her as her inner muscles fluttered against his velvety length. Between her body, and the feeling of her orgasm through their bond, he was coming inside her with a shout only a few heartbeats later.

She wrapped her arms around his back, peppering kisses across the top of his Jaka. "You said ten minutes, we have at least five more."

Von snickered, still hot and thick inside of her. "Utterly insatiable," he growled, but it wasn't a complaint. He began to move again, long slow thrusts that had her toes curling and her back arching up and off the bed. Time lost all meaning as they worshiped each other with their bodies.

Ten minutes had come and gone a hundred times over before they finally made their way out of bed, and then out of the Palace. The future might be uncertain, but with her Mate at her side, there was absolutely no way she'd ever be bored.

Ronan let the note fall to the floor with a disgusted snort.

"I can't believe they just left the rest of us here."

"You can't?" Reyna asked with an amused lift of her once again perfect brow. Helena had made a point to personally heal Reyna, removing all traces of the General's corruption. Ronan almost missed the scars. Scars were proof that you had fought and won. Reyna was a powerful woman; she would have borne her scars with pride.

His lips twisted in a wry grin. "All right, so maybe it's not that hard to believe."

Von and Helena had left a note saying only that they were going to be out of touch for a few weeks and that Ronan was in charge in their place. They didn't even leave a way for Ronan to reach them if something came up.

"I think she's earned her rest," Ronan finally said. No one in the Circle had spoken about the fact that Helena had come face first with the darkest parts of her soul, or that she had nearly succumbed to it. They also hadn't brought up her transformation, at least not in front of her. Whether it was a skill Helena still had access to, no one was certain. The popular belief was that the leftover power gifted to her by the rest of the Chosen had allowed her body to make the transition in response to her need to defend her Mate. It was just one more thing, in an already long list, that made Helena the most impressive Kiri the Chosen had ever seen.

Reyna murmured her agreement and made to stand as a knock sounded on the door. They shared a curious look as Ronan went to open the door.

Alina stood there, wringing her hands nervously. "A letter has arrived; it's addressed to the Kiri."

Ronan frowned, holding out his hand. "I'll take it."

Alina looked relieved as she handed it to him before bobbing a curtsey and scurrying away.

The thick green velum was expensive, and the scrawling text on the front was unfamiliar.

Without waiting, Ronan peeled back the seal and quickly read the text, his amusement fading with each new sentence.

Reyna read over his shoulder, her expression a twin to his own.

"We've been summoned," Ronan said.

"What do you think it means?" Reyna asked, already walking with him as they went to find the remaining Circle members.

Ronan shrugged. "Effie wouldn't have sent it if she didn't need our help. It can't possibly be good."

"That's what I was afraid of," Reyna said with a sigh.

Ronan lifted his brow. "You don't have to come, Night Stalker. This is Circle business."

Reyna scowled at him. "As if I would let you wander around Bael unprotected."

"Worried about me?" he asked with a smug, purely masculine smile.

Reyna rolled her eyes, calling over her shoulder as she walked away, "I already told you, Shield. I'm not done with you yet."

Ronan's smile grew as he watched Reyna's swaying hips. After a moment, he shook his head, pulling himself out of his reverie. Following her, he let out a low whistle before muttering under his breath. "Mother's tits, this is going to be fun."

EPILOGUE

*T*he Triumvirate stood overlooking their favorite cliff, their faces tilted up toward the stars.

"The pieces are finally in place."

"Is she ready?"

"The first step has already been made."

Their cloaks billowed around them as the wind swept up.

"There is much she must learn."

"We will teach her."

"She is stubborn and unfocused."

"She doesn't trust us."

"It doesn't matter; she is where she was destined to be."

"The rest will soon fall into place."

The scrape of a boot against a rock had the three figures twisting toward the mouth of the cave.

"What are you doing out here?" an annoyed voice snapped.

"Daughter." As always, it was impossible to tell which of the three figures was speaking.

Effie grit her teeth, her blonde hair flying around her in the breeze. "I told you to stop calling me that. I am *not* your daughter."

The central figure shrugged. *"And yet here you are."*

"Because you promised you'd teach me," she shouted, frustration and grief twisting her face. It had been weeks since she'd joined the Keepers and she was no closer to understanding her visions or fighting off the horrible side effects. All she felt was more desperately alone than ever.

"Then perhaps it's time we begin."

WANT TO FIND OUT WHAT HAPPENS TO EFFIE AND LEARN MORE ABOUT THE MYSTERIOUS KEEPERS? NOW'S YOUR CHANCE!

THINGS IN THE CHOSEN UNIVERSE ARE JUST GETTING STARTED. EFFIE'S STORY CONTINUES IN THE KEEPER'S LEGACY, BOOK 1 IN THE KEEPERS SERIES.

READ ON FOR A SNEAK PEEK!

SNEAK PEEK

THE KEEPER'S LEGACY

*M*inutes.

That's all she had left before leaving the last of her old life behind. Effie straightened, the straps of her knapsack falling from limp fingers as she turned to face the beige colored cloth that would mark the official death of the girl she'd been. Once she stepped through that flap there'd be no looking back. How was it possible for such an innocent looking scrap of fabric to hold so much power?

With a sigh, Effie turned away and went to work triple checking that she'd packed everything she might need in the days to come.

You're doing this for your friends. To save them.

Letting out a shaky breath, Effie reminded herself that she was lucky to even have those she could call her friends. It wasn't all that long ago she didn't even have that.

It was an unfortunate side effect that the only way she could help them was to leave. The Mother only knew if she'd ever see them again . . . if she'd ever make it back to the Kiri's camp . . . if they'd still be standing once this was over.

Effie started to shove items into her bag with more force than necessary, her eyes burning with tears she refused to shed.

Some memories she'd be glad to leave behind: the beatings, the jokes, the indifference. Those she would gladly bury. No one wanted reminders of all the ways they failed simply by being born.

But others . . .

Grief stabbed at her heart, and Effie's breath caught. It was hard enough to say goodbye to the living, but she was still working on how to say goodbye to the dead. Her memories were all she had left of them. She should be better at letting go by now; it was something she'd had to do a lot of recently. First with her lover, and then her grandmother.

Eyes squeezing shut, Effie pushed their faces from her mind. It was not the time or place for ghosts. Not when all they would do is torment her.

There was a war raging. One she now played a part in, if not on the battlefield itself, perhaps in its outcome. So long as she could learn to control what had lain dormant within her all these years. A legacy she inherited after her grandmother's death.

Visions.

Prophecies.

Nightmares masquerading as some obscure version of the truth—a truth she must learn to interpret if there was any hope.

Effie snorted, her eyes flying open. *What a joke.* Who would ever believe that the fate of the Chosen rested in part on her shoulders?

She was little more than a mouse. A nothing girl.

Ungifted.

The shame of the word still coiled in her stomach, choking her with its venom. Even though it was no longer true.

There was nothing worse for the Chosen than being overlooked by the Mother or her blessing; to have none of the magic that would mark her as one of them. If the Mother didn't want her, why should they?

Growing up, the only person to treat her as if she mattered was her grandmother. Not even her parents wanted her once it was clear she couldn't claim any magical ability. It wasn't until just under a year ago when she'd met the Kiri Helena and the rest of her court that others started to look at her the same way. There was something ironic about the fact that the Mother's Vessel, her living representation in this world, saw Effie as an equal, but her Chosen hadn't.

Her life had not been kind, but it was the one she'd been given. One she'd made peace with a long time ago. Now, even that hard-fought peace had been taken from her.

Nothing in her twenty-six years had prepared her for this, for being a Keeper. Effie had no clue how she was supposed to hold the weight of the future—in all its various iterations—within her mind. Nor did she have the skill to accurately distinguish the nuances hidden within those visions—distinctions that would either save or damn them all.

It was an impossible task. One she could not do on her own. It's why she had to go, why she needed the Triumvirate to teach her. As the leaders of the Keepers of Prophecy, there were no three beings in Elysia more qualified to train her.

But none of that meant Effie had to be happy about leaving behind everything she'd ever known to go with them.

All she wanted was to learn enough so that she didn't make any more mistakes. She knew now what happened when she misinterpreted the messages contained within the visions. Too many people could get hurt—or worse—if she was wrong again. A shudder traversed down her spine like tiny pinpricks of ice as she recalled just how close the Chosen had come to losing everything the first time.

The reminder of her failure did what nothing else could. Determination pulsed through her with each beat of her heart, like a tiny war drum calling her to action.

It was time to go.

Grabbing her bag, Effie took a deep breath and lifted the heavy flap, sealing her fate.

They were already waiting for her when she stepped outside of her tent and into the early morning darkness. The three hooded figures stood at the edge of the camp in perfect stillness. Their cloaks did not so much as ripple in the gentle breeze, which only further cemented them as *other*.

"Daughter." The spectral voice, equal parts breathy whisper and serpentine hiss, echoed in her mind.

Effie froze mid-step, no longer certain she wanted to go with them. Once she left the safety of the Kiri's camp, there would be no turning back. Swallowing back a wave of nausea, Effie clutched the bag in her sweat-dampened hand. Cautiously, she dipped her chin in a nod of greeting, her wide eyes never straying from their obscured faces.

No part of their skin—skin she knew to be covered in intricate snaking runes—could be seen beneath their signature crimson fabric. Nor could Effie find any trace of their gruesome visages beneath their deep hoods. For that she was grateful. The Triumvirate were terrifying at the best of times, but now, surrounded only by darkness, they would have embodied her worst nightmares.

She'd only seen the three eldest Keepers de-hooded once before, and it was more than enough as far as she was concerned. She could still vividly picture their gaunt, hairless faces, with bottomless black pits where eyes should have been, and the thick cord that stitched their mouths shut. She shuddered. The memory alone had goosebumps racing along her skin.

There was a ripple of red cloth, and Effie's eyes dropped down to the middle figure's long sleeves, waiting for one of his inhumanly long fingers to make an appearance. She could hear the rush of blood in her ears as her heart began to race. Her breath caught as she recalled the feeling of his paper-thin skin pressing against her forehead as he'd pulled one of her visions into himself, allowing him to witness what she had Seen.

Was it only yesterday he'd touched her?

The central figure tilted his head, studying her as she remained suspended half-in and half-out of her tent.

Heat crept up her neck and bloomed in her cheeks as Effie realized she had been caught staring. Clearing her throat, she completed her step and let the heavy cloth fall closed behind her.

"Do not be afraid."

As always, when communicating with the Triumvirate, it was

impossible to know which of the three was speaking. Instinct told Effie it was the one in the middle, whom she'd always assumed was the leader, although she would not have been able to explain what gave her that impression.

"I'm not afraid. You merely caught me off guard," Effie lied, taking two more hesitant steps toward the trio.

The trees rustled, and Effie could have sworn it was the Triumvirate's laughter. She would have been insulted if she hadn't been on the brink of bolting back into the tent. Pride be damned. There had to be another way for her to learn how to control and interpret her visions.

A quick glance at the large tent in the center of the camp filled her with resolve. Helena was counting on her.

Pushing her fear into the furthest recesses of her mind, Effie steeled her shoulders and closed the distance between them.

"Well, what are we waiting for?"

After another rustle of branches, all three figures twisted to the side and held out their right arms, gesturing for her to precede them.

Mother's tits, they want me to walk in front of them? How am I supposed to know where we're going? It seemed that there would be no easing into the head games. If this was some sort of test, Effie was desperate not to fail. So rather than giving voice to her question, she obeyed their silent command.

Gulping, she moved forward on shaking legs, taking great care to ensure no part of her touched any part of *them*. If they could pull visions from her mind with a mere touch, Mother only knew what else they could do. She had enough issues dealing with her own visions. No need to risk overseeing any of theirs.

The only sound Effie could hear over her racing heart was the soft brush of her boots over the forest floor. The Triumvirate were utterly silent behind her. If she closed her eyes, she might be able to pretend they weren't even there—if it wasn't for the hair on the back of her neck standing on end to remind her of their presence.

Nothing about the three of them following along behind her

provided any measure of comfort or reassurance. If anything, it only served to make her jumpier.

The crack of a branch had Effie reaching for the small dagger the Commander of the Kiri's army had given her the night before. Ronan's words echoed in her thoughts.

'Remember what I taught you. If you're in danger, stab first and ask questions later. Better to beg forgiveness than risk your life.'

Without any power to protect her, Effie had taken the lesson to heart and had no qualms gutting a man if it meant she or her friends would live to see another day.

The dagger bit into her skin where she held it in a death grip. Realizing what she'd been ready to do, Effie closed her eyes and let out a heartfelt curse. *You simple-minded fool. Don't go stabbing one of the most revered men in all of Elysia in your first handful of minutes together. You'll likely not live to share the tale. What good would you be to Helena then?*

Shame flooded her. She needed to be stronger than this. There was no one left to count on to protect her, save herself. Did she really want to be a timid little mouse for the rest of her life? It seemed like the fastest way to get herself killed.

Swallowing the ball of emotion that had lodged itself in her throat, Effie forced the fingers gripping the handle of her dagger to loosen and fall back down to her side.

"It's not much farther."

"We need only leave the protective barrier of the camp."

Stumbling at the unexpected voices, Effie's arms flew out to catch her balance, but there was nothing to support her. A vise-like grip on the back of her cloak was all that kept her from falling face-first to the ground.

Humiliated, Effie's eyes squeezed shut and a lone tear rolled down her cheek. It hadn't even been a full fifteen minutes since she'd joined them, and she'd already managed to make a complete and utter ass of herself.

"Breathe," one of the spectral voices ordered.

Effie didn't hesitate. Following orders was second nature after years spent in the service of others. She sucked in the pine-scented air, holding it deep in her lungs before it burst back out of her.

"Again."

More controlled this time, Effie took another deep breath. As she let the air out, her heart began to slow back down to something resembling normal—or at least as normal as it could get given her present company.

The hand fell away from her back and Effie braced herself for chastisement, certain that one or all of them would berate her clumsiness. When none came, she slowly turned back to face the trio. They were closer than she'd thought, their misting breaths mingling with her own.

"This is far enough."

Startled, Effie glanced over the right one's shoulder, where she could still clearly see the scattering of tents through the trees. They'd barely gone any distance at all.

"H-here?"

The Triumvirate's synchronized nods were her only answer.

Confusion added itself to the list of emotions spiraling through her. What made this patch of the forest any different than the rest?

As if he could read the question in her eyes, the left figure lifted his hand and let his long fingers unfurl to reveal a glittering purple stone lying in the center of an unfamiliar rune that covered his bone-white palm.

The stone, at least, Effie recognized. It was a Kaelpas stone, and it was the first thing that had made any sort of sense all morning. The small stones were very rare and did much to explain how the Triumvirate always managed to appear as if out of thin air. When activated, the stones allowed the holder, and anyone else that made physical contact with them, to travel anywhere they desired within the realm—so long as they'd been there before. The stronger the stone, the farther one could travel, and the more people that could accompany them.

This was going to be a shorter trip than she'd initially thought. Travel by Kaelpas stone was instantaneous, but also incredibly disorientating. Effie prayed that she didn't embarrass herself further by puking on one of the Triumvirate once they arrived . . . wherever it was they were going.

Heavy silence stretched between them before Effie realized the trio was waiting for her to reach out and touch them so that they could be off.

A flicker of annoyance brought a scowl with it. The least they could do was give her a bit more direction instead of letting her fumble around and make an ass of herself. Their mouths might be sealed, but they clearly had no trouble communicating when they wished to. Which only made their silence all the more damning. It was intentional. Meaning this was very much a test.

Effie grit her teeth, not appreciating the realization one bit. She might be a mouse, but she refused to be a plaything.

When her hand lifted, it was steady. Chin tilted high, Effie stared at the central figure, imagining that she was staring him straight in those pits that served for eyes. There was another rustle of branches, but Effie barely had time to note it before her palm made contact with the surprisingly soft fabric of his robe and the ground was yanked from beneath her.

The breath was pulled from her lungs and her body felt like it had been turned inside out. The feeling passed as quickly as it appeared, but even so, Effie was on her hands and knees when the world finally righted itself again. Swallowing back waves of nausea, Effie silently sent up heartfelt thanks that she'd manage to hold onto that small measure of dignity.

An outstretched hand came into her field of vision, and it was all she could do not to flinch. It still took her longer than she would have liked before she could bring herself to willingly touch the inked skin.

"Thank you," she mumbled when the hand closed around hers and pulled her to her feet. For as delicate as those bony fingers looked, their grip on her was strong . . . and warm. Effie frowned at the unexpected discovery. Perhaps there was a smidgeon of humanity to be found in the trio after all.

"Welcome to your new home, Daughter."

Tearing her eyes away from the hand that still held hers, Effie managed to catch a glance at the maw of darkness yawning before her. That was all it took before her final shred of dignity was lost.

In the midst of her blood-curdling screams, Effie couldn't find it in herself to care.

FROM THE AUTHOR

If you enjoyed this book, please consider writing a short review and posting it on Amazon, Bookbub, Goodreads and/or anywhere else you share your love of books.

Reviews are very helpful to other readers and are greatly appreciated by authors
(especially this one!)

When you post a review, send me an email and let me know! I might feature part, or all, of it on social media.

XOXO

♡ Meg Anne

meg@megannewrites.com

ACKNOWLEDGMENTS

Writing this book terrified me. I had to find a way to say goodbye to characters that had become as close to me as family in the last couple of years. On top of that, I desperately wanted to do them justice. Not just for me, but for the people that invested their time and money to read my words. (I still can't believe that happened. You guys are freaking amazing.)

These words have been thoughts inside my head for so long, when it came time to finally share them I was paralyzed more days than not. It is with no small bit of humility that I admit this, but it's important because it means that these thank yous are truly well deserved. Without the following people, I would probably still be staring at pages of notes and a blank computer screen.

For my family (even those of you that are not readers) that made a point to ask how it was going and listen to me geek out on specifics of fight scenes, jokes that weren't funny to anyone but me, or my detailed explanation of the newest M. Night Shyamalan twist... thank you.

Gabe... there are no words for what your support means to me. Trust me... I've searched for them. Thank you for being my person, and for loving all the wacky sides of me. You are the other half of this author, even though your name isn't on the cover.

Fran, Jess, Laura... I love you ladies. Thank you for always being there to listen and offer your support or share a bottle of wine... or both. <3

For My Chosen... thank you for reading my words. Every email, every message, every kind word is cherished and saved for me to revisit on the tough days. I keep writing because of you.

Hanleigh, Lori, Dominique... thank you for sharing your talent with me. Here's to another job well done.

ALSO BY MEG ANNE

High Fantasy Romance

The Chosen Universe

The Chosen

Mother of Shadows

Reign of Ash

Crown of Embers

Queen of Light

The Keepers

The Dreamer – A Keepers Story

The Keeper's Legacy

The Keeper's Retribution

The Keeper's Vow

Paranormal & Urban Fantasy Romance

The Gypsy's Curse

Co-Written with Jessica Wayne

Visions of Death

Visions of Vengeance

Visions of Triumph

Cursed Hearts: The Complete Collection

The Grimm Brotherhood

Co-Written with Kel Carpenter

Reaper's Blood

ABOUT MEG ANNE

USA Today and international bestselling paranormal and fantasy romance author Meg Anne has always had stories running on a loop in her head. They started off as daydreams about how the evil queen (aka Mom) had her slaving away doing chores, and more recently shifted into creating backgrounds about the people stuck beside her during rush hour. The stories have always been there; they were just waiting for her to tell them.

Like any true SoCal native, Meg enjoys staying inside curled up with a good book and her cat, Henry . . . or maybe that's just her. You can convince Meg to buy just about anything if it's covered in glitter or rhinestones, or make her laugh by sharing your favorite bad joke. She also accepts bribes in the form of baked goods and Mexican food.

Meg is best known for her leading men #MenbyMeg, her inevitable cliffhangers, and making her readers laugh out loud, all of which started with the bestselling Chosen series.